THE WEEKEND RETREAT

A NOVEL

TARA LASKOWSKI

GRAYDON
HOUSE

GRAYDON
HOUSE®

Recycling programs
for this product may
not exist in your area.

ISBN-13: 978-1-525-81145-6

The Weekend Retreat

Graydon House
22 Adelaide St. West, 41st Floor
Toronto, Ontario M5H 4E3, Canada
www.GraydonHouseBooks.com
www.BookClubbish.com

Printed in U.S.A.

PRAISE FOR *THE MOTHER NEXT DOOR*

"A polished and entertaining homage to *Big Little Lies* and *Desperate Housewives*... The denouement is bonkers, but satisfying."

—*New York Times Book Review*

"Suspenseful, compulsively readable... Extremely fun to read."

—*Shelf Awareness*

"A witty, wicked thriller packed with hidden agendas, juicy secrets, and pitch-perfect satire of the suburban dream."

—ANDREA BARTZ, *New York Times* bestselling author of *We Were Never Here*

"Tara Laskowski's brilliantly paced tale of perfect-suburbia-until-you-scratch-the-surface is as compelling as it is twisted."

—HANNAH MARY McKINNON, bestselling author of *Never Coming Home*

"A scintillating suburban thriller... *The Mother Next Door* promises to mix its feminist sensibilities with plenty of entertaining camp."

—*CrimeReads*

PRAISE FOR *ONE NIGHT GONE*

"A subtly but relentlessly unsettling book."

—TANA FRENCH, *New York Times* bestselling author of *The Searcher*

"An evocative and beautifully crafted tale of suspense."

—*Publishers Weekly* (STARRED REVIEW)

"Laskowski is a truly gifted storyteller. Spectacular."

—JENNIFER HILLIER, bestselling author of *Things We Do in the Dark*

"A heart-wrenching and suspenseful novel of betrayal and revenge. A stunning debut!"

—CAROL GOODMAN, award-winning author of *The Stranger Behind You*

"The talented Tara Laskowski, with her confident hand, beautifully drawn characters, and unique style, is sure to be a major voice in crime fiction."

—HANK PHILLIPPI RYAN, bestselling author of *The House Guest*

Also by Tara Laskowski

Novels

One Night Gone
The Mother Next Door

Short story collections

Modern Manners for Your Inner Demons
Bystanders

For my brother Mike, who's absolutely nothing like the siblings in this book. (Thank god.)

W-JKA BREAKING NEWS

Tragedy strikes at Van Ness Winery

SUNDAY, October 15—Multiple people have been reported dead at the Van Ness Winery after an altercation late Saturday night, our Eyewitness Team reports. Police were dispatched around 1:00 a.m. on Sunday morning after a 9-1-1 call from the estate's main house, but they were delayed hours getting to the scene because of the torrential rainstorm that flooded Rte. 8 and many of the small roads leading up to the winery.

Our news team is on-site but has not been able to verify details with officials, who are still investigating the scene. It appears the damaged substation in Parnell affected power to the estate as well as a number of neighboring homes and businesses in the Finger Lakes area.

This tragedy is the latest to befall the Van Ness family, whose matriarch, investor and philanthropist Katrina

Van Ness, died earlier this year of pancreatic cancer at the age of sixty-eight.

The Van Ness winery, known for producing high-quality, award-winning wines, has been owned by the Van Ness family for several generations. The family started the business in the 1950s, after selling their Arizona-based copper mining company founded by Benson Van Ness. The 985-acre winery and estate is now managed by the Van Ness siblings, who live full-time in New York City. Their family investment office owns interests in multiple different real estate holdings and industrial and manufacturing enterprises. The siblings are believed to have been visiting the estate for the weekend for a family celebration.

We will report more as details are confirmed.

THURSDAY

Two Days before the Party

LAUREN

Ever since Zach told me about The Weekend, it's all I've been able to focus on. Most people would naturally be at least a little nervous to meet their significant other's family for the first time.

But most people aren't dating a Van Ness.

"Earth to Lauren." Zach snaps his fingers, grinning over at me. He left work early to get on the road sooner and didn't have time to change, so he's still wearing his suit, purple tie slightly askew but knotted even after hours of driving.

"Sorry," I say, tugging the ends of my hair. "Zoning out."

"You look like I'm driving you to your death," he says, then grabs my hand and squeezes. "Don't worry. I promise it'll be fun. Even if my family's there."

All I can see out my window are trees and fields and cows, my cell phone bars ticking steadily down. We must be close. Zach is taking care on the steep, curvy roads. One bad turn could send our car into a deep ditch or crashing into a thick tree trunk.

It's so beautiful up there, my best friend Maisie said when I told her about the invitation. She had that wicked look in her eye. *All the rolling hills. A vineyard. Starry sky. Super romantic. Perfect place to propose.* My stomach flips at the thought, and I breathe in deep. This weekend is not about us. It's a birthday party for Zach's older siblings, Harper and Richard, the twins, an annual tradition to celebrate at the family's winery. I can't get ahead of myself.

We drive up a winding gravel road, through patches of dense trees. Taller ones have already gone barren for the winter, but some of the smaller trees arch over the road, their branches meeting and entangling like fingers, blotting out the remaining light.

"Ladies and gentlemen, we are now approaching the famous Van Ness estate," Zach says in a booming voice as the car's headlights flick on. "Please, no photographs, and keep all hands and feet inside the moving vehicle at all times."

Zach told me the estate is large—a thousand acres—but I didn't grasp what that meant until the tunnel of trees ends and the view opens to a sprawling expanse of green fields and rolling hills, stretching endlessly against the purple-hued sky. We cross a small stone bridge that extends over a stream, then bump along a rocky road. The vineyards creep closer to us now, eerie in their precise organization, each plant in a perfect row. We're inching toward winter, and all the grapes must have already been picked for the season, pressed and bottled, because the vines are bare and withered.

When I first moved to New York and waited tables at an Italian restaurant, we served the Van Ness wine. I remember those dark purple labels, the name stamped big and bold on the front. A brand that said, *We are too good for you.* But Zach is nothing like that, like the Van Nesses you read about online. Sometimes I forget he's part of that family in the day-to-day rhythm of our lives. He doesn't talk about them much, offers the scantest of information, or cracks a joke, or completely changes the subject when I bring them up. All I know of them is from the press, fleeting and superficial, like the pages of a glossy magazine, but hazy enough that I can imagine slicing open my finger on the sharp edges if I'm not careful.

"Tell me about them," I say now, when there's no evading the topic.

He glances over at me. "My family? What more do you need to know?"

"I don't know. How can I win them over so they all love me forever and ever?" I say, trying to hide my nerves.

He laughs. "They're impossible to win over."

"Oh perfect," I say. "That makes it easy then."

"Nah, they aren't that bad. They're…particular is all."

We head up a slight incline. To the right, there's a gravel path marked Private—Staff Only. We pass it and stop in front of a large metal gate. Zach rolls down his window, fetches a key card from the glove compartment. "We had this installed years ago for extra security," he says. Once the machine reads his card, the gates swing open soundlessly. I turn to watch them rotate back and slam into place.

As we round a corner, I finally catch a glimpse of the house, a stone mansion, stoic on the hill. The long driveway curves up to an overhang in front, flanked by a series of round potted trees.

"Here we are," says Zach as we pull up. He shuts off the car, taps the digital clock on the dashboard. "And on time for dinner, too. Elle will be pleased."

My stomach does another flip.

Breathe deep.

Project confidence.

They're going to love you.

I get out. The air is chilly—it's dropped at least ten degrees since we left the city. I wrap my arms across my body.

The massive wooden front door opens, and an older man walks out, gray hair and beard, a deep purple polo shirt with the Van Ness logo stitched on the pocket, two flutes of sparkling wine in his hands.

"Bill! You are the man." Zach trades him the keys to the car for the glasses. "Lauren, Bill and his wife Linnet have been taking care of the estate—and us—since I was a snotty-nosed kid."

As Bill heads for the trunk to unload our baggage, I survey the house. My eyes follow the three short steps up to a wide entryway with pillars, to the archway above the door, and then outward to the wings on either side. Greenery climbs up the stonework between the windows, and I imagine Bill must trim it often to keep it so nice. I touch a pillar next to me and feel its cool smoothness.

"Where's everyone else?" Zach asks Bill. For him, this is business as usual. I doubt he even notices the grandness anymore.

"Oh, they're around," he says. "Miss Elle says dinner at 6:30, and you can all meet in the library."

I smooth down the gold silk top Zach picked out for me, hugging and hiding in all the right places, like expensive clothes do. What would my parents say if they saw me? They would never guess I'd be weekending with a famous family like this. They never thought I'd make it in New York, thought I'd come crawling back begging to return to my night shift writing obituaries at our small-town paper.

But I'm never going back.

I take a sip of the sparkling wine. The bubbles pop, cold and hard against the back of my throat.

HARPER

I gaze at myself powering away on the bike in the mirrored wall of the gym. I always loathed the way Mother designed this gym—who wants to watch herself sweat?—but it turns out it can also be validating to see yourself, no filters, all angles.

"You definitely do not look thirty-five," I say to myself.

"You're modest, too," calls Lucas, upside down, from across the room.

I climb off the bike and pat my face with a towel as I walk over to him. My quads are burning, but I squat down next to my husband anyway, run my finger along his stubble.

He's hanging in his gravity boots for his spine decompression therapy. I like when he's like this, tethered up and vulnerable. How easy it would be to pick up one of the weights and slam it down on his neck, crush his windpipe.

I stand. My murderous thoughts have definitely been on an uptick lately. Part of it is being back here at Mother's house. The heavy drapery and the gold statues, like we are throwback 1680s French royalty. Everywhere with the Herend ceramic cats and dogs, Versace vases gathering dust, thick Persian carpets. Even the gym can't escape gold-plated spotlights in the ceiling and a goddamn chandelier.

This house is a behemoth, needy and wanting, and Mother always enjoyed feeding the monster. But it's angry and sullen without her, listless, the shadows in the corners deeper and longer.

"You need to get out of those things. It's nearly time for dinner," I tell my husband.

Lucas pulls himself up, unlatches his boots from the pole, and flips himself down and upright. His face is beet red, his eyes puffy.

"I don't know how you can stand that," I say.

"Good for the back." He stretches upward. I hear the crack. "Besides, these boots are the closest thing I'll get to skiing this weekend."

I ignore his comment. He's still not over the fact that I canceled the ski trip he'd planned for my birthday. It didn't matter that *he's* really the skier. *You seriously would rather go there?* he'd asked me. *With your family?*

Of course, I said, but he knew I was lying. He knows how I feel about this place. My brothers love the estate, but my memories of summers here are complicated. All these walls do now is remind me of Mother's games, challenges that were always impossible for me to win, as if she'd set them up that way.

When she was alive, it was a tradition none of us could break—one long birthday weekend at the estate. We'd sometimes bring friends from the city, one or two each for Richard and me. Mother always tried to plan a few surprises for us. When we were kids, it was horseback riding or boat rides or, one year, a full-on circus with a tent and acrobats and a baby tiger we all got to pet until it tried to bite my friend's arm. As we got older, casino nights or live bands. And always, the nighttime games and fireworks. Once Mother got sick, though, the birthday weekend was a quieter affair, with Mother telling stories about traveling around Europe and doling out too much wine and unsolicited advice.

I'd planned on stopping it this year.

But then things changed.

I move closer to the mirror and pull the collar of my T-shirt down. In the reflection, the bruise is nearly gone now, just a faint greenish-blue outline that will barely be visible when I wear my jumpsuit tonight.

"Wear your navy suit to dinner. It'll complement my outfit," I say as I trace the bruise with my fingers.

"I still don't get why I have to wear a suit at all," Lucas says, holding a push-up. "It's just your family."

"Because it's tradition," I snap and turn away from the mirror. "We always dress up the first night for dinner."

He knows this. It's part of the package, putting up with our families' various persuasions. I put up with his family's annual beach white-out parties and cornhole tournaments. Looking nice for dinner for mine hardly seems like a big ask.

Lucas raises his hands. "Fine, fine. I just hope we get some time to just chill. You know how Elle gets about these kinds of things…"

He doesn't need to finish that sentence. My sister-in-law has always been a type A perfectionist, desperate to please—and anxious for control. This is her element, planning events, making a list and checking it twice. She prides herself on being detail-oriented, and for everyone around her, it's exhausting as hell.

I'm fine to have drinks and dinner, and I'll even smile cheerfully for the inevitable group photo. But she can't expect us all to hang out every second and sing songs by the fire. If this weekend is really supposed to be about relaxing, then we shouldn't have to deal with one another the whole time. What I need is the escape, and if Mother's house is good for anything, it's at least good for hiding away.

ELLE

I thought I forgot to pack my pill case, but here it is, under Richard's toiletry bag in our suitcase. With relief, I unroll it, pull out the CBD tincture, squeeze a few drops (and then a few extra) under my tongue. It should take effect before dinner. The edge should be good and gone by the time Harper gets her forked tongue going.

Yes, this and just a little bit of wine and I'll be good to go.

While Richard's in the shower, I run over my mental checklist again. Family time tonight and tomorrow, the big party on Saturday. We all deserve a little fun. Especially Richard. He's taken it extra hard losing Mom, burying himself in work. I want this birthday to be special, as she'd have made it. I've been in this family long enough to know there's nothing more sacred than a Van Ness tradition.

I step over to the window. Clouds are gathering, though it's not supposed to rain tonight. Bill says a big storm is coming, that the main road out of here might flood over. I'm hoping it'll hold out until after the party, and we'll be able to leave Sunday morning before it gets really bad. I would hate to have to move everything inside. I have a vision for how the terrace will look, how the food and drink stations will flow, where everyone will gather. And with our friends coming from the city, I want to show off the spectacular views, make sure the drive is worth their while.

I pick up the CBD tincture, a few more drops on the tongue, and turn from the window as Richard steps out of the bathroom, steam drifting behind him, towel wrapped around his waist. I slide the bottle quickly back into my pill case and pop a mint in my mouth. I've been using my CBD more and more lately and I don't want him to ask questions.

"Zach's here," I say brightly. I'd spotted his car in the driveway.

But Richard doesn't answer. He's using another towel to dry his hair, whistling a tune, grabbing for his phone. He probably has work on his mind. He always gets ideas in the shower, rushes out to make notes before they dissipate with the steam.

Richard's the steady one of the family—the steerer of the ship. It's what drew me to him, his stability, his predictability. We work well together. Everyone can rely on us, always. For the most part, this is how I prefer things—I know Richard will do what I expect him to—but sometimes I wish we were the spontaneous couple who showers together before dinner and shows up late holding hands, laughing, much to everyone's irritation.

Richard locks his phone and walks it over to the charging station. "You forgot to pack my new shaving cream."

Dammit.

I encircle him from behind, lay my cheek against his back. He's still damp, but I don't mind. I like the smell of his body wash, woodsy and masculine. "I'm sorry."

"I knew I should've done it. I've been breaking out from the other one," he says. Which I know, because I'm the one who recommended the new brand—free of dyes and fragrances that irritate his skin. His comment is somewhere between a rebuke of himself and of me. He's always too hard on himself. I offered to pack for him so he'd have more time to work. He's taken on most of the responsibilities of the family business this past year. But I won't let him start out on the wrong foot this weekend.

"Did you think any more on the candle thing?" I push the error aside and lean into his weight. "I know you like to make a wish, but I just worry it's going to ruin how beautiful the cake looks."

"I'd be fine without candles, but it's whatever Harper wants."

Harper. Of course. This is how it always is when they're together. We have to endure their meaningful looks across the room and all the stories about how they can read each other's minds. I don't know how Zach's lived with it all these years.

Richard steps away, opens the closet, and tugs his pants off the hanger. I made sure to have them delivered to our town house yesterday, freshly pressed from the cleaners. "You invited Victor and his wife to the party, right?"

"If I left them off, I'd never get invited to another one of Alicia's Sunday brunches," I joke. I would be perfectly fine if I never had to sip another mimosa with Alicia Hastings and her friends, but Victor is on the board of our investment company, so we must keep in their good graces.

"Now that would just be a *tragedy*," Richard says with a small smile as he swipes his deodorant, always three times under each arm.

"I'm so glad we're reviving the old birthday tradition," I say, fiddling my diamond earrings through their holes. "So many surprises in store for you."

"And Harper," he adds, picking up his phone again.

"And Harper," I repeat.

He tucks in his shirt, zips up his pants, and threads a leather belt through the loops. Whisks a comb through his hair and slides his wallet in his back pocket, always on the right-hand side. He'll wait to put on his suit jacket until he's heading downstairs so it doesn't wrinkle. And then he'll take it off halfway through dinner and hang it carefully on the back of a chair.

My husband is a creature of habit, a man of rules and regulations. I've been with him long enough that I know them all.

He fetches his glasses off the nightstand, slips them on, blinks as his world comes into focus. He nods his approval at my short black dress and long hair, which I've blown out into loose waves the way he loves it. "You look gorgeous, as usual."

"Thank you, my darling." I kiss his cheek, ignore the red blotches from the shaving cream.

I check my watch. "About time for drinks?"

I've also been in the Van Ness family long enough to know all their rules, traditions, quirks, desires. I know which flavor cakes to buy, which china patterns to use, which political issues they approve of, how to properly let a bottle of wine aerate. I know how to get under their skin and when to dodge the bullet. I know their sensitivities, their soft spots, their weaknesses.

I know their secrets, too.

THE PARTY GUEST

I like driving in the country. The long, quiet roads, especially at night. Gives you plenty of time to think as the miles pass with nothing but your headlights to guide you through the shadows.

And I have a lot of thinking to do.

I've waited patiently for this moment. Another person might've rushed things, acted too soon, but that would've been a mistake. I knew I had to hold out for just the right time, the right place, the right moment—there's a comfort in the plotting. A pleasure in slipping into their world, learning all about them. Gathering evidence and information.

And now here it is. This weekend. The birthday party.

Some people hate birthdays. They don't like the reminder that time, tick-tock, is clicking steadily forward, always moving, and they can't escape it. They loathe the thought of getting old, of things failing them—their eyesight, their joints, their mind, their beauty.

Me? I've always loved birthdays. A tradition, a milestone. A reminder of how far you've come and how far you've yet to go.

Another year ahead to right the wrongs that have been committed around you—to you. Because no matter how much you try to be good, no matter how hard you try to go about things honestly, there are always people who just can't play nice.

It's so dark up here in wine country. I must go slow, watch out for wildlife that could dart into the road. Anything can be lurking in the darkness, ready to lunge out. Terrible things happen in the blink of an eye. One moment everything's fine, and the next, the world comes crashing down around you.

But I'll drive carefully. I'll arrive safe and sound.

There's a big storm coming, and I've got everything I need— rain boots, raincoat. Night-vision goggles.

Finally, the last item, right here next to me on the passenger seat, wrapped and ready to be delivered—the birthday gift.

For what's a party without gifts?

The Van Ness family knows how to throw a good party. They love to flaunt their wealth. They'll pull out all the stops. Good food, good wine, decorations, hospitality. All the details accounted for. They'll have planned for everything.

Well, nearly everything.

HARPER

It's when I'm grabbing the lipstick I left in the car that I see them: several dozen silver and purple balloons in an arch above the front door. A giant banner reads HAPPY BIRTHDAY RICHARD AND HARPER! The astronauts in the International Space Station could spot it, but that wouldn't be enough for Elle.

Someone's left a white box propped against the stone next to the door. It has a simple gold ribbon tied around it and the tag says *Happy Birthday!* I take the gift inside before Elle can appear and fish for compliments about the display and follow the voices to the back of the house.

Zach and his girlfriend are in the library, sipping wine and murmuring to each other near the crackling fireplace like they're in a Jane Austen novel.

"Well, well. The prodigal son returns."

Zach turns, sees me, and grins that grin of his that has allowed my baby brother to get away with so much in life. "Harper!" He hugs me, then steps back and introduces her—Lauren Brady—all glowing skin, dark eye shadow, and brown wavy hair.

She's petite, but her handshake is surprisingly strong. Zach said she's new to the city, a writer or PR person. I hope she appreciates all the perks of being with him while she can; Zach will tire of her soon.

"What time did you get here?" he asks. He doesn't make a motion to sit, so we all stand around the fire, watching the wood char and blacken. "And where's Lucas?"

"We arrived early this morning, up at the crack of dawn because my darling husband is allergic to traffic as much as he is to tree pollen." I roll my eyes.

"That's right, I am." Lucas's voice, from the doorway. He's cleaned up nicely in his navy suit, as I knew he would. He stops next to me. "Did you see the balloons out front?"

"Is it possible to miss them?" For that, Lauren gives me a small chuckle.

After more introductions, Lucas heads to the bar cart in the corner. It was important to Mother to have all the necessities to make a drink no matter where you were in the house. Zach and I once counted, and there are twelve bars or liquor cabinets on the main floor alone.

"Where are we dining?" Lucas asks, concentrating as he pours scotch into a glass.

"Outside, I think." Zach checks his smart watch, then rubs Lauren's shoulder. "I hope you won't get cold."

"Don't worry," I tell her. "Between the alcohol and all the heat lanterns, you'll be as snug as if you crawled into the entrails of a recently killed bear." I smirk. "Speaking of alcohol—" Lucas returns from the bar cart with a nip of scotch as if we've choreographed the whole thing.

With a little whiskey in me, I can face the ghosts in this room. The library still smells like Mother, her lotion, her perfume, permanently settled into the upholstery. It feels like she's going to waltz in at any moment and toss a silk scarf around her neck. Snap at us all impatiently to start the party like she always did. *Where's the music? Where's the booze? Where's the life?*

Lauren glances at me. She's got a shy smile, but her eyes are shrewd. "Zach told me we weren't supposed to do presents."

I look down at the gift still tucked under my arm. My fingers have been playing with the ribbon, I realize. "This? I have no idea what this is. Found it outside."

"Oh." Those eyes flick away. She doesn't believe me. She thinks I'm just trying to be polite.

I set the gift down on a side table and join Lucas, who's browsing the bookshelves. He sniffs, blinks his eyes. "It's all the dust," he says quietly.

"The books," I say. "You're allergic to all this...knowledge."

"Har har."

There are a lot of books. Some are mine, Zach's, and Richard's, but it was Mother who really loved to read. Mysteries, biographies, true crime. She lived abroad for much of her childhood, and as a teenager read Beat poetry and drank wine in cities along the Mediterranean, flirting and generally getting into trouble before returning to the States in her early twenties.

"Who's the hunter?" Lauren's staring at the deer head mounted on the wall between the windows.

"Oh, that's Mother," I say and walk over. When she looks at me, I add, "I mean, she didn't *kill* it. She bought it somewhere."

"She hated deer," Zach says. "They like to eat the grapes. So this was her revenge."

My husband steps under the deer and peers up at it from all directions. "Yeah, that's real." He says to Lauren, "Guess you didn't grow up around hunters?"

Lucas loves to pretend he's rustic, like some lumberjack from the backwoods, because he grew up in a godawful town in the middle of nowhere Pennsylvania before his parents moved to DC. If I didn't make him wear a nice suit to dinner, he'd be in his usual uniform of waffle shirt or a flannel, like a wannabe J.Crew model. The man can't boil a pan of water to save his life, but sure, he's a hunter.

"Actually, yes," Lauren says. "I'm from Delaware, and I knew lots of people who lived for hunting season." She shivers. "Not for me, though."

So she grew up around people who boost their egos by shooting unsuspecting wildlife. Couldn't Zach at least have dragged home someone interesting, like the vegan karate expert, or the militant accountant he once dated who gave us good pointers about tax breaks?

"Delaware, eh?" Lucas says, and I can tell he's going to start grilling her about things literally no one else cares about, so I cut him off.

"What part of the city do you live in?" I ask. She's too sweet for the East Village, but not polished enough for the Upper East Side.

"Oh, we—" she begins, but Zach butts in, thrusting his arm out and nearly sloshing his drink on the carpet.

"Is this twenty questions or what?"

"I thought I heard you all in here!" Elle's voice grates as she appears, Richard in tow. She's wearing a little black dress that does nothing to enhance her flat chest. Her face lights up when she spots Zach and Lauren, and the room must endure the sugary introductions and hugs again. I don't have much choice but to partake when Elle lunges for me. "Come on, come on, I have to hug you again, too." As if we are the best of friends. As if she doesn't despise me.

She feels like a piece of bamboo furniture, giving a little here and there but mostly just rigid and awkward. When we pull apart, she leaves a coat of floral perfume on my shoulders.

"Isn't she so cute?" Elle says about Lauren when we once again converge in front of the fire. "So little and sweet."

"She's a person, not a teacup," I say.

"Oh, Harper." Elle has a tinkly little laugh she makes when she doesn't actually think something's funny. "You always do know just the right thing to say." She takes in my navy blue jumpsuit, plunging neckline, tiny belt, diamond stud at my throat.

I toss her my most charming smile and resist the urge to poke and prod the fire—too much meddling will suffocate the flames.

Richard looks sharp in his dark gray Armani bespoke suit. At least he's arriving into our next year in style.

We lock eyes. Wait. Wait. Wait. Wait. Wait for it. He blinks first.

I always win.

Richard walks over to the bar and selects a bottle of wine. "Lauren, my sister is much more fun when she's drunk."

"Aren't we all?" asks Zach with a wink.

This weekend has hardly begun and already I'm nauseated. When can we start stabbing each other in the backs and rewarding ourselves with long naps? I nudge Lucas, who has tuned us all out checking his phone for sports results.

"What?" he asks, annoyed. "This is the first time all day I've had good service."

"Cell signal is spotty out here," Zach tells Lauren.

"Dead zone," Lucas mumbles.

"But it must be kind of nice to get away from everything, to have all this land? When was this house built?" Lauren asks, petting the back of one of Mother's chairs like it's a cat.

"No idea," I say, but Zach pipes up.

"In the late 1800s. It was a Gilded Age mansion, built by some financier for his second wife. Our great-grandfather bought it in the early 1950s. That makes us the fourth generation."

I set down the nasty scotch. Richard's opened a special reserve pinot noir, and I pour myself a glass, swirl the wine around until a little hurricane forms.

"Why don't we sit?" Elle suggests. "Still a bit 'til dinner."

Zach and Lauren take the velvet sofa, Elle perched next to

them, Lucas and I in the black, hard-backed Victorian chairs I've always hated. Only Richard remains standing, hovering behind us like a poltergeist, holding his wineglass like a prop.

Zach rubs his palms together. "So, what's on the agenda this weekend?" he asks Elle.

"Oh, lots of things," Elle says mysteriously. She's enjoying this a little too much, performing for her audience. "There will not be a moment of boredom."

I can feel Lucas's *Make it go away* stare on me. My husband hates organized fun. He told me one of the reasons he was motivated to start his own business was so he'd never have to endure another work retreat with skits and trust falls.

"You really don't have to go through any—" I break off as Richard warns me with his eyes. *Be nice. You owe me.*

"It's no trouble," Elle says. "I'm just excited the whole family is back together again."

I nearly spit out my wine. This is how she bills it? All back together? Like we're a band going on a reunion tour?

"We're not," I say flatly. "In case you forgot, Mother's dead."

Elle flinches. For a moment that smile flickers, dims.

The room goes silent, only the crackling of the fireplace fills the space.

Finally, something interesting is happening.

"Yes, we know that, Harper," Zach jumps in, putting an arm around Elle. "But Elle's right. It's nice being back here, having something to celebrate. Let's focus on that."

Elle throws him a grateful look.

"She's been planning this for months. We're in good hands," Zach says with plenty of that golden-boy charm to go around. Always the talent for smoothing things over.

"What's this?" Richard nods at the gift I set on a side table.

"Oh, I almost forgot," I say. "Which of you assholes broke the rules and brought that? I thought we said no gifts."

No one admits guilt.

I raise my eyebrows. "Really?"

They all shake their heads. Zach says, "Maybe someone dropped it off?"

"It was probably a courier," Elle says. "Sometimes they come up the vineyard road since that's the bigger entrance."

"But those gates are locked."

Elle frowns and tilts her head in a way that makes me think of a parrot. "I left them open. We've got a lot of people coming to set up things for the party."

My hand instinctively goes to the bruise fading on my collarbone. Lucas notices, and his jaw tenses. I jerk my hand down, swallow the rest of my wine.

"We need to close them," I say. "For security. We can't have random people wandering around the estate."

The gates are there for a reason. If Elle's going to act like this is her house, she needs to follow the rules.

"Anyway, why don't you open it?" Zach gestures toward the gift. "Solve the mystery."

But Elle snatches it first, wiggling her finger. "No. Not now. Don't you know? It's bad luck to open gifts before your birthday."

LAUREN

The terrace has a magical feel. Fairy lights wrap around a white trellis, and the oval dining table is set with china. Long tapered candles stand at the center, the flames flickering in the crystal wineglasses positioned at each place setting.

The view is equally stunning, at least what I can see of it in the dying light. The stone terrace overlooks a manicured garden, paths leading from several directions to an elaborate fountain. Lanterns make the bushes and plants glow and scatter shadows over the lawn beyond.

"It's beautiful, isn't it?" Elle saunters up next to me and hands me a fresh glass of wine. She tosses her long dark hair over her shoulder and stares out at the grounds like this is also her first time glimpsing them. "We're lucky to have Bill. He spends so much time out here tending to the gardens. Sometimes I catch him talking to the plants, like they're his babies."

I smile politely as she leans against the cold wrought-iron railing, dangling her own glass over the edge, rolling it between two fingers like it's a child's plastic toy, not an expensive vessel that will shatter into a million pieces if it falls onto the stone below.

"I trust your room is all good?" she asks. "Linnet is around if you need anything extra—linens, towels, whatever. We want you to feel like this is your home this weekend."

Our bathroom—which is nearly the size of a one-bedroom apartment—already has an entire cabinet stacked with plush towels. Before dinner, I spent thirty minutes probing in drawers, uncapping shampoos and lotions and gels. The sage green soaps, stamped with the Van Ness initials, so smooth and flawless I had the urge to bite them. I ran my arm under the hot water of the massive claw-foot tub until my skin turned pink and blotchy.

"I'm good," I say. "Everything is just great. Perfect."

She doesn't respond but takes a long sip of wine. The wind picks up. There are heat lamps around us, and something is pumping warm air near my feet, but the cold whips through my hair and under the skirt of my dress.

"Are you ladies plotting our demise?" Richard asks dryly as he and Zach join us. He gives Elle an obligatory peck on the cheek that barely grazes her, but she seems pleased by it.

The brothers look so similar—the same square jaws and those dark eyes, though Richard's are framed by large black glasses. I'd easily believe they were the twins.

"We're discussing how amazing the view is," I say. "I'm sure you never tire of it."

"Get sick of all the maintenance bills, though." Richard laughs and combs his hand through his hair.

"Here we go," Zach says. "It wouldn't be a party without Richard obsessing over the cost of something."

Richard's mouth twitches, but Elle slides a manicured hand over and squeezes his arm. A warning? The tension falls as quickly as it rose.

"Speaking of this view," Elle says, "I can't look at it without thinking of you, Zachary Van Ness, and that time you ran through the gardens dressed as a Greek god and nearly scared your poor mother half to death. Have you ever told Lauren about that?"

"No, he hasn't," I say, smiling at the thought.

There's still so much I don't know about him. What was he like as a child? What's his favorite Christmas present? Has he ever broken the law? This weekend is the chance to fill in the gaps, surrounded by the people who know him best.

"I need more wine in me if you're going to start telling embarrassing stories," Zach says, but he seems to enjoy the attention.

Elle laughs, kisses his cheek, then loops her arm through Richard's and walks toward where Harper and Lucas are talking at the built-in bar against the house. She beckons us to follow.

"Don't we all just look divine?" Elle asks the group. She plucks at the skirt of my dress, rubbing a finger over the velvet pattern, and gives me an approving look.

It's a dress I would never have chosen for myself—so intricate and luxurious, I would've never thought I could pull it off. But when I tried it on after Zach found it on a rack at Bergdorf's, I felt like a movie star. Sleeveless, deep blue velvet, mesh lace sheath. The pattern of vines twists around my body, gathering in a pool of more deep blue velvet at my ankles. When I turn, the skirt billows out, revealing the layers of cream lace underneath.

"Divine," Harper says coolly, lazily, like a cat yawning and stretching.

Beside her, Lucas finishes typing on his phone and slides it in his pocket. He towers over all of us, glances around like he's just noticing we're here, and his gaze lands on me.

"Not much of a drinker, eh, Delaware?" He nods at my still-full glass.

I hold it up. "Actually, this is already my second—or is it third?" I say, suddenly feeling the effects of the alcohol. "Guess you need to catch up."

As he laughs, the sound deep and satisfying, I can feel Harper's eyes on me.

Zach tilts his glass at Lucas. "Better watch out. She's not messing around."

"You're right," Lucas says. "Small-town girl knows how to hold her own."

"I just love small towns," Elle says, leaning into Richard. "What was yours like, Lauren?"

I try to imagine Elle walking down First Street in Maurville, all the closed businesses with FOR LEASE signs in the dirty windows. What she'd think of the checkered paper table-cloths at Duke's, the fanciest restaurant in town, or Candy, the middle-aged woman who marches miles each evening carrying a tuba and playing music for anyone who will listen. What any of them would say if they walked through the front door of my parents' house and saw the thin carpeting, the brass fireplace doors, my father's Elvis lamp prominently displayed next to the sofa.

"It's what you'd expect," I say, looking down at the new navy blue heels that are starting to pinch my toes. "Very quaint."

"I bet," she says. "We spent a month once in this tiny village in Tuscany, and my god it was wonderful. The air was completely different. Fresh and clean—it was a dream. And our housekeeper baked fresh bread and bought cheese every day. She knew everyone in the village—you know how that happens. Small towns have a nice charm about them."

I don't correct Elle and let the conversation continue around me. Maurville is about as different from Tuscany as you can get. I couldn't wait to leave, and I can't wait to never go back.

Zach smiles down at me. "Having fun?" he asks, but before I can answer his eyes flick to something over my shoulder, and his expression changes. "Check that out," he says, low, and I turn to where he's pointing, off in the darkness.

I see it then, a short gray animal and two green eyes just off the terrace, staring at us through the vertical columns of the railing.

"What is that?" I whisper.

"Probably a coyote," Zach says into my ear, so close I can feel his lips on my skin. "He senses you. He's coming to get you…"

The animal trots off, but the idea sends a shiver through me. All the gates and protection can't keep out the wild creatures prowling in the woods.

Zach has evidently moved on. He addresses the group. "Okay, everyone. Time for a toast."

"Ooh, great idea." Elle holds up her glass.

"To my favorite twins, Harper and Richard," Zach says. "Happiest of birthdays, and many more to come."

We clink glasses. Harper whispers something in Richard's ear and he laughs, glancing over at Zach and me. I take a step back, and my heel gets caught on the stone tiles. A hand steadies me. It's Lucas, his palm lingering on my side as he laughs down at me. "Whoa, there, Delaware."

Zach is too wrapped up in his toasting to notice. He makes a slight bow toward Elle. "And to my favorite sister-in-law, for planning this weekend and giving us a much-needed chance to catch up and chill out."

"Oh, it's nothing," she says, but her expression suggests otherwise, and she blows Zach an air kiss. "You know I'd do anything for you. For any of you."

"To family," Zach says, raising his empty wineglass. He sweeps an arc with his hand, indicating the gardens, the house, all of us. "Let's enjoy each other—and all this—the way Mom would've wanted us to."

Everyone grows silent. This is their first time back here since Katrina Van Ness died earlier in the year. Even I get a little emotional at the weight of the moment.

But then Zach does what he does best. "That is—she'd want us to get completely blitzed."

Everyone chuckles except Richard, who has drifted back, his expression dark. As the others resume conversation, I follow his gaze to a spot just above us, between the poles of the trellis, where a large barn spider has crafted a web in front of the motion sensor light. It moves toward a stink bug, slowly, carefully, spinning it in circles, wrapping it in a silk prison.

THE PARTY GUEST

When you've got so much, it can be hard to keep track of it all. Take the Van Ness estate, for example. It's so large, acres and acres of vineyards and endless stretches of woods. Even if you had an entire team of security guards, they couldn't cover all the territory. You wouldn't be able to train surveillance cameras on every square foot of the grounds.

There are many areas that could prove dangerous. Loose, rocky inclines where someone could trip and fall. The lake, snaking through the land, with waterfall currents strong enough to pull you off course. One could get lost for days without a map.

It attracts everything, this kind of place. Weeds, wildflowers, spiders, mice, skunks. Deer, foxes, or coyotes who prowl and stalk their prey all through the night where the grass grows wild and the trees have taken over.

But with a little knowledge, you can maneuver around more easily. Slip into parts only a few people know exist. Keep yourself entertained until the real festivities begin. When they do, they'll be sure to end on a big bang. The Van Nesses would have it no other way.

ELLE

I take my place at one end of the table and unfold my cloth napkin, deep purple and monogrammed with VN. Through the flickering light of the candles, I admire the view of everyone chatting and drinking and settling in. With Zach and Lauren on one side, Harper and Lucas on the other, and Richard at the head across from me, there's a symmetry with six of us again, balance.

Zach, the gentleman that he is, made a show of waiting for Lauren to sit and pushing in her chair, as Richard had done for me. But Harper sneers at anything of the sort. She wants nothing to do with traditional chivalry, claims it's anti-feminist. When I changed my last name to Van Ness, she told me I was caving to the patriarchy. But I didn't change it because the world expected me to. I changed it because I'm part of a family now, a unit, and I wanted to make sure they knew I was all-in.

Now I have a second daughter, Mom had said to me after Richard and I took our vows. She insisted I call her Mom—and so I did. She made me feel more loved than my own mother ever did. And now it's my job to carry out her wishes like I know she would've wanted, to keep her traditions alive.

I clear my throat to get their attention. "Before Linnet brings out the dinner, does anyone have any questions about the party on Saturday?"

"We really have to turn thirty-five on Linnet's cooking?" Harper mutters to Richard.

"We'll be having scallops and steak—Richard and Harper's favorites—and a fresh garden pesto pasta for the vegetarians in the group. Catered, of course"—I stare pointedly at Harper—"so you don't have to worry about Linnet's cooking, which is perfectly fine, by the way."

"Niiiice." Lucas draws out the word to several syllables.

"And in addition to the cake—which is being delivered tomorrow—I've ordered fresh fruit, sorbet, and chocolate truffles with edible gold flecks on top."

"I just hope you didn't clean out our bank account for all this." Richard laughs at his own joke.

"Don't you worry, honey," I say sweetly. And then add, still in my best light tone, "Besides, you'd know if I did."

Richard's in charge of the finances. He obsesses over budgets, keeps intense track of expenses, investments. He's never complained about my spending or tried to limit my access to any of our accounts, but every once in a while he'll make a comment—"So you and Lacey like that new tapas place?" or "What book caught your eye now?"—that reminds me I'm essentially living in a fishbowl, every twist and turn I make on display.

"Is anyone famous coming?" Lauren asks, then laughs awkwardly and takes a big gulp of wine to cover it up.

"I told her about that time Richard conned Matt Damon into showing up at your Fourth of July party," Zach explains with a shrug.

"For all of ten minutes," Richard adds. "Until Elle's friend threw herself at him and scared him away."

"Well, I'm sure everyone will behave themselves this time," I say. Maria wasn't my friend then, and Richard knows she isn't now. Her father is a major hedge funder so we had no choice but to invite her. "And there are no Matt Damons on the list, sorry, Lauren." I smile at her.

"None of our friends on the list, either, apparently," Harper says.

None of them will be there because up until a couple of weeks ago, Harper and Lucas weren't even supposed to come. But when they changed their minds, I improvised the best I could.

"Don't worry, Harper," I say. "I'll make sure this birthday is unforgettable."

Linnet brings out the appetizer, three butternut squash ravioli in a light brown butter sauce, topped with crispy walnuts and sage. With the exception of Lucas, everyone eats slowly, savoring each bite. The evening has a nice haze about it. Even Harper's jab passes over me and evaporates into the air. Actions have consequences, and if she wants to spend her life being bitter and backstabbing, karma will eventually catch up. I do believe that.

I rest my chin on my hands and gaze at Lauren next to me. She's tuned into the conversation, but content to sit back and observe, a good complement to Zach, who was born for the spotlight.

"Lauren, why don't you tell us more about yourself? You're a writer?" I ask. "I've always wanted to write, but I've never found the time."

She seems startled at her name. "I'm actually a journalist."

"Can you even make money in journalism anymore?" Richard asks.

Zach rolls right past the comment. "She writes for the *Times*."

"I can't read or watch the news these days," I say. "It's so depressing."

"And magazines. She's written for a ton of places. Like *GQ*."

Lauren, however, seems embarrassed by the attention. She

tugs at the ends of her hair. "Well, just a movie review," she says quickly.

"So you freelance?" Harper asks.

"Something like that." Lauren dabs at her mouth, leaving a swipe of red lipstick on the purple cloth of her napkin.

"She's freelance for now, but someone's going to snatch her up soon," Zach adds.

"You know, Lauren can answer for herself," Harper says dryly.

"Thanks. It's all good. I'm trying to find my way, I guess."

"We all are," Harper says. "I knew nothing about starting a company. I just had to go for it because I believed in it. Believed in me. And now, here we are."

I lean over and fiddle with my shoe strap so my face doesn't betray my feelings. When Harper starts talking about her business prowess, it takes immense restraint to remain polite the way I was taught in cotillion classes.

"That's great," Lauren says. "You've accomplished so much in so little time."

"She'd accomplish a lot more if she learned how to let someone else do more of the work, let go of all the control," Lucas says. "Build it up, then hand it off, that's what I say."

"What can I say? I'm a workaholic. I could never just sit around all day with nothing to do." Here Harper throws a smug look my way. "My business gives me strength."

My restraint begins to slide away. "Speaking of, how's it going with VNity's new product line?" I can't help but linger on her company name whenever I say it—pronounced "vanity," it's so fitting for Harper. "It wasn't doing so well, I heard? Any better luck?"

Richard shoots me a warning across the table, but Harper's expression doesn't slip, not even a bit. "That was just a small blip," she says. "It's on track to be our best yet."

"And what about that woman who was posting about how

you test your products on animals? It was just so terrible what she was saying about you." I glance around the table. "Do we need more wine?"

No one's glass is empty, but I reach over and top off Lucas's and Lauren's anyway.

"That was a pathetic attempt to get attention," Harper says sharply. "A technicality. One ingredient in one line of lip booster went through a testing lab, which we didn't even know about, and she's all up in arms. You know how it is."

Lauren nods in understanding, and Harper continues. "People are always jealous of you when you're successful. They want a piece of the action. One had the nerve after Mother died to claim Mother had been sending money to them—for no reason—and she thought we should keep doing it."

"For no reason?" Lauren's attention is fully turned toward Harper, clearly drawn into her orbit. I can understand why. I used to admire Harper's sass, her confidence, the way she took what she wanted, no apologies. I was born trying to please, trying to measure up to my parents, a doctor and an attorney always out saving the world and making sure everyone knew about it. I thought I could learn something from her. And I did. I just learned it the hard way.

"No reason, no proof." Harper leans in. "They just throw darts in the dark, hoping to hit a target, any target."

"So what did you do?"

But it's Richard who answers Lauren with a shrug. "Ignored it. You can't open the door even a sliver with these people, or they'll slip right in and refuse to leave."

HARPER

Six beautiful people around an elegant table on a crisp fall night, celebrating a birthday. That's how it appears. The second course has been served, the wineglasses have been filled and refilled, and there's a feeling of promise in the air.

But look closer, and you'll find that Zach's too drunk, that his glass has been refilled more than the others. That Lucas and I haven't had sex in months. That my twin is exhausted. That Elle is trying too hard to fill the void Mother left.

We're all good at faking it, at pretending, at covering it up.

I wonder what Lauren thinks of us, the Van Nesses, if she can tell what we're all hiding.

Zach addresses Richard and me. "Thirty-five years, huh? That's a big one. How *are* you two feeling about it?"

Richard adjusts his glasses. "It's just a number. Isn't that what we're supposed to say?"

"Or, 'You're only as old as you feel,'" I add.

"Ah, you two. I love you guys." Zach's words are slippery from all the wine. "I love this wine, too. And this house."

Richard shoots me a look, but there's no way Zach knows. He just gets sappy when he drinks. "This house is ridiculous," I say. I never understood why Mother was always so adamant about keeping it, and the wine business, when it's entirely impractical.

"I have to disagree," Zach says. "It's big and has a flair about it. Like we're in that old *Clue* movie."

Richard's lips twitch up just a little. "Harper Van Ness, on the terrace, with the butter knife."

"I prefer a fork, actually. Right in the eye."

Zach groans, then tilts back in his chair and points out to Lauren the English ivy clinging to the sides of the house.

"So vicious," Richard says to me, brushing back his hair, which has gotten longer and curls slightly at the end. There are circles under his eyes. My twin hasn't been getting much sleep. "I think poison is more my style."

"But who would you kill?" I ask him, tapping my cheek thoughtfully.

As if on cue, Elle's voice trails down from the other end of the table. "What are you two conspiring about over there?"

I raise an eyebrow at Richard and pick up my fork. He could bristle at me for joking about his wife but instead he laughs. Hard.

Elle glares at the sound.

"Just admiring the silverware," I call down to her.

Richard laughs again.

At the other end of the table, Lucas has started rattling on about smart homes. "We could really make this place wired. Blinds, thermostats, appliances, music. It would be intense." I could save them, but Elle is sitting in Mother's old place and acting a little too comfortable about it. "Why bother to do something that a computer can do ten times faster? Man, in a few years, we'll all have robot maids who can cook this food for us," he's saying.

Once we finish our dinner, Richard brings back two more bottles of wine from the bar. He removes a small silver corkscrew from his pocket, twists it into one of the corks. One confident tug, and the cork escapes, releasing a small, satisfied sigh.

"Oh wow, the twenty-year?" I ask, checking the label. "This *must* be a special occasion."

"Only the best for you, my favorite sister." Richard hands me a hefty pour.

I bring the glass to my nose, inhale black cherry, pepper, hints of tobacco. I swirl it around, creating small waves, observing them lap the sides.

Lauren drinks from hers and immediately sets it down. I can see her fighting back a cringe, and I hide a smile as I sip mine. Port isn't for everyone.

I savor its finish and gaze out beyond the table, the terrace, where darkness has pressed its way in from the gardens and grounds. We are the only light for miles, our little dinner party sticking out like Las Vegas in the desert.

Anyone could be out there.

But no one is, I remind myself with another sip. The estate is far from the city, from the mobs of people zipping past each and every day, from the cloud of dread that's been hovering over me for weeks now. I came here to de-stress after VNity's latest product line failed, to get away from the pressures. I haven't been myself since Mother's death, and it's starting to take its toll. I tell my followers all the time they have to listen to their bodies, their souls, know when to pause. This weekend in the middle of nowhere is *exactly* what I need for me—and for the brand. I'll have to write about the importance of self-care for our site and use this retreat as an example.

My name tugs me back to the conversation. Zach is staring at me expectantly, illuminated by the candlelight.

"What?" I ask.

"The dessert wines. They're always your favorite," he says.

"Is it time for a tasting?" I ask.

To be a true sommelier, Mother always told us, we had to

sharpen our nose, exercise it like a muscle. She would walk us around the estate, tell us to focus on the smells. Call them out one by one. Soil, sap, flowers, spice.

It worked. I can close my eyes, sip the wine, sift everything out like a fucking magician—tobacco here, raspberry there, ladies and gentlemen, let me take a bow.

"Is it ever not?" Zach asks.

On cue, the patio door slides open, and Bill and Linnet come out to clear the table. "Done, miss?" Linnet asks me. Her face is neutral, but she takes it personally when we don't finish our food, always has. She loved our mother, was loyal to her, but she would've been perfectly happy to do without us kids. Linnet's not the warm, loving second-mother type—she treated us like unruly pets. Of course, we weren't always the sweetest children. Zach used to sneak up on her when she was vacuuming and scare her just to hear her curse, and Richard and I once put a worm in her socks. Still, they should both be grateful we've kept them on.

"Yes, you can take it. And can you check the filter on the refrigerator? This water tastes stale."

"Of course, ma'am."

"Switching to water already?" Richard asks, skeptical.

"No, but you can never stay hydrated enough," I say, invoking my sales persona. "Your skin is an organ. You have to take care of it so it will take care of you."

My words echo back at me—*take care of it so it will take care of you*. I make a mental note to remember that line for a future VNity video. I wonder if there's a National Hydration Day we can take advantage of. If there isn't, we'll create it. Hashtag WaterIsLife.

Zach nods at Lauren's glass, which is still full. "Babe, if you don't like the wine, don't drink it."

It's quiet for a moment. Lauren shifts in her seat, but she

shakes her head. "No, no, it's fine," she says, then makes a show of sipping it.

I smile to myself. It's always interesting to observe people's relationship to wine, the way they react to a sophisticated blend versus an overly saturated strawberry "hot tub" wine, if they sip or slurp, what labels they gravitate toward. All of it can tell you a lot about how well they were bred. And yes, we all notice. Richard broke up with his girlfriend Jennifer because she put ice cubes in her wine the first time he brought her here.

"Let's break into some of Mother's private collection," I say, pressing my palms to the table. "It's a special occasion, after all. They aren't my favorite, but Lauren might enjoy the ice wines. They're sweet."

"That's our specialty. Sweet as sweet can be," Zach says to Lauren. "Like you."

To her credit, Lauren rolls her eyes and takes a larger gulp of wine. This time, she swallows it down like a pro.

"Zach's right. Dessert wines are our best business. Especially the ice wines, which are made from grapes that have frozen on the vine." Richard pushes up his glasses, which reflect the dancing candlelight. "It's cold up here. We're almost too far north for grapes to thrive at all. So we work with the toughest grapes. The ones that have adapted to their surroundings to survive."

"Too much chatter," Lucas says, as if he's not been blabbering on all dinner. "Let's get to these wines."

Lauren laughs once and fiddles with her necklace, and my husband gives her a big wink. Apparently Lucas has decided to make the new girl feel right at home.

"Let's send Lauren down to pick one out," I say. "Like a challenge."

Elle furrows her brow. "Oh, come on. You don't want to send her down into that dark cellar all alone."

Zach laughs. "Nice try, Elle. But Lauren's not afraid." He elbows her. "Right, babe?"

I can't help but enjoy the variety of emotions flashing on Lauren's face. She's worried about picking the right wine. She wants to impress all of us. But underneath all of that, there's something else, too. Something I can't put a finger on. A weird kind of confidence, like Lauren knows something I don't, something I should.

"Sure, I can do that," she says.

LAUREN

At the end of a hallway, Zach unlocks a massive dead bolt and throws open a door to reveal a stone staircase descending into darkness. My palms itch, the way they did as a kid whenever my mother forced me to go down into our basement to get a spare lightbulb or can of vegetables. Wispy spiderwebs in my face, strange noises in the corners.

I catch Zach's eye.

"Don't worry, no one's going to bite you," he says.

"She seems nervous," Harper says, cocking her head as she surveys me.

"Lauren?" Zach waves his hand in dismissal. "Nah, she's a good sport. Aren't you, babe?"

He's grinning, but I can tell that he's counting on me. And I *had* been the one to ask him what I could do to fit in, to make his family love me.

"I'm good." I try to mimic Harper's confidence. "Just tell me what I'm looking for."

Zach presses a button on the wall and lights illuminate the stairwell, which curves around so I can't make out the bottom.

"The dessert wines are at the back," Harper says with a

smile. "You'll see them. The bottles are smaller. Whatever suits your fancy."

"When you say the back, do you mean—"

"And don't take any bottles from the first three racks," she adds. "Some of those are worth thousands of dollars."

"A bottle?" I ask.

She looks at me with disgust. "Just avoid those. Now, go."

Her tone is commanding—*Fetch, little girl. Fetch*—and I feel myself getting prickly. I shake it off and start my descent.

The stone steps are uneven and worn down, like they've been traversed thousands of times, and a constant draft curls around my ankles like a needy cat. I wobble in my heels, my knees tangling in the fabric of my dress, and set my palms against the walls for balance. They're cool and seemingly miles thick. Someone could scream down here and you'd never hear them.

At the bottom, the staircase opens to a large room with at least a dozen racks of wine. I run my hands along the ones in the first rack, wondering just how much money I've touched, then move farther back like Harper instructed. She's right—I wouldn't be able to tell a thousand-dollar bottle from a fifteen-dollar one—but I'm guessing the Van Nesses don't keep drugstore quality wine in their private stash anyway.

I walk past rows and rows of bottles. On the end of each rack is a large thermometer to track the temperature. It's a balmy fifty-five degrees, but in my dress, it feels more like forty. I stop between the last racks and tug out a bottle. Then another. Are they smaller than the others? None of them seem to be dessert wines. The labels mean nothing to me. I'm the girl who selects her wine by the cutest animal on the logo. And yet here I am, and they're all upstairs waiting for me, and it feels like this is a test.

"If you're going to cut it in this family, Brady, you need to step up your game," I mutter to myself. My voice sounds strange down here, like the shadows suck up all the sound, and where the racks stop and the cellar continues in the dark, there's a slow, rhythmic dripping coming from that darkness and a small blinking red light.

I pace up and down the rows, forcing myself to ignore the noises, and finally, within the second-to-last rack, I find smaller bottles labeled "dessert wine." I pick one with a five-year-old date that has a gold-embossed Van Ness logo, instead of the usual deep purple.

As I turn to go, I notice a portrait hanging on the wall, a painting of a man with tense eyes and a thick mustache, sitting on a large formal green armchair, a pointer dog resting on his lap. The plate underneath reads Benson Van Ness.

I step closer, peering into his eyes, trying to decide if Zach looks like him at all, and relieved that he doesn't.

"Mean-looking bastard, isn't he?"

I jump, the bottle slipping from my grasp. Miraculously, it doesn't break, but it thumps to the ground and rolls under a rack.

"Sorry, I thought you heard me." Lucas kneels down, fishes for the bottle. "They make these things pretty durable."

He gets up and stands beside me, rolling the bottle in his hands. He's taken off his suit jacket and tie since dinner and rolled up his sleeves. His dress shirt hints at the defined muscles beneath.

He angles his head and examines the portrait, raps it with his knuckle. "This here is their great-grandfather. The dude who started this whole place. Harper says he was a holy bastard. He hated Harper's grandmother, his daughter-in-law. Thought she wasn't good enough for the family." He rubs his beard and laughs bitterly. "Probably turning over in his grave over me."

"Why?" I ask as he passes me the bottle, the warmth of his hand against mine surprising in the cold of the cellar. I read the recent article in *The New York Times* business section about the sale of Lucas's second tech start-up to Microsoft a few months ago. If Lucas isn't good enough for the Van Nesses, then I haven't a hope or a prayer. "You're incredibly successful," I tell him.

He stares at me then like he's just seeing me. "Doesn't matter," he eventually says. He gestures again at the painting. "That's why they've got the bloodline thing."

"The bloodline thing?" I say, looking to him for an explanation.

"This guy," he whispers, leaning in so I can smell his cologne, "hated his daughter-in-law so much he made it so only bloodline family can inherit the land."

"Really? What did she do?" I whisper back, unable to resist a good story.

Lucas squints at the painting as though Benson Van Ness might answer himself. "Nothing, far as I know. He thought she was a gold digger, out for their money. But Harper says it was her grandfather who was the irresponsible one—horse racing, mostly."

He moves closer. I step back into the corner, my hair snagging on the rough stone next to me. Lucas reaches out an arm and for a dizzying second, I think he's going to pull me to him.

But his arm flies past, and his hand slams against the wall.

"Cricket," he says softly, brushing off his palm.

HARPER

We're in the library when Lauren returns from the cellar. I expected her to pick one of the ice wines that will make everyone's teeth hurt, but she found one of our hand-harvested Riesling dessert bottles that is one of my favorites.

"Looks like you survived the cellar…" My words trail off as I see my husband behind her, wiping blood from his hands. "I thought you said you were going to the bathroom," I say with a cocked eyebrow as he sits next to me on the couch.

"I did. But then I figured I'd save Lauren from the crickets, you know, be my charming self." He's acting casual, as if daring me to challenge this version of events.

I look between him and Lauren as he settles onto the couch. He's quiet, studying her carefully, like he's rooting for her. He always does like to bet on the underdog.

Bill has tended to the fire, and Linnet brings in a tray of fruit and petit fours before we dismiss her for the evening. Lauren takes the hard-backed chair next to Zach's.

The fire cracks, snaps, like it's a whip goading me. "I think Lauren needs to do a tasting. The Van Ness way."

Lauren tugs at the ends of her hair and smiles nervously. Maybe she thought her work here tonight was done.

"What's the Van Ness way?" she asks, glancing at Zach, but he's busy opening the wine she brought up.

I motion for her to move her chair closer to the coffee table. She drags it forward then sits again, tentatively, like the chair might bite. Smooths down her dress, rubbing her thumb across one of the velvet leaves on the skirt.

Richard is the one who says, "Zach, please do the honors."

Zach finishes uncorking the bottle and frowns. "Ah, come on, Richard. Maybe we should just drink and chat."

"Where's the fun in that?" Richard says, gesturing to Lauren. "You know this is the way we always do things."

Zach hesitates, but then he caves, like he always does, eager to please us, his older siblings. He moves behind Lauren, massages her shoulders briefly, then puts his hands over her eyes.

"I've always been terrible at pin-the-tail-on-the-donkey," Lauren jokes, biting her lip.

"Relax," Zach says. "You'll be fine."

Once I'm sure she can't see, I fetch the bottle of our sparkling grape juice I stashed under the couch while Lauren was in the cellar. I put my finger to my lips to signal to the others before pouring it into a sherry glass.

"When you're blindfolded, your smell and taste are enhanced," I say somberly.

I walk around the table and grasp one of Lauren's hands, guiding the glass into it. She tips the juice toward her and smells it slowly.

Elle's standing off to the side, arms crossed, her mouth a thin line. She doesn't approve of my game, but she won't say anything because Zach agreed. His hands are tight against Lauren's eyes, making sure she doesn't peek as she tilts the glass up to her mouth and takes a sip.

"Let it sit on your tongue," Richard says. "Tease the sugars out."

"It's good," she finally says.

I bite my hand, then say, "Any flavors, smells, stand out to you?"

She takes another sip. "Maybe honey?"

"Good. Honey notes," Richard says. "What about the bark? Do you get any of the bark on your palate?"

"Yes," she says automatically.

A laugh bubbles up—I can't help it—and Elle finally bursts. "Enough." She stomps over and bats at Zach's hands, pushes them away from Lauren. "Stop it."

Lauren blinks, confused. Part of her eyeliner on one eye has smeared, making her look off-kilter.

"They're messing with you, Lauren," Elle says, holding up the grape juice. "Because they are mean."

Lauren turns bright red.

"Ah, come on, Elle. Just a joke," Zach says. He kisses the top of Lauren's head. "Lauren's a good sport."

Elle picks up the tray of desserts. "I'm ready to turn in. Plenty of weekend ahead," she says testily. "No need to use up all the *fun* in one night." She stretches out a hand for my glass, but I ignore it and pour some of the dessert wine Lauren brought up from the cellar.

Despite the long drive, I'm not tired. I could ask Lucas to watch a movie with me in the theater, but he's being distant again, as he has been lately, pulling away at random moments. After today's trip, he would probably drift off twenty minutes into it anyway.

"Richard?" I lift the bottle, but he shakes his head and yawns.

"Zach? You'll stay up with me, won't you?" I cross the room, edge between him and Lauren, and top off his glass, throw him my best sad eyes.

He rubs his face, probably tired from a day of work and the travel, but Zach's never been good at saying no. "Sure, we can hang with you for a little while," he says, looking to Lauren.

"It's fine if you want to stay up," she says, casual, but she's trying to hide that the prank rankled her. "But I've got one more thing to do for work."

"You can follow us up, Lauren." Elle loops arms with her. "It's easy to get lost in all those hallways."

I watch them leave the room, talking low like they are old pals.

Already sides are being taken.

Once everyone is gone, I set the wine bottle on the coffee table in front of Zach and draw the blinds closed. The fire's dying, and I'm too lazy to throw on another log, so I grab a soft plaid blanket from a basket in the corner.

He stretches, sighs. "It's good to be back here."

"Yeah, you said that at dinner," I say, and it sounds crabbier than I intended. But already I can feel the effect of being inside these walls. Zach has such starry-eyed memories of this place, of being a kid here, running wild and free. But all I remember are Mother's judgments. I keep expecting her ghost to emerge from the tapestries with a list of all her grievances and a hat to hide my head of unruly hair.

"You don't think so?" he asks me.

I stare into the fire. "It's complicated." The Riesling has warmed me, and I find myself being more honest than I normally would. Not that Zach will pry further. He loves avoiding complications, not entertaining them.

He flips through Mother's records, slides one out, and holds it with two fingers at the edges. "Let's do some classic vinyl, shall we?" He sets it on the turntable and the needle arm moves, descends, as the table starts spinning. Aretha Franklin's soulful voice wafts low through the speakers.

"So what do you think of Lauren? Do you think Mom

would've liked her?" He kicks off his shoes and rests his legs on the coffee table, leans back into the couch and hums along to the music. He's unbuttoned the top of his shirt.

"Oh, I'm sure they would be already linking arms, skipping around the gardens, sharing secrets and dreams together."

He snorts. "Bullshit. Mother would've put her through a three-part stamina and mind test just to see if she's okay to walk through the front door."

"Only three parts?"

"She could be tough, couldn't she?" Zach closes his eyes, so he doesn't see the disbelief on my face.

Tough? Mother let him get away with everything. *I* was the one she pushed, judged, criticized, but Zach and Richard walked down easy street. Especially Zach, Mother's golden child. He could set fire to my hair and she'd just rap him on the back of the hand and tell him to stop playing with matches.

"But yeah, I think Lauren's a keeper," he says.

I poke him with my foot. "Don't you say that about every girl?"

He smiles briefly, but then his expression turns serious. "Nah, this is different, Harper."

"Okay, well, don't go investing all *my* life's savings into this girl yet." I use my sarcastic tone, but I'm only half kidding. That's all we need is for Zach to get too in his head and do something reckless this weekend.

He runs his fingers through his thick head of hair. He's got the same effortless looks as Richard, chiseled features, bright eyes, great metabolism. We all inherited Mother's long nose, but it's more forgiving on the men. When my brothers turn eighty-five, no one will think to call them old or out of touch or ugly. No one will give a half second's thought of saying anything as horrible as some of the stuff people post online about women every day right here, right now.

"Just no more hazing," Zach says. "I feel bad about the grape juice thing."

"You don't seem too torn up about it," I say, and he smiles. "Besides, someone has to give her the stamina test now that Mother's gone."

"Go easy on her at least. This should be a relaxing couple of days. No drama. Promise?"

I take one last sip of my wine and set the glass on the table. "Who, me? You think I would dare to ruin your perfect weekend getaway?"

But Zach is distracted now. At first I think he's just intently listening to the music, but then he points to my phone on the coffee table. "That thing keeps lighting up."

It's only now I notice it, a string of notifications from Instagram, one piling on top of the other like a terrible game of Mahjongg. Somehow I know it can't be good. And the cloud of dread that's been following me around for weeks suddenly starts pouring down rain.

THE PARTY GUEST

Everything is more daunting in the darkness. All our problems seem worse late at night, when we should be in bed, when we should be sleeping, tucked safe and warm on feathers.

It's then we can't see clearly. It's then we meet our demons.

Aren't we all the same in this way? We get lonely, fearful, depressed. We wake from terrible dreams we can't quite remember. We dwell on our mistakes and our flaws. Even the Van Nesses have troubles, worries, that make them punch their feather pillows at 3:00 a.m., sweat between their Egyptian cotton sheets.

But they would never compare themselves to someone like me. They can't see our similarities, and even if they did, they wouldn't admit it, or care.

I'm invisible to them. I'm a shadow in the darkness, a flicker of movement in the corner of their eye. Right there, but not important enough to really look at, to notice.

This weekend, though, that's just fine by me. Because being invisible can also have its benefits.

ELLE

I'm surprised Richard came upstairs instead of staying with Harper. He seems wide awake, hums under his breath as he unbuttons his dress shirt and throws himself across the bed in a T-shirt and boxers. I'm glad to see him relaxing.

"Why don't you put on that slinky silk nightgown I bought you and come over here?" he says.

"Are you kidding? It's too cold up here. I'd be freezing."

He rolls over on his side and props his head up on his hand, watching me change into my pajamas.

"Lauren seems nice," I say as I remove my earrings and put them away in the monogrammed travel jewelry case Mom bought me one year for Christmas. I rub the batch of shea butter body lotion I made a few weeks ago into my arms and chest—making my own creams and soaps has been a hobby of mine since I was a teenager. "Zach seems smitten with her."

"Does that make you jealous?" Richard asks.

"What? No." My spine stiffens. I glance back at him, search his expression. "What a silly thing to say," I tell him before turning back to the mirror. "You all are hilarious with your jokes. You should take them on the road."

When he closes the bathroom door, I slide into bed, feeling

the cool satin against my cheek. I pick my phone up off the nightstand to scroll through social media. I'm sure Mallory has posted photos of our girls' night earlier this week and has noticed I haven't commented on or liked them yet.

But it's a photo of Harper that pops up when my feed refreshes. A heavily filtered selfie—the background is white, so I can't tell when or where she took it—with the caption, This is 35. Hundreds of comments already, including one from the official VNity account that says, Happy birthday to our amazing CEO and founder! You're an inspiration to all women.

"You've got to be kidding me," I mutter. I open the rest of the comments just to eye roll at all her loyal followers gushing about how beautiful she is and how she's changed their lives.

But another type of comment catches my attention.

FRAUD!

There are a flood of similar ones, and my heart starts racing.

Whatta bitch!

Step down now.

#CancelHARPER

And then one with a long URL that says, That may be 35, but THIS is horrifying.

I copy and paste the URL into Safari and find myself at the latest post on *Van Nessity*, an anonymous blog dedicated to our family.

Harper Van Ness: World's Bitchiest Boss?

Uh-oh! Seems our favorite girl HVN is trending again.

An anonymous friend of *Van Nessity* has sent us video and

workplace chat room messages that don't put Ms. Harper in the best light.

In the video, which we've also posted to Twitter, HVN is standing in the middle of the VNity headquarters with a megaphone, calling employees to attention. Yes, you heard that right—a megaphone.

She goes on to tell her 100 percent female workforce that they need to understand the brand of VNity and "live it, even if it means you are on call 24/7. This isn't a job, it's your life."

We've also got screenshots of an internal VNity chat room that show HVN requiring employees to work overtime, mocking an intern's Southern accent, and warning people to watch what they eat. "If I catch one whiff of fast food grease in this place, I will conduct a witch hunt."

It seems, my friends, that VNity—which, as we all know, touts to all that it's a feminist company—is actually an incredibly toxic work environment. (Like, that black sludge you find crusted to the pipes of toilets kind of toxic.)

Our source tells us she's "tired of all the smoke and mirrors. VNity is the opposite of a health and wellness organization, and Harper Van Ness needs to be held accountable for her actions. She's a hypocrite on the grandest scale."

HVN has been having a bad time of it lately. We reported a couple weeks ago when she disappointed her fans—popularly called "ambassadors"—by being a no-show at one of their VIP events. She later posted an apology and a photo of herself with a nasty bruise near her collarbone, claiming she was "sorry to disappoint everyone, but thankfully I'm okay and that's all that matters." Penny Pearson, VNity communications assistant, later issued a vague statement that Harper was accosted on her way to the event, though no details were released. I'm getting some interesting emails about that but can't spill any beans quite yet.

I'm pretty sure the ambassadors of VNity will come out in droves to defend their fave. But I want to hear from you! What side are YOU on? Should we cancel Harper Van Ness? Or are we all being unfair to our beloved beauty mogul? Email me your thoughts!

Posted by Kat Sparks

I scroll through the blog comments. Sapphire_999 wrote, Cancel her! She'll never admit guilt, and I can't help but quietly laugh to myself. It is, as my friend Mia says when she orders a peanut butter strawberry smoothie at the gym, a "guilty pleasure."

My pleasure grows the longer I scroll. Harper brings out the worst in me. She's a two-faced liar, pretending to be humble and care about female empowerment for all her fans but in reality treating the women she's closest to like trash. Everything about her is fake, all the little stories she shares about her life are polished for her *image*. Even after she was attacked at her office, she seemed more interested in posting about it and gaining sympathy than she was in finding the person who did it. I'm only surprised she's fooled everyone as long as she has.

"What are you so engrossed in over here?" Richard suddenly plops down into bed next to me and looks over at my screen.

"Nothing," I say, trying to close out the tab.

His smile disappears. "You're reading that trash site?"

"There's something new. About Harper." I hesitate, knowing how defensive of her he can be. "You should probably see it."

He pushes my phone away. "Nothing but lies. After everything she's been through lately, they can't leave her alone?"

The double standard has always gotten to me. If I have one

too many glasses of wine at a party, Richard's on me for weeks about it. But Harper can single-handedly destroy an empire and it's all, *Give her a break, she's had a rough day.* Still, I'm betting if the comments and shares keep coming like they are, the rumors will hit bigger publications tomorrow and it will be harder for Richard to ignore.

"I just think it's important to keep up on what people are saying, Richard."

He takes my phone and sets it on the nightstand and nuzzles my neck. "But when you click on it, you just give them more traffic," he whispers in my ear.

He kisses me, tentatively, a quick peck, and then again, harder, when I don't protest. Our first kiss had been here, at the estate. *Would you mind if I...?* he'd said, and pointed at my lips, like he'd forgotten the word for it, or was too afraid to say it. It was charmingly formal, strangely sweet, and even though it wasn't a sweep-me-off-my-feet kiss, I liked the way Richard saw me in that moment, that he was nervous. I was good enough—no, better than good—in his eyes. Richard's admiration that night made me feel like I'd finally been seen.

I accept the kiss but gently push him away. "I'm just really tired, hon. Tomorrow?"

I switch the light off before the disappointment floods his face. I'm sure he assumed we would have sex tonight, especially given our talk about trying for kids soon. But I have too many things on my mind right now, too many thoughts racing around. How big is this story going to get? Why did it post tonight? Has Harper seen it yet?

There's silence for a moment, and then rustling as Richard gets up. I hear him pull on pants. The door clicks open, shuts. When I'm certain he's gone, I pick up my phone to scroll again.

LAUREN

I wake from a bad dream, panting, and take a deep breath. Zach's snoring lightly next to me. I check the time on the clock on the nightstand, just after 1:00 a.m., and fling Zach's leg off me. He doesn't even stir.

It's too cloudy for the moon to shine through the window. We are in the middle of nowhere—nothing outside but the dark and the coyotes. But a small green glowing night-light under a desk helps guide me to the armchair on the other side of the massive room. I move all the clothes Zach tossed there and sit, pulling a small flannel throw over me. I don't feel great about the evening. Harper's mocking laugh. The three Van Ness siblings grinning once Zach took his hands away from my eyes. The drink Harper handed me *had* tasted like grape juice, but I couldn't very well say that. If I said it tasted like grapes, it would have been an insult. They backed me into a corner. It had all been a setup.

When I mentioned it to Zach before bed, he brushed it off. *A little family hazing is all. They wouldn't tease you if they didn't like you.*

I'm not sure I believe him.

I slide my leg across the plump footrest, run my fingers down the gold buttons of the chair's seam. Unplug my phone from the wall and see a text from Maisie.

How's it going? Call me tomorrow! Want deets!

I know the details she wants. If she hadn't planted the idea of a proposal in my head, I would've never thought it. Zach and I have only been dating for six months. I never thought we'd last this long, that we'd get serious so fast.

There were hundreds of people at the party the night we met. Models in sequined dresses or crop tops, celebrities, influencers—everyone pulsing to the music, drinking cocktails, swapping pills and joints. Somewhere in the crowd was Maisie, an "atmosphere model," paid to be a living, breathing, gorgeous decoration to complete the mirage. I'd looked her up immediately when I moved to New York early in the year, and she'd been helping me find a job, get a room. She'd been a senior when I was a freshman—smart, beautiful, homecoming queen. I knew she'd get out of our shitty town and go on to greatness. And when we met over cosmopolitans at a breathtaking rooftop bar, she told me, *There's enough money to go around. You just have to find it.* She introduced me to a different world.

That night, the reporter in me was intrigued by this slice of life, these people, but I was in over my head, out of my league. I slipped outside on a balcony for fresh air, and when I turned around, Zach was standing there in the shadows. *Do you hate these things as much as I do?*

It was easy enough to get swept away in the grand charm of Zach Van Ness. Even if I expected him at any moment to move on to someone else, there was a small part of me that wanted to believe in fairy tales and happily-ever-afters. But I haven't told a soul back in Delaware about us, including my parents, and Zach doesn't ask questions about my family either. Sometimes, I think he doesn't want to know, and maybe that's for the best. But it's like we're living in a delicate bubble, floating around, waiting for it to pop.

The longer we're together, though, the more complicated things get. I squeeze my eyes shut. *What would you do if he did propose, Brady? What would your answer be? And would you tell him the truth about you?*

I put my phone away. That kind of light isn't going to help my brain go back to sleep, and I already worked enough when I came upstairs after the tasting prank.

I tug on my oversized sweater and slippers to go get some water. The house is quiet as I step into the hall, my slippers softening the sound of my footsteps on the hardwood floors.

At the bottom of the stairs, the grandfather clock ticks in the entryway like it's judging me. *Tsk, tsk, tsk, tsk.* The heavy gold pendulum like a head shaking that I just won't do. Trust me, I already know, I want to tell it.

The kitchen is dark except for a small light over the range, but in that dim glow I can tell everything's been cleaned from dinner. The countertops are shiny and immaculate, a fresh bouquet sits in the center of the island. I find a glass in one of the overhead cabinets and fill it with cold water. The refrigerator kicks on, whirring and humming, and there's a crunch as ice falls into the freezer tray.

Zach had briefly showed me one wing of the house before dinner, but not the other. I finish my water and make my way to it, awake enough now that I won't be able to go back to bed anyway. Maybe I'll learn something new about Zach, or about the family, how to get in their good graces, or not.

This side feels less lived-in somehow. It's colder and mustier, and more doors are closed. I open a few, the slight creaks of the hinges feeling magnified in the silence. Some of the rooms are like a museum, adorned with beautiful artworks, antique furniture, but in others, all I make out are large forms draped with cloths like ghosts.

On the way back to the main staircase, a small stained-glass lamp catches my eye in a room closest to the entryway. It casts a soft gleam in the formal sitting area, like the room is awaiting visitors. I step inside and jump, thinking someone's there before realizing it's just my reflection in a large mirror on the wall to the left.

As I walk across the room, I run my fingers along the ivory keys of the grand piano, not daring to press any of them, trace circles in the velvet upholstery of an armchair, imagining Katrina Van Ness entertaining senators, presidents, billionaires here.

I've always been drawn to things that aren't mine. The tendency comes from my dad, from observing him take all the stuff people would bring to his pawnshop, things they didn't want to part with but had to, the looks in their eyes as they left empty-handed. When they were gone…how it felt just to hold the diamond rings or the glass vase or the gold watch.

To pretend they were mine.

Just before I step back into the hall, I hear a voice in the foyer.

I freeze. I thought everyone was asleep. I move back into the room and wait inside the doorway.

"I can't believe this." Harper's talking rapidly, her voice up and down in pitch. She's agitated. "Honestly…it's all a bunch of *lies*." My pulse quickens. I wonder if she's on the phone, but then I hear a man's voice—Richard.

"Shh," Richard says. "You want to wake the whole house?"

"They're all drunk anyway," she says.

They continue their conversation in low murmurs, and I only hear random words. "Fucking trolls… I would never…" I stand perfectly still, willing them to leave until a loud bang startles me.

Harper curses. "God, there's too much junk! I hate this house. The sooner we're rid of it, the better."

"Speaking of"—Richard's voice is suddenly loud enough for me to hear again—"have you talked to Zach?"

My body tenses at the mention of Zach's name. I shift forward, watching the hallway outside the door intently to make sure I don't cast a shadow.

"Not yet." Harper says something else I can't hear, then laughs.

"So I always have to be the bad guy?" Richard asks.

Her voice fades out and in again. "…so good at it."

"He's going to hate us. If this deal—"

Harper cuts him off with a harsh whisper. She says something else I miss. Their footsteps echo as they climb upstairs, their voices getting farther and farther away.

I wait, holding my breath, my thoughts fighting with each other. Does this mean what it sounds like? They're selling the house? They're cutting out Zach from the decision?

A moment later, silence descends once more.

W-JKA BREAKING NEWS

"It's a birthday gone bad," reports neighbor as scene unfolds at Van Ness winery

SUNDAY, October 15—Details of the tragedy at the Van Ness family estate are still unfolding this morning, but early reports confirm two deaths. Officers on the scene have not released the identity of the deceased or the manner of their deaths, though one source told us a gun was taken into evidence. Officials also reported an abandoned car on the estate that does not appear to belong to the Van Ness family.

Attempts to contact any of the siblings—Richard, Harper, or Zachary—have been unsuccessful.

Local residents we talked to say the Van Ness annual birthday celebration, while not open to the public, was one they looked forward to each year because of the elaborate fireworks displays. Representatives from Private Pyrotechnics, Inc., confirm that the show was canceled this year due to the weather.

"I guess this is a birthday gone bad," one community member commented when she heard of the tragedy. "Let's just hope it isn't any worse than it appears."

Stay tuned as we continue to report on this tragedy.

FRIDAY

The Day before the Party

ELLE

We all slept in. In the kitchen, Linnet left a large platter of bagels and pastries, with fresh lox and dips and spreads in the refrigerator. I take another peek at the cake from the best bakery in the Finger Lakes, delivered this morning in a big pink box. Sculpted flowers surround a bunch of blown-sugar purple grapes in the center, so perfect they look like the most fragile glass, ready to shatter at any moment. It's a work of art.

I make myself a latte with extra hot foamy milk and a pinch of caramel and settle on one of the stools at the kitchen island with my laptop. I need to check in with the fireworks guys to ensure they're on track for the party. Food, music, dancing. The terrace, decorated with tea light candles. And then the grand finale fireworks display, lighting up the sky with a boom. It's going to be an unforgettable evening.

Zach pushes through the swinging doors, mid-conversation with Richard. "…even you have to admit her last album wasn't up to par."

They're followed by a freshly showered Lauren, her hair still damp.

"Morning, beautiful!" Zach says when he spots me.

My heart skips at the compliment. I turn to the sink and wash my hands so the others can't see my smile. "There's a raspberry Danish there with your name on it," I say.

"You think of everything." He snatches up the pastry like I knew he would. "I hope Richard knows how lucky he is."

"Of course I do," Richard answers.

I dry my hands and tilt open the blinds above the sink. "I trust you all slept well?" Sunlight streams through the window. It looks like the weather is going to hold out for us.

"I was dead to the world," Zach says. "Until this one gets a call from her editor early in the morning on her day off."

Lauren scrunches her nose as she surveys the tray of pastries. "I'm sorry. She had a question about what I sent her last night. I didn't know my ringer was on."

He kisses the top of her head. "I'm just teasing. She sounded very pleased with you, anyway, so that's a good thing."

"I hope you don't have to work too much while you're here," I say, shutting off the faucet.

Richard smirks. "Better watch out, Lauren. If Elle catches you working too hard, she'll take a ruler to your knuckles."

Zach and Lauren fix their breakfast and cozy up in the nook while Richard pops a sesame seed bagel in the toaster oven, tapping his knife impatiently on the counter as he waits. He opens the refrigerator door and starts rummaging around.

"There's a pitcher of mimosas in there," I say, teasing, because I can tell by the sag under his eyes that he's still feeling the wine from last night. When he finally did come back to bed, his sleep had been restless, tossing and turning, the sheets damp from his sweat.

He groans, grabbing a large bottle of spring water and chugging nearly half of it before recapping it.

"You're getting to be such an old man," Zach tells him.

"Right?" I say, poking Richard in the side. "If you don't watch out, I might even beat you at skeet shooting this morning."

That won't happen—he's way too good, even hungover—but I do love to watch the guys slide on their earmuffs, set up their rifles, every muscle tense and ready right before they yell, *Pull*. I know how much they enjoy pulverizing those clay pigeons, the satisfaction of finding the target, getting the kill.

"Oh, about that," Richard says. He leans against the counter, picking stray seeds from the cutting board and eating them. "Harper wants to take you ladies on a boat ride instead."

"A boat ride?" I repeat. The plan was for all of us to go skeet shooting, have a picnic lunch, stop at the winery for a tasting.

Richard nods, fishes his bagel out of the hot toaster oven with his fingers, and sets it on his plate.

"I feel like Lauren would enjoy skeet shooting, though," I say lightly, trying not to sound difficult. "Plus, it's something for all of us to do together."

Richard carefully stacks the lox on top. "I'm sure she'd also enjoy a boat cruise on the lake."

Yeah, but I won't, I think, but bite my tongue. The last thing I want to do is go out on the water with Harper. I don't know what she might be planning. This estate seems to bring out a wicked side of her. Like the time she stranded Richard and me on a tiny island on the lake, leaving us to get eaten alive by mosquitos, blowing it off as us being stick-in-the-muds when we got mad at her. But Richard always forgives his sister.

I glance over at Lauren, hoping she'll back me up. She's nibbling on her blueberry muffin, but she nods, slowly at first, then more confidently. "Sure. Either sounds fun."

My shoulders grow tight. Of course. Of course Harper wants to change the plans. If I say it's daytime, she'll say it's nighttime. But I should let her have this petty little win. She's grasping at anything to feel in control, since the rest of her life is slowly crumbling. I checked this morning when I got up, and the video of her yelling at her employees is spreading. Even *Cosmo* picked it up in their online buzzworthy news section.

"Okay, then," I say brightly. "I'll make sure Bill gets the boat ready."

"Already have." Richard grabs extra napkins and his water bottle. "I've got to shower and send a couple of emails, look over a few contracts."

I make a face, point my thumbs down.

"I won't be long," he adds, gives me a quick kiss, and heads off, nearly bumping into Lucas on his way out.

Lucas barrels through the doors, yawning, like a bear stumbling out of his cave after hibernation. His hair is sticking up, and he's wearing blue pin-striped pajama pants and a T-shirt that says ALL HAIL OUR A.I. OVERLORDS. He stops at the edge of the island and stretches. He's so tall he's practically eye level with the pans hanging on the rack overhead.

"If I don't eat something soon, I'm going to throw up," he says.

"Help yourself," I say, but he already is. He picks at the pastry tray, touching everything, selecting a bagel on which he spreads an inordinate amount of cream cheese. He gnaws on the bagel, flecks of cream cheese smearing in his beard, puts it down right on the counter, pours himself some orange juice, splashing it. I'd shoot Richard if he acted like this.

I've always thought it strange that Lucas and Harper ended up together. Lucas so into tech, always off on exotic skiing trips around the world, and Harper so into...well, herself, her business summits and wellness retreats. I remember when they were dating long-distance—Lucas in California, Harper in New York—flights back and forth for a couple of years. I assumed it would fizzle out eventually, that one of them would find someone more convenient to be with, but then Lucas surprised us all and moved back east to be with her.

It turned out that they have more similarities than I often give them credit for. Intensely competitive, self-absorbed, driven. I wouldn't trust either one of them as far as I could throw them.

Lucas lets out a massive sneeze and honks into a paper towel. "Something in the air up here. Messing with my sinuses."

"Hm," I say. "Probably ragweed."

He pours a giant mug of coffee and disappears with the promise to take a shower. As I dab up the coffee he dripped on the counter, I glance over at Zach and Lauren, who are whispering to each other.

"So what are you two lovebirds up to this morning?" I ask casually, tossing them a winning smile.

"I told Lauren I'd show her the waterfall."

I prop my elbows on the island. "Oh, that is the best spot on the estate, isn't it?" I considered hiring a professional photographer for the party, let the guests get their photos taken with some of the scenic backdrops. The waterfall would've been perfect. But it's too remote, the path muddy, bug-filled, treacherous. It would be dangerous to hike there in party gowns and heels.

Lauren rinses her plate and mug and stacks them in the dishwasher, leaving no mess. She excuses herself to go get proper walking shoes.

When she's gone, Zach joins me at the kitchen counter. He knocks into me playfully with his hip. "Hey, do me a favor, Elle, will you? I think Lauren's intimidated by everyone. Can you just make sure she feels welcome? Take her under your wing. You're good at that."

"Of course. Absolutely."

He squeezes my arm in thanks, takes one final swig of his coffee and leaves, and I realize I've agreed to something I don't necessarily want to do. Take Lauren under my wing? I don't need another project. But maybe I should help the poor girl out. She needs an ally, someone to make her feel like she belongs. I know what it's like to be alone. There wasn't anything "collective" about my own family growing up, so I found belonging where I could—Girl Scouts when I was a kid, or my Theta sisters in college, and now as a Van Ness.

I load the dishes in the dishwasher, wipe the counter, and slip a CBD oil pill between my lips, washing it down with the rest of my latte. I still remember the birthday weekend the year Richard and I were married. How different it felt coming here as legally part of the family. Lying on a blanket, staring up into the black sky while fireworks burst with color right above me, I felt like the luckiest girl in the world. The Van Nesses had their faults. They had their peculiarities. But I finally had a family like the one I created in the giant dollhouse in my childhood bedroom. I knew I couldn't lose it.

That's why it's so important we're all here this weekend. Without family, without traditions and memories, what are any of us, really?

The perfect weekend is just the beginning.

THE PARTY GUEST

Secret's Edge. That's the original name of this house.

It brings up questions. What is the edge of a secret? Edges can be dangerous. They are places from which you can dangle, fall, slice your skin open.

Secrets, too, can be dangerous. If you keep one for too long, it can hold you hostage, warp and change you. You can become obsessed with keeping it. Do anything to make sure no one discovers it.

What secrets do you have, Richard? What vices are you hiding, Zach? What will you never admit regretting, Harper?

I like to imagine that George Maxwell, the man who built it in 1884, had his own secrets. That he wanted this massive estate in the middle of nowhere to hide inside, to bury them.

The house has been renovated over the years, but the bones remain the same. I've studied the blueprints, seen the way each piece of the house fits with the others like a jigsaw puzzle. From the map of the estate, I know all the roads and paths, the way the lake wraps around one corner of the property like a snake.

I can use it all to my advantage.

HARPER

We forgot to close the drapes. The sun might as well be a flashlight in my damn eyes. I roll over and reach for my phone, only to remember last night, lying in the dark watching it light up, ping after ping until I turned it off. Fuck.

I need to call Penny.

I know she's probably driving herself mad trying to decide if she should call me. I told her not to bother me this weekend unless the company headquarters was literally on fire.

If I'm going to face the vitriol, I at least need to be clean. I shower with the hottest water, the highest massage pressure, scrubbing and scrubbing until my skin is red. I wish people would see how much good we do in the world, all the women we've helped, and not focus on all this ridiculous drama. Whose lives have *they* changed? How many people have *they* employed?

When I get out of the shower, I sit down at the desk in our room, brace myself, and finally check my phone.

It's not as bad as I thought.

It's worse.

The video of me yelling has gone viral. There are already memes, GIFs. *PopSugar* has it as a top feature. The culture editor at *The New Yorker* tweeted that I'm a "modern-day Cruella de Vil," which has gotten more than ten thousand likes and a bunch of comments. There's an avalanche of DMs from strangers spewing hate, including one especially chilling message that says, *You're gonna die, bitch* and a knife emoji.

When Lucas opens the bedroom door, I jump half out of my seat.

He raises his eyebrows.

I don't say a word, just trade him my phone for the mug of steaming coffee in his hand. I take a big gulp. Black and bitter, just the way I need it.

Lucas barely reads the messages before rolling his eyes and handing my phone back. "It's all bullshit. Ignore it." He sits in a chair next to me, tilts it back, and props his long legs up on the bed. "People suck. I'm not trying to make light of it, but there are a lot of assholes out there who, for whatever reason, like to sit in their dark basements with their laptops and write hateful shit to people they don't know, just for kicks. They don't act on it. They just troll around. Maybe it gets them off. Maybe it's a rush of power. I don't fucking know. Who cares? Point is, you're bigger and better than all this. You owe them nothing. Ignore."

Sometimes Lucas's blow-it-off attitude can be irritating, but right now I appreciate the perspective. This is when I love him most—when he no-nonsense has my back. He used to butt heads with Mother defending me like that. He was the only one at a Thanksgiving dinner with enough guts to call bullshit when she said she thought VNity was frivolous. *She just broke 2.5 million in sales, Katrina. How is that frivolous?*

And yet, when I shared the photo of my bruise to my followers, he got pissed. He doesn't think I should be personal, show vulnerability online. He thinks it's unsafe, asking for trouble. He doesn't understand that the following, the brand, the *feeling* people get from a product, is equally, if not more, important.

"Agree," I say. "The question is, who's the rat? Who the hell leaked that video?"

Eliza Andrews, one of our sales reps, has been bitter since I turned down her request for a raise. Was it her? Or the intern I fired after I found out she lied about having COVID so she could go to the beach with her boyfriend? Or Rachel King, one of our models who desperately wants to be the spokesperson for the brand? The bitch even hinted to Penny that I was getting too old to hit the demographic we wanted.

Phones are constantly out at the office, in our palms, on our desks. Anyone could've secretly recorded me.

After Lucas leaves to go shower, I head to the office, where there's better cell service. I sit at Mother's massive desk and call Penny. It's nearing 10:00 a.m. She should be getting ready for the weekly staff meeting.

"Harper, I didn't know if I should call..." I can picture her pacing, clicking a pen open and shut, eyes closed, that thin pointy chin of hers sticking out as she clenches her jaw.

"Who videotaped me?" I ask evenly, trying to keep the rage at bay.

"I have no idea," she says. "But we will find out."

Her confidence soothes me even more than Lucas's did. One of my greatest decisions was plucking her from the temp world and bringing her to VNity. She, at least, has a brain between her ears, unlike most people, and a thread of ruthlessness that makes her willing to go the extra mile to get the job done.

"Watch Rachel," I warn. "She's been getting a little too cocky for her own good."

"I've got eyes and ears everywhere, Harper."

I smile. What am I worried about? Penny's handling it. She'll get answers.

"What's everyone there saying?" I ask.

A long pause. I can almost hear the gears turning in her head. "Well, I had a quick Zoom meeting with them all this morning"—Penny's working remotely this week, I suddenly remember. I special approved it. Some family thing. Terrible timing, of course, but I bite my tongue—"and naturally, everyone is a little worried."

I imagine the VNity office right now, all the women gathering around the smoothie station gossiping under the guise of concern when they should be working, selling and marketing the lifestyle so everyone forgets about this mess. That's what I'm paying them for.

"Perhaps they should, I don't know, worry about their work instead?" I have a hard time keeping the snark out of my voice. Most of my employees are naïve, clueless about how the world works. They think because they are beautiful, things should just float to them, that they don't have to put in any hard work.

Still, I don't need more unflattering videos popping up right now.

"Okay, that was uncalled-for," I force myself to say. "Tell them all to take the afternoon off. Do self-care. My treat." *And make sure they tell everyone about* that.

"Got it," she says. "And I'll handle this. You enjoy your birthday and don't worry about it."

I start to hang up, but she stops me. "One more thing. We need to confirm the date of the next ambassadors event for the caterer so I can book it."

"I thought I told you to cancel the ambassador event."

There's a brief silence. "You were serious?"

"Cancel it."

I close my eyes, but all I see are the rabid VNity ambassadors in our headquarters, all that need on their faces. The need to be close to something important. To have a little taste of this life. We ask them to be obsessed with our products and they are. But I can't face that crowd yet.

I realize I'm massaging my bruise again.

"Just say something about the attack," I add. "I'll write a blog post or something, and they'll feel bad for me."

I picture Lucas's disapproving look and push it out of my mind. He doesn't understand what it takes to be a female entrepreneur. I've seen women get destroyed in this cancel culture for a lot less than one angry moment in an employee meeting. It's a vicious world out there, and people love to pile on the hate. You have to do what you can to keep them on your side.

"But they won't be happy. They look forward to these events. It's why they push our products."

"It's not—hold on." I hear footsteps in the hall. There's a click as the door opens and then Elle backs in, quiet as can be, like she's hiding from someone. She doesn't even bother to turn around until she closes the door, scanning the room, and nearly jumps out of her skin when she sees me.

I can't help but smirk.

"Look, I've got to run," I say to Penny. "But thanks for the update. Post something about the new face cream."

"Harp—"

I hang up. Elle's frozen, staring at me.

"Playing hide-and-seek?" I ask.

"Absolutely not." She frowns. Her long hair is pulled back into a high ponytail. "In fact, I was just looking for you. Richard told me about the change in plans. I had no idea we were going out on the boat today."

"Like you said, this weekend is full of surprises." I smile. "We'll have to make sure Bill has prepped the boat. Last time I tried to take it out there was algae staining all over the bottom."

"I'm sure he's on it," she says. "Anyway, I meant to tell you, I was cleaning out Mom's bedroom upstairs"—*of course you were, always inserting yourself where you don't belong,* I think but say nothing because the thought of dealing with Mother's things myself is as appealing as a bikini wax—"and found some stuff in the back of the closet that I know you'll want to save. I left it downstairs in the sitting room for you to look over." She stops, bites her lip. "There's a jade necklace of hers that will look fab with your eyes."

I lean back, surprised at the compliment. "Thanks. I'll look later."

Elle hesitates, opens her mouth, then closes it. Finally, she says, "Are you doing okay? You know, after...what happened?"

Her eyes flick to my collarbone.

"I just...know it must've been scary."

For a second, I feel nostalgic for our former friendship, all those long lunches when we both worked at *Beauty Plus* and bonded over our authoritative parents. We liked to shop, too, and Elle would always find the perfect accessory for my outfit or my hair, telling me why one skin cream or another would work better for my type than the last. I, in turn, helped her hone her sales skills, negotiate for a promotion. We'd been good friends once.

But then she became more interested in my family than me, slinking her way into Richard's life, taking sides with Mother. And now she likes to act as though *she's* the one who was betrayed.

"All good." I stand and shove my phone into my back pocket.

"Terrible what they're saying about you online," Elle says quietly, not leaving.

I don't make eye contact. "I appreciate your concern, but it's being handled. Just part of the deal when you're a powerful and successful woman."

She twitches like she's just touched a hot stove. Narrows her eyes. Before I can say anything more, she turns on her heel and leaves, slamming the door behind her.

LAUREN

The ground is rougher on this part of the estate. It's more wooded, roots poking out, steep inclines. I have to concentrate on my steps as Zach forges ahead.

"Let's go, let's go." He seems determined to get there as fast as possible. I barely had time to finish my coffee before he was dragging me out the door into the cold morning, dew still glistening on the lawn.

It's a brand-new day. Zach's family seemed nice enough at breakfast, especially Elle. I'm still not thrilled about the joke they played on me last night, but maybe Zach was right that it was harmless fun. And even if it wasn't, karma has a way of sneaking back up on people—I'm sure by the end of this weekend, they'll realize I can hold my own. In the meantime, I am in a beautiful place, and there is much to look forward to.

As we walk, Zach tells me about the property, about the different types of grapes they grow, stories about skeet shooting and archery, he and his siblings riding ATVs in the backwoods. He doesn't normally open up like this, and the picture he paints of his childhood is fairly sweet, but it makes me wonder about the other side of the story. It can't all be perfect.

"So where do you bury the bodies?" I joke.

He raises an eyebrow. "Ah. If I tell you that, you'll have to join them."

When we clear the trees, I take a moment to look up from my feet. The sun peeks through the clouds, and mist billows through the vineyard like spirits. The wind is fierce, but it feels good on my face, invigorating after a night of drinking. I spin around slowly, trying to imagine what it would be like to grow up in such a place. For your backyard to be as big as a small town.

"My mom was big into flying," he says. "She had her pilot's license. At one point she looked into creating a runway and hangar for her plane here, but there's too much uneven terrain." As if to prove his point, the path ahead takes a steep route upward.

"I'm imagining the three of you as kids, running around all this land, getting into trouble," I say.

Zach chuckles. His shoulders are thrown back and there's a flush to his cheeks. He's settling into his role as my personal tour guide.

"Oh yeah. Our parents used to say we turned into savages." Zach was young when his parents divorced, and from what I gather, his dad's out of the picture, remarried and living somewhere in Canada with his new family. It's not like I call my dad every day—in fact, I haven't spoken to him in weeks—but it's sad to think of Zach and his siblings as basically orphans now. "Maybe we'd come in for meals. Maybe. Or to sleep, though sometimes Richard liked us all to camp out in the woods. I think I know this place better than anywhere else in the world."

"Sounds like you really love it," I say, recalling the conversation I overheard last night. The thought of the two older siblings making important decisions without him, selling this place, rubs me the wrong way. "Do your brother and sister feel the same?"

"Yeah." He looks surprised I'd even ask. "Of course they do. Harper was just playing around at dinner. She won't admit it, but this place is special to her too."

"I ask because—" I begin, but Zach cuts me off, tugging on my arm.

"Come on, there's still a bit to go and I really want you to see this view."

Since when is the man who enjoys leisurely Sunday afternoon strolls around the Village, stopping for gelato, petting everyone's dog, in such a hurry? He's relishing the outdoors, but there's also something jittery about him, the way he keeps patting his pockets, chewing on his lip, walking fast like he's trying to lose someone tailing us. It's making me nervous.

He continues on like this, determined, until we finally near the water. I hear it first, the crash of the falls like loud static on a car radio, and then I see them tumbling above us, violent and powerful. Near us at the bottom, the moss grows fuzzy on the stones; white froths of water pulse in the river.

He takes my hand. "Come this way. It's a better view."

Zach steps out onto flat rocks sticking just over the water's edge like turtle backs and leads us out to a larger plateau a few feet from shore. We can watch the falls head-on now. Their roar sounds like a warning not to get any closer.

"It's intense, right?" Zach shades his eyes with his hand. "The Van Nesses don't do anything small scale." He drops down. "Ouch," he says, digging into his sock. "I've got something in my shoe."

I bend to help and notice something wiggling. "Oh shit, Zach. There's a snake." It's brown, almost the same color as the water, slithering quickly toward our rock.

"You're not scared are you? He's harmless."

But suddenly I feel vulnerable. What else might be lurking below the surface?

"Lauren, my foot really hurts." Zach keeps wincing.

I eye the rocks we used to hop over here. They seem smaller now, too close to the water's surface. "Do you need to take your shoe off?" I look around nervously. I've lost sight of the snake. It could be anywhere.

"Wait. I think feel something." He tugs his hand out of his sock. Then he whirls, still on one knee. "I've got it. It *was* a rock. A big one."

He's holding a small crushed black velvet box. He opens it, and I catch a flash of sparkling light in the middle.

I sway back, nearly slipping into the water. The roaring in my ears is as loud as the waterfall.

"I was thinking, Lauren Brady, that maybe we should get hitched." He's smiling shyly. "What do you say?"

The back of my throat is dry.

I'm not who you think I am, Zach.

But I can't form any words. All I can do is nod as Zach puts the biggest diamond I've ever seen on my shaking finger. I clench my hand into a fist, staring down at it.

"What's wrong?" he asks as he rises back onto his feet.

I take a breath to give myself time to recover. "Nothing. It's—perfect. It's all perfect. It's just—" I pause, trying to figure out how to put it without revealing the real reason. "There's just…so much we don't know about each other."

He laughs. "We have our whole lives for that."

"Right, but—I don't even know…do you want kids? How many? When? We haven't even had a Christmas together yet. And in the—"

He kisses me, stealing the questions from my lips.

"Please don't spiral eighteen steps ahead of yourself. Next you'll be asking if I want to be cremated. Enjoy the moment— nothing else matters right now."

I believe he believes that. And I want to, too.

I hold out my hand, this time unclenched. The ring winks at me in the sunlight, as if it's in on a joke I don't yet know. As if it's saying, *one day you'll be dead and buried, Lauren Brady, and I'll still be here.* It'll all still be here—the ring, the pounding waterfall, the snakes and the rocks.

"We need a picture. Let's get a picture." Zach pats his pockets, his smile dying.

"What?" I ask.

"I was so nervous, I forgot my phone."

"Do I always have to be the responsible one?" I joke as I pull out mine, squeeze tight next to him.

"Let's not tell anyone yet, okay?" he says when we've taken a few selfies. "I don't want to overshadow the birthday celebrations. We can tell the others before we leave on Sunday."

I'm nodding, trashing a photo where I'm squinting, when a text message pops up.

Got anything for me yet?

I almost drop the phone. No, I quickly respond, then delete the text. Another pops up almost immediately after.

Keep those eyes and ears open!

"Lauren?" Zach says.

I shove my phone away, then grab his face for a kiss. Despite everything, despite my bad choices that might take it all away, now that the moment's come, this is what I want. I feel a little thrill at the idea of keeping such a big diamond tucked in my pocket.

"Yes, of course," I say. "It'll be our little secret."

***VAN NESSITY* BLOG**

Zachary Van Ness: World's Most Eligible Bachelor?

Ok, friends, we talk a lot on here about HVN and her wellness ideas and beauty hacks and, let's face it, ability to cause a stir, intentional or not. But let's for today turn our attention to her hunky brother Zachary. Yum yum yummy in my tummy. ZVN is quite the glass of milk.

Word on the street (from you, my loyal readers and commenters) is he's *quite* the partier. ZVN frequents the best clubs, the best restaurants (ones most of us don't have access to, sad face).

He also seems to always have a different woman on his arm.

So tell me, friends, who's the current lucky lady? I rely on you, my eyes and ears, for intel. Post it here or email me all

your delightful gossip about ZVN, last letter of the alphabet
but first in my heart.

I know, I know. It's those dimples of his that do it. Le sigh.

Posted by Kat Sparks, 35K likes, 583 comments

ELLE

"Were you able to find those waterproof camping blankets?" I ask Linnet as she follows me through the house, notebook in hand. "That's what we always lay out on to watch the fireworks."

"Yes, ma'am, but just so you know, Bill says they're predicting the storm sooner now," she says. "I'm not sure if—"

"Oh, stop being such a downer." I swat at her. "Storm this, storm that. That's all I hear from you two. We'll be fine. We'll make it work. Just find those blankets. And don't worry the others about it."

We climb the stairs to the second floor, and I stop her in the middle of the hallway, lowering my voice. "So right here is where I want you to do the photo hall in the morning." We had childhood photos printed up and framed of all the twins' previous birthday celebrations. "If you can go in chronological order, starting from their rooms? So as they walk down the hall, they can see each year after year, you know? I should've ordered another arch if I'd thought of it." I pinch my lip, thinking. "Well, just do balloons and streamers."

I give her a few more to-dos, making sure she writes it all down, and send her on her way to check on the party tent being set up outside. The caterer won't arrive until tomorrow, but I wanted the tent up early to avoid any delays.

It's hard to decorate such a large house. There are so many details to consider. You have to put yourself in the shoes of the ones experiencing it, try to see what they'll see. Still, I do love this place. Endless rooms to sit, hide away in, always something new to discover. It was one of the things Mom and I bonded over—our mutual love for this house and its history, all its secrets and surprises, nooks and treasures. There are still signs of her everywhere, the house untouched since she died, a museum, preserved in time. Now that she's gone, it's my responsibility to maintain it, ensure it's taken care of and loved the way she did. Especially because the others won't.

None of them seem to care about the house—or Mom for that matter—as much as I do, which is why I get so upset whenever Harper posts about Mom on her social feeds, acting like she was the one who took care of her when she was sick. Thinking of my mother, today and always, with hashtags about #strongwomen and #familyfirst. Using her as some pawn for her fake VNity persona.

When I was the one who did it all. Classic Harper, claiming credit where credit isn't due.

Before Mom died, we spent several weekends up here together, just the two of us. My own mother had written me off once I married into the Van Ness family, claiming Richard was a spoiled brat, that I was throwing away my life and all my hard work for a tabloid family, so my relationship with Mom was that much more special to me. She saw my potential, whereas my own parents only ever saw my deficits. Here at the estate, we'd talk over tea (spiked with a splash of bourbon as she liked it) and play strategy games that involved her invading lands and hoarding resources and joyfully starving my people to death. She'd tell me stories about her teenage days abroad in Europe, each anecdote allowing me to see a different facet of her, like twisting an opal to find all the dazzling colors.

I wish she'd told me more.

But she told me enough.

I've got a little something no one knows about at all, Elle. Not even my children. In case of an emergency, she said a few times. *A nest egg, if you will. Hidden in this house.* Her lips would curl into that smile I never knew how to read, and then she'd throw back her head and laugh.

I don't know if she was serious. It's been eight months since she died, and her words have burrowed in the back of my mind, but I haven't had the guts to search. It's always felt greedy, unpleasant, to look for it, like I'd be taking advantage.

"But now I *need* it, Mom. Surely you can understand," I whisper as I slip into the office again.

Thankfully Harper is gone, so I can take a look around in peace. Mom's office is one of my favorite rooms in the house. Grand and elegant, with French doors that open to a balcony overlooking the vineyards, the lake in the distance.

I wonder just where that nest egg could be, or what it is. In this office, there's the embroidered tapestry on the wall that Mom brought back from Morocco. A model of the first Cessna she owned, hanging from the ceiling. A pewter rabbit on the desk along with three tiny glass tigers crouching in various positions. A clay vase on a wall shelf. A pair of Chinese relaxation balls, painted with hummingbirds, nestled in a painted box on the desk. I grasp them, roll them around in my palms. They make a lovely, light, musical ringing.

None of these are what I'm looking for.

It's encased in blue velvet, Mom whispered to me last summer. We were outside on the terrace, an unusually hot day for this far north, but neither of us minded the heat. *Hidden in plain sight.*

This weekend is my only chance to find it. I need the money *now*, before the weekend is up. And if I try to withdraw a large amount of cash from our account, Richard will notice and there will be questions I can't answer. I never was a good liar.

"Give me a clue, Mom." It feels strangely soothing to talk to her. Of course, she'd be disappointed in me for what I've done. Or would she? Katrina Van Ness often surprised me, and she was a woman you did not cross and get away with it. Maybe she *would* understand.

I scan the highest shelves now. The objects on top must be dusty, the most forgotten. I drag the desk chair over and carefully stand on it. A porcelain vase, a crystal parrot. I lift the parrot by its hefty beak.

Finding nothing of note, I step down and slide the chair farther down the wall and climb up again, but there are just lines of books and a small box of matches.

"What are you doing?"

Too late, I hear the whoosh of the patio doors opening. I nearly tumble off the chair. "My god, you scared the living daylights out of me, Richard." I set the matches back on the shelf and get down.

Richard closes the door behind him, but not before letting in a burst of cool air and the faint whiff of cigarette smoke. He watches as I move the chair back behind the desk.

"It's so dusty up there. No wonder Lucas has allergies. I'm surprised all of us aren't sneezing our heads off. I really need to talk to Linnet about making sure these rooms are actually cleaned." I pause to take a breath. Smile. Finally look Richard in the eye. "We also need to tell her to make sure all the beds are made. And to grab any used towels in the bathrooms. I want everyone to feel completely pampered this weekend."

"Aren't we supposed to be relaxing?" He raises an eyebrow. "Not cataloging items?"

"I was just looking for something to put some flowers in," I lie.

He picks up a nearby Tiffany vase and examines it. "Like this?"

"Perfect," I say, accepting it from him, then change the subject. "Did you get all your work done? I can look at something if you need me to."

Richard's stressed, and when he's under pressure he withdraws, refuses to ask for help. That's when mistakes are made. He knows I'm good at reading contracts—my lawyer father's idea of bonding time with his daughter—and since Mom died, I've pitched in more. It's in good part because of me that Richard even finished the strategic plan for the board.

But Richard is very protective of the family investments, just like Mom was. He shakes his head. "I've got it under control."

HARPER

There's still some time to kill before the boat ride, and I don't want to spend it on my phone. I pay Penny to doom scroll for me.

Besides, there's no point in reading all that noise, anyway. It's like acid—it eats away at you, poisons you, and I have no time for it. I have always been good at bottling up my emotions, a magician's trick I learned from my mother—cast all the fear and rage and sadness down into a dense silver sword and swallow it whole. *They will never take you seriously if they see you cry*, she'd say, and she was right. Some people perceive that as cold, severe, but they're wrong. It's a more efficient way of navigating life. Emotions don't change anything—they just get in the way.

I put my phone—and my rage—aside and find Lucas in the game room, sprawled out across the couch watching a YouTube video on his laptop.

"Are you ready for skeet shooting?" I nudge his long legs out of the way and drop next to him. This has always been his favorite room in the house. It has the best bar, a large-screen TV mounted to the wall, and when she was alive, Mother never spent much time here.

"Richard'll win," he says from behind the computer screen.

I reach over and press down on the screen until it closes. "What happened to your vicious competitive streak?"

Lucas grunts, slides the computer off his chest and onto the floor. He loves to act chill, too cool to care, but underneath that persona is someone intensely driven. It's how he methodically masters the most difficult slopes at every ski resort he visits, how he built and sold two companies before he turned thirty-five.

Lucas and I met at a blackjack table in Vegas. I had been lucky that night, and I could see the guy with the scruffy beard on the other side of the table was noticing. He was hot in a rugged way, like he reveled in his masculinity rather than trying to shave or trim it away like so many of the frat boys I was used to from my college days. When I got up from the table, scooping up my winnings, I knew he'd follow.

Are you always that lucky? he'd asked, setting down a whiskey next to me at my slot machine.

I'm always that good, I said, smiling, taking a sip of the drink, enjoying the slow burn down my throat.

I was there covering a beauty convention for the magazine. He was a keynote at some tech conference. By the end of it, we'd blown off both events and spent most of our time gambling or getting room service in his hotel suite.

I crawl on top of Lucas now, tug on his bottom lip. I need him to look at me the way he did that night in Vegas. "Let's have uninhibited sex right here on the couch. Like old times."

He turns his face away, rolling his eyes. I dig my fingernails into his armpit as punishment, and he jerks, pushing me off him.

"Quit it, Harper."

"So this is where the party is." Richard saunters in carrying his coat, an hour early according to Elle's schedule. He hasn't shaved in a few days and the stubble makes him seem brooding. "Am I interrupting something?"

"Just Lucas throwing a tantrum." I rest my arm against the back of the couch.

"Just Harper being overly aggressive," Lucas counters.

I pick up a decorative dish from the table next to me—one of Mother's Murano glass treasures—and twist it in my hands, restless.

"We need to give her something to do," Richard says. "When Harper's bored, we all suffer."

"I'm looking forward to being on the water," I say, putting the dish back down. The power of the boat's engine, slicing through the water, the spray on your face. It's always been self-care for me. "Lauren and Elle are just an added bonus."

Lucas wags a finger at me. "I like the new girl. I think you underestimate her."

Richard walks over to the fireplace and fusses with the fire. The wood spits and sparks. One log breaks in half and crumbles in black ash to the brick bottom. A twirling piece rises and flits out, drifting under a chair, still burning. I think of us as kids, using Mother's magnifying glass to set fire to ants, the little wafts of smoke drifting up from their twitching bodies as they tried to get away.

"You're going to burn this house down." I move the chair to check to make sure the spark didn't catch the carpet on fire, and that's when I spot it, the gift from yesterday, shoved behind the chair against the wall.

I fish it out, a white box with a simple gold ribbon. "We should open this thing."

I balance it in my palms and hand it to Richard. "You do the honors."

"Now?" He cocks an eyebrow.

I recall Elle's comment that it's bad luck to open a present before your birthday.

"Yes, now."

After another stare-down, Richard drapes his coat over a chair and snatches the box from me. He wobbles it in his hand, testing the weight. "It's substantial."

"Hm. So no one gifted us Elle's attention span," I say.

Richard sits across from Lucas and me, resting the box in his lap. He's one of those: He carefully unknots the ribbon, then slides his finger underneath the tape to free it. Lucas could start a new tech company and sell it off to the highest bidder in the amount of time it takes Richard to remove the paper.

The wrapping reveals a small plain box. Richard slowly lifts the lid.

"Well?" I ask.

He pushes aside tissue paper and pulls out the gift. It's an hourglass, filled with black sand, protected by a silver frame. He unfastens a card taped to it and then passes the hourglass to me. On the edge of the frame is an engraved message:

A house built on lies will crumble like sand.

"What the hell is that?" Lucas says over my shoulder. He snatches the hourglass from me, flips it so the grains start sifting through, hissing as they hit the bottom.

"Who's this from?" I ask Richard.

But he's busy tucking all the tissue paper back in the box.

I frown. "Where's the card?"

He looks up. "There isn't a card."

I grab the box from him and fish through it. "I swear there was..." I trail off as Richard's eyes meet mine. A jab of electricity passes between us. Our twin connection. He's warning me.

Don't push it.

Lucas runs his thumb along the base where the message is etched. "I think it's kind of cool."

Richard's phone dings. His jaw tightens as he reads the notification and sticks the phone back in his pocket. "It's Victor. He wants to call an emergency meeting to discuss your...situation."

"My *situation*?"

"He says the investors aren't happy. They want you to issue an apology."

An apology? For what? No way in hell I should cater to those trolls online. I'd love to see them try to run a multimillion-dollar company for one day. "Bullshit. Tell them no. It's my company. Has nothing to do with them."

I elbow Lucas to back me up. Those were his words this morning, anyway. He nods, still studying the hourglass. "Agree. Harper should lay low. Let it all blow over, the way these things do."

"I think Victor has a point," Richard says in his know-it-all voice. "You're still a Van Ness, and he's the board president of our family's company. This could hit our wallets hard." He lowers his voice. "It also could make selling this place harder. Business owners don't want to be associated with someone who can't behave."

I laugh bitterly. "Behave? I'm not a fucking poodle."

I hate that Richard is caving to the board. VNity is a completely separate entity—they have no right to police me.

He sighs. "You know what I mean, Harper. This isn't a time for drama. Last time I checked, you're not a Kardashian."

I scoff. He thinks because he was born a whole three minutes before me that he can boss me around. And he's wrong. He's not the only one working hard to uphold the Van Ness name.

"*I'm* the one being dragged through the mud online. *I'm* the one being targeted. They should be backing *me* up." I rise, impatience beginning to vibrate through me. "Blood is thicker, Richard. Family is the most important. Make sure you remember that."

At that moment, Zach and Lauren waltz in like they just came back from a Disney cruise. Holding hands, Zach whistling. Lauren's cheeks are pink. I eye her suspiciously. No one has ever smiled that much in this house.

"Here you guys are. We thought you were hiding from us," Zach says.

Richard uses the interruption as an opportunity to excuse himself. He points at his phone. "I have to go deal with this." He disappears.

Zach rubs his hands together. "So what are we going to do before our big activities?"

"Drink." Lucas stands, sets down the hourglass, cracks his knuckles. "It's not too early, right?"

"It is actually," I say. "But that's not going to stop you."

Lauren takes it all in. The dartboard, the jukebox, the pinball machine, the pool table in the center. She brushes her hand across the felt of the pool table, picks up the cue like it's a stress ball and squeezes it in her palm, then tosses it lightly in the air and catches it with her other hand. "This is a really nice table," she says wistfully.

I walk over to it, flick on the overhead light. "We've been shooting eight ball ever since we were old enough to see over the table," I say. "I aced geometry in school."

Lauren sets the cue ball down on the black dot. "Want to play?" she asks me.

Her face is friendly, but is that a challenge in her gaze? Payback for yesterday? Maybe this is exactly what I need. Another win.

"Sure." I point at the hourglass, the black grains drifting down. "We've got all the time in the world."

LAUREN

The wall behind the bar in the game room hides a small room with a refrigerator and storage.

"What would you like, m'lady?" Zach asks.

There are at least five different types of microbrew beer, some hard cider, and any kind of soda your heart desires. I choose a dark beer, and Zach pops the top off with a KVN-monogrammed bottle opener affixed to the wall. He heads back to the game room but I linger behind, pull the ring out of my pocket. The way it glitters, even in the dim light, makes my heart race.

Lauren Brady Van Ness.

I slide it onto my finger and splay my hand out to snap a close-up for Maisie. She'll look gorgeous in a bridesmaid's dress, something light-colored, yellow maybe. Flower wreaths in our hair. I picture the photos on Instagram—the vivid green of the vineyards contrasting with the white of my dress, wine toasts, deliberate blurs of twirls on the dance floor.

And then another, less pleasant image: my parents in the front row, looking lost. My father will use the wedding as an excuse to splurge on a tuxedo. He'll buy my mother a new necklace, which she will bitch about but wear anyway because she secretly likes it, hoping she can return it afterward. My father will be oblivious, smoking cigars with Zach before, wanting everyone to have a good time.

I tuck the ring back in my jeans pocket. *Let's not tell anyone*, Zach had said. I'll need to stash it somewhere safe before we go out on the boat, but for now, I want it close to me.

When I return to the room, the others are chalking up their sticks.

"So how good are you?" Harper asks. Her tone is light, but after last night I don't trust her. I asked her to play so I could beat her, to prove to all of them I'm not just the brunt of their jokes.

"I used to play back home, but it's been a while." I set my beer down on a high-top near the rack of cue sticks, select one, and join the others at the pool table.

Harper rests her stick against the table and places her hands on the edge. "Lucas is probably the best player of all of us, and I'm second-best." She looks to Zach as if expecting a reaction out of him, but he doesn't bite. "So why don't we do Lucas and Lauren on one team, and Zach and me on the other?"

Lucas saunters over and throws his arm around my shoulder, pulling me toward him protectively. "We're about to kick their asses, Delaware," he says, then swigs his beer once. It takes a second too long for him to let me go, but it's not an entirely unpleasant feeling, the way he's on my side filling me with confidence.

"What are we playing for?" Zach asks as he racks the balls. He's in a good mood. I wonder if he likes keeping such a big secret, or if he's simply relieved the proposal is over.

Like anyone could ever say no to Zachary Van Ness.

"Let's go big," Harper says. "It's my birthday. Let's bet the house."

"What?" Zach rolls the cue ball across the table to Lucas, who scoops it up.

"The estate." Harper smacks the table. "The winery. All of it."

She's not serious, but the comment reminds me of her whispers with Richard last night. *The sooner we're rid of it, the better.* Could Harper and Richard really be planning to sell behind Zach's back? Surely they can't cut him out so easily.

Diane's text message from earlier pops into my mind: Got anything for me yet? I push it away and focus on the moment.

"Why not our whole inheritance?" Zach jokes. "And Richard's, too."

"Oh, I love that idea," Harper says.

Lucas rolls his eyes, sticks his thumbs through the belt loops of his dark jeans. "How about fifty bucks?" he asks Zach.

"Deal."

Lucas breaks, a powerful shot that sends the balls scattering across the table. They bounce around, but none fall in the pockets. The table's still open.

Zach gestures toward it. "Ladies first," he says to Harper.

She surveys the table and settles on a short corner shot with the three ball. She makes it easily. She sinks two more before screwing up an angle and nearly popping one of our balls into the side pocket.

"We have low balls," she says to me from the other side of the table.

I slide my stick into the space between my thumb and forefinger, testing it out. Then pick up the cube of blue chalk and run it across the tip, blow off the excess dust. I assess the table. The cue ball is blocked by a bunch of their balls. I can feel Harper gloating. I don't have much of a shot.

Zach sets his beer down on the table and walks over to help. "Not much you can do there, Lauren. You can't hit any low balls first or the shot doesn't count."

I don't need his advice. It's been years, but the muscle memory is still there, everything my father taught me, when we played each other for quarters at the pool hall.

"You can just whack it and see if you get lucky," Zach says, taunting me.

Lucas holds up a hand. "Now, now. Don't tell my teammate what to do. You just want her to scratch." He hovers over my shoulder, examining the table. "You might be able to just slip it through those two balls there."

Above me, a long, rectangular stained-glass lamp stretches almost the length of the table, casting light over our play. I lean down, close an eye, and line up.

Clack.

Perfect bank shot, and the eleven ball falls definitively into the corner pocket.

Everyone's frozen for a moment, and then Lucas hoots.

My eyes meet Harper's across the table.

"Lucky shot," she says coolly.

"Lucky, my ass," Lucas says. "Looks like you're about to get smoked."

The mood shifts then. I can feel it, like barometric pressure dropping. Zach looks surprised too. He wasn't expecting this. He likes being the expert—teaching me the ropes, showing me how to do something. And it turns out he's a terrible pool player, not spending the time to line it up, forgetting to chalk his stick, flubbing easy shots with too much power. The harder he tries, the worse he does. He scratches twice, cursing, and Lucas takes advantage of it each time, sinking at least two balls each turn.

Lucas isn't helping the situation. Every time I make a shot, he has to point out how good I am. "Delaware! You're a hustler!" There are high fives and fist bumps, and after a particularly hard shot, a bear hug, his breath hot in my ear as he says, with a slight slur, "I love you."

"Looks like you and Lucas make a good team," Zach says, mouth pinched, when I return to the high-top between shots.

"Not as good as you and me," I say, placing my hand on his.

He accepts the gesture, but I still feel tension in the air between us. We perch on the stool at the table, sipping our beers. The stools are wide and soft, with a generous back. They feel like the eel-skin wallet my father bought me on my thirteenth birthday, so unlike the cheap cracked red leather stools at Mackey's back home that would pinch the backs of my thighs in summertime.

A slight smile plays on Harper's face as she walks over to Zach, elbows him. "Lauren's just full of surprises, isn't she?"

Zach makes an irritated grunt and chugs more of his beer.

"What other surprises do you have for us, Lauren?" She moves back to the table and starts spinning a coin on the edge, which irks Lucas as he's trying to line up a shot. He nudges her out of the way with his stick.

"*Many.*" I try to say it in a mysterious tone. If only she knew the half of it.

"Ignore her," Lucas calls to me from the table. "She's trying to distract you. She hates losing."

But it works. When it's my turn again, I miss, adding one of their balls to the pocket.

"Looks like your luck's running out," Harper says and high-fives Zach.

After a few more turns, Lucas sinks our final ball, leaving only the eight ball to finish off.

Zach and Harper still have three balls left to play. Harper misses a shot and curses.

Lucas nods with assurance. "Alright, Delaware. You can do this."

It's a long shot across the table—not my strong suit. We win the game if I make it.

I get low, lining it up as best as I can. Everyone's watching, and I hear my father's advice: *Don't take your eye off the cue ball.*

When I release it, the shot is on point, and the ball sinks beautifully into the hole. Lucas throws his arms up, then rushes toward me, grabbing me and lifting me off my feet.

Harper rolls her eyes. "How mature."

"What? You're jealous we kicked your ass?" He grins at Harper, still holding me close.

After all the stress since I've arrived, the need to be liked, to make an impression, to belong, I get caught up in Lucas's excitement, in his embrace and the way it makes me feel. "They are definitely jealous," I agree, pressing into his side and laughing.

Too late, I realize, pulling away from Lucas, that even though Zach's smiling, shaking Lucas's hand, his jaw is set as he tosses a fifty-dollar bill on the table. "Nice playing, Lauren," he says.

Before I can respond, Elle pops in the doorway. "Ahoy, ladies. Who's ready for a boat ride?"

THE PARTY GUEST

The main road leading to the Van Ness estate is lined with trees. The dense foliage provides good cover even this time of year for a car you don't want anyone to find.

Some trees are old and thick and tall; others lean and young, fighting for space. It doesn't take long for me to find one perfect for my needs. It sits ten feet back, the trunk two feet in diameter, and leans slightly like it's listening for something. It's splotched with green patches of fungi, and thick slabs of bark have peeled off in places—signs of decay.

I pat it with my thick rubber gloves, whisper *sorry* before lowering the safety goggles around my eyes.

It takes a few tries for the chain saw to kick on, and when it does, the sound cuts through the quiet like a gunshot. I make the notch like my father taught me years ago, two cuts, one straight across and one angled on the side where I want the tree to fall. The wood spits, chunks fly into the air. The blades sputter at one point, and I worry the chain saw is going to get stuck, but it holds up like a champ.

When I'm finished, there is a nice wedge cut into the tree. Not enough to fell it, not right now. But there's a storm coming. High winds, heavy rain—one big gust and this guy's going over, blocking the road.

None of the party guests are getting in or out.

LAUREN

I would not picture Harper as someone who knows her way around the water, the work involved, but here she is at the end of the dock, uncoiling thick ropes in a slick black raincoat, plaid scarf, and rubber boots.

As we approach, she steps into the small boat and starts the motor. There's room enough for the three of us but not much more. The boat sways as I board, pushing me ungracefully forward. The water slaps against the sides, like all it would take is the right movement, the right angle, and it would rush over the top and suck us all down.

At least I have some time away from Zach. Some breathing room. It's not like him to get annoyed over a game of pool. But I know family can bring out the worst in people.

We ride in silence as Harper guides the boat toward the middle of the lake. Across from me, Elle's hair whips like a flag in the cold wind, giant sunglasses hiding her eyes.

We glide along the water, past large wet rocks that dot the shoreline, white foam crashing against them. The landscape of the Van Ness property seems to alternate between lush hills and jagged, harsh drops. Luxurious and dangerous at the same time.

After a few more minutes, Harper cuts the motor and the

boat slows, creating ripples that cascade outward on all sides of us. She twirls around, the captain in her chair, the queen on her throne, scarf billowing violently, like a trapped bird. "Hardly anyone ever sees the estate from out here on the lake," she tells me. She's relaxed, in command of the boat, the game of pool forgotten.

"Mom always loved this view," Elle says. She tilts her chin up to the sky. "I had an artist paint a landscape of it for her for her birthday one year."

"Yes, you do think of *everything*, don't you?" Harper mutters. Elle smiles to herself. "Someone has to."

I shade my eyes with my hand to take it all in. It's chilly, but the sun is bright enough to sting. It's hard to believe the forecast is calling for rain this weekend. The scene in front of us is like a postcard. Gentle rolling vineyards tucking into one another, flanked by giant purple mountains in the distance. I can't fathom anyone giving up all this. The Van Nesses have no idea how much they have to lose.

"Well, it's about time for lunch, isn't it?" Elle pulls out a cooler I hadn't noticed before and withdraws wrapped sandwiches and a bottle of wine. "Lauren, Zach told me you like chicken salad?"

I nod as she passes out the food and napkins. The others seem to take for granted how prepared Elle always is, how much she thinks ahead. I wonder if she resents that.

"Hope the boys are enjoying themselves," Elle muses, wrangling her thick head of hair into a ponytail to keep it from blowing into her face while she eats. She hands me a small glass of Chardonnay, which I balance along with the sandwich in my lap. "Would've been nice to join them."

"But then we wouldn't have this girl time together, bonding. Learning *all* about Lauren."

Harper is clearly imitating Elle, but Elle focuses on recorking the wine. "Did Zach buy you that necklace?" Harper asks me suddenly, and I realize I've been nervously zipping my vest up and down, exposing the amethyst pendant around my neck.

I grasp it. "He did. How did you know?"

Harper shrugs, tosses a thin slice of tomato from her sandwich into the lake. "He likes to buy things for all his ladies."

The necklace slips out of my fingers. How many other of Zach's girlfriends have sat on this very boat, undergone Harper's judgment?

"Harper!" Elle shakes her head. "That's rude."

Harper raises her eyebrows defiantly. "That's rich, given that you didn't even want Lauren to come here this weekend."

I work hard not to wince. I knew I wouldn't just blend right in with the Van Nesses, but I didn't expect them to be so blunt about it.

"I never said that." Elle turns to me. "That is not—I was just concerned. This was the first time we'd all be back since…" She lets the rest of her sentence trail off, unfinished.

"Who's the liar now?" Harper leans back, satisfied, like a lioness who just found a warm patch of sunlight.

Elle's face is bright red.

"Were you afraid Zach wouldn't give you all the attention?" Harper jokes, but the words have an odd edge to them. She addresses me. "I sometimes think Elle might've married the wrong Van Ness brother."

I don't respond. The idea makes me uncomfortable, but the reality is, Zach is nice to everyone. It's one thing I love about him.

"Cut it out, Harper." Elle tries to brush it off, but I can tell she's furious. "Do not listen to her. I'm thrilled you're here," Elle says, patting me on the arm.

"It's fine." I wave her off, wishing they'd just drop it.

Elle busies herself cleaning up, stuffing our trash back into the cooler, then pours us more wine. I hope we'll head back now. I'm done being trapped in a small space with their snip-ing, their fake-polite tones, smiles like daggers.

But Harper seems to have no interest in starting the motor, which means we're drifting downstream. There's a low hiss in the distance, a churning white noise gradually growing, the breeze picking up.

The waterfall.

"Chilly?" Harper asks, watching me.

"It's much colder on the water," I admit.

She leans over the side of the boat, drags her fingers through the water. "Can you swim, Lauren?"

"Why?" Elle pipes up. "Are you going to throw us in?"

Harper ignores her. "You know Zach can't swim, right?"

This surprises me. Zach seems capable of anything. I can't imagine him not knowing something so basic, especially with all the summers he spent here.

"It used to drive Mother crazy," Harper said. "She thought he was faking it. So one day, she brought us out in the boat. She cut the motor and told Zach he had to jump in and swim or she'd let the boat go over the falls."

The falls had been a beautiful sight as Zach proposed, but now, as we float toward the top, all I can think of is our little boat cascading over the edge, crashing on those flat rocks at the bottom.

Elle twists an unruly lock of hair from her cheek. "That's ridiculous. Mom would never do that."

"I was there. He was like, I don't know, ten? Eleven? It was literally sink or swim." She stops, looks out at the vineyards as if replaying the moment in her head. "He jumped. No one said no to Mother. And then he sunk. I had to dive in and get him. He was thrashing around. Whacked me in the jaw. I thought he was going to drag us both down."

We're only fifty feet from the top of the waterfall now, pulled nearer and nearer like the waterfall is playing an invisible game of tug-of-war, and our team forgot to tug. I feel a twinge in my gut, thinking of Zach, just a little kid. The shock of the cold water, his wet clothing weighing him down, air bubbles dancing around him.

"Mother was a mess. I've never seen her like that. We managed to get him back in the boat, of course, and the whole way back she was white as a sheet." She shrugs, like she's talking about the breakfast menu and not a childhood trauma.

"Harper! That's awful," Elle says.

"Honestly?" Harper pushes her shoulders back. "Sometimes I wonder if he did it on purpose, knowing how it would wreck her. I don't know, playing the long game? Because after that day, Zach was always untouchable. Her favorite."

"He was ten," Elle says. "More likely he was trying to save all of you. That's a horrible story." She draws her hands over her chest, as if to ward off the unpleasantness.

"Possibly. But we Van Nesses can be a vindictive little bunch." Harper drags her fingers through the water again. "What about you, Lauren? If I told you to jump or we'd all go over the falls, would you do it?"

I meet her gaze and don't like what I see there.

She thinks you wouldn't do it, Brady.

She thinks you're afraid.

"I'd call your bluff," I say.

We can barely hear one another now, the roar of the falls louder as we near the edge. I can feel the mist on my face, curling my hair.

But Harper won't look away from me.

It's a game.

She knows nothing about me. She thinks she does—she believes she can toy with me—but she underestimates me. When I left Maurville nine months ago for New York, I promised myself I'd do what it takes to succeed. I'd leap into a freezing lake if I had to. Or *not* leap—if the situation called for that.

I will myself not to break eye contact, not to worry about the water violently churning before us.

Harper laughs once, then finally presses the ignition. The motor chugs to life, and she turns the wheel, our boat breezing in a wide arc, rotating back the way we came.

HARPER

When we return to the house, there's a blue Audi in the driveway, its trunk open. The car is faintly recognizable, but a gust of wind whips my hair into my face as we approach, preventing me from seeing whoever is entering the front door. The arched balloons jostle back and forth, bouncing off each other like they're trying to warn me away.

"Oh!" Elle says. "He's here. Just in time."

In the front hall, voices echo off the high ceilings. The guys must've just returned from shooting because Richard is still in his peacoat, joking around with Lucas like two men filming a Brooks Brothers commercial, not a care in the world.

Zach's talking to another man whose back is to the door. As we enter, they both turn. The man's eyes take all three of us in, but his gaze rests on me. Those piercing dark eyes. That hint of stubble, the crew cut. He's wearing a fitted black T-shirt that shows off his muscles, two tentacles from his octopus tattoo peeking out from the sleeve of his left arm.

You've got to be fucking kidding me.

A smile lights up his whole face.

"Guys, surprise! This is Todd Christie," Elle says. "Our personal wellness coach this weekend. This gathering is supposed to be a retreat, an exercise in relaxation and reconnecting, and Todd's going to help us with that."

He removes his hands from his black jogger pants, taps at his smart watch a few times, and meditative pan flute music begins to play from a wireless speaker on the circular entryway table. He folds his hands and bows.

Elle takes her sweet time making introductions. She saves me for last. "And of course, Harper." She puts her arm around me, squeezes tight.

"The one and only," Todd says, looking me up and down, and I stiffen.

"You know each other?" Lucas asks.

I shrug off the question before he starts pawing at the ground and grunting like a bull. My phone buzzes in my pocket, but I resist checking it. Mother despised our over-reliance on technology, especially phones. She thought we were weak in our addiction to immediate gratification, *slaves to the little electronic boxes*, she'd say. She hated people who had no self-control, bullied us into not jumping at every whim. I hated it, and yet here I am, doing exactly what she wanted.

"They recorded a few wellness videos together," Elle says, laying it on thick. "That's how I found him. I mean, if Todd's good enough for Harper, then he's got to be *spectacular*."

Todd simply nods. "She's a pleasure to work with."

"I bet she is," Elle says, and shakes my shoulders vigorously. "Harper really throws herself into her work. I admire that so much."

Lucas rubs his beard, like it might give him some answers. "Why don't I remember this?"

I pull away from Elle before I stab her. "I don't know. Maybe you were busy gambling cryptocurrency away in your fantasyland."

My phone buzzes again. I wonder if it's Penny with information about who leaked that video. Or if Todd is sending me a spiritual tip via his smart watch. Or if one of the Van Ness board members wants to chat about crafting my ladylike apology.

"Just what kind of wellness are we talking?" Richard asks. My brother is not exactly a woo-woo guy.

"Oh, I have some wonderful things planned for us," Todd assures him. "This evening, we'll have a quick chakra cleansing and meditation. Tomorrow we'll indulge in outdoor yoga and a nature walk, weather permitting, of course. I'll post a sign-up for personal massages as well, where we can work on deep tissue massage or general relaxation. Oh, and many other pleasures await, which I won't spoil now."

"There's a virtual reality headset," Elle says to Richard. "You can use it on the bike or the treadmill to make it feel like you're in all these different places."

Richard still seems skeptical, but he thrusts out his hand to Todd. "Well, welcome. Elle's a great host, but let me know if there's anything you need."

"Virtual reality?" asks Lucas with a raised eyebrow.

"There's a cross-country skiing one for the SkiErg," Todd says. "Harper told me you love skiing, am I right?"

"She did, did she?" Lucas gives me a look, and I tug at my scarf. I'm still wearing my raincoat and boots from the boat ride and it's too warm in here.

As soon as I can, I escape to the sunroom. When I'm sure I'm alone, I dig my fingernails into my palms and silently scream. Of all the people Elle could choose to hire for this weekend, she picks Todd? Does she know—no. She can't know. Even she wouldn't stoop so low. Still, I'd be doing the world a service if I just strangled her with one of Lucas's woolen ties and dragged her out into the middle of the woods for the coyotes.

But I cannot let her—or anyone else—know I'm bothered by Todd's presence. I breathe deeply and finally check my phone. It's a text message from a number I don't recognize.

What did you think of your gift?

I stare at it for a few seconds before remembering the hour-glass, the black sand. *A house built on lies will crumble like sand.*

Who is this?

I look out the wall of windows in the sunroom, but of course no one's there.

In the front hall, Todd laughs, his voice bouncing off the high ceilings. I think about Elle leaving the security gates open. We used to get random people wandering the property. People who couldn't read signs that said PRIVATE or STAFF ONLY BEYOND THIS POINT. Who thought they could take a little hike around the vineyards, bringing their trash and their germs, plucking off a grape here and there.

It's incredible how entitled people are.

After one too many times, Mother put the fence up.

I'm starting to think you aren't very grateful.

A light-headedness overtakes me, and I hold my palm to the wall to steady myself.

The social media trolls' words echo in my head. You entitled bitch… Step down… Eat shit… You're ugly…you're old…you're going to die, bitch.

And then one more text comes in.

Remember, I know where you live.

A chill goes down my spine. This is different from the on-line threats. This is my phone. The gift was sent to *my house.*

I rush upstairs to Mother's bedroom. Someone's shut the

vents to redirect the heat elsewhere, and it's cold in here. *Like a tomb*, I think before I can stop myself.

Mother always believed in being prepared, in taking precautions just in case. Richard didn't approve, but I'm beginning to understand why she wanted to feel safe, to protect herself. Her home. Her family.

I cross the room, around to the far side of the four-poster bed to the nightstand, praying it's still there. I yank on the jewel-handled top drawer, which slides open silently.

There are her reading glasses. Her phone charger. Her pill box.

And tucked safely in the back, the object I'm looking for.

I reach inside and press my fingers against the cold metal of her gun.

THE PARTY GUEST

My dad had a beautiful hourglass he kept on a high shelf in the den. It was a gift from his sister. The sand was a deep orange, reminded me of sunsets, and the glass was thin, so delicate I held my breath every time he turned it over for me.

And then one day, I accidentally knocked it over in my haste to turn it. A small fissure appeared in the glass, the whole thing cracking. The orange sand rained onto the floor, the grains worked their way into grooves and cracks.

One moment, it was there, one piece, whole.

The next, destroyed for good.

Barriers so fragile are bound to break. And you can't save all that's inside from spilling out.

That doesn't keep some people from trying, though.

I slide the key into the lock and twist. Access isn't just for the wealthy—when you're resourceful, you can open doors too.

There are a few ways to get rich quick in this world. One is to be born into it. Another is to get lucky—win the lottery, marry a billionaire, become famous. And yet another is to cheat and steal. Whichever way it happens, once they're rich, the rich like to stay that way. They'll do whatever necessary to get more, whatever it takes to eliminate the people in their path.

The Van Nesses are no different.

The trouble is, their wealth? Their power? Their influence? It's built on lies.

All it will take is one simple push to topple their empire over.

ELLE

It's turned out to be a glorious day. I don't know what the weather forecasters are saying about a storm, but the sun is out, the temperature just warm enough to be enjoyed.

I leave Todd in the gym to set up and steal Lauren away from Zach—"we girls need our girl time," I say with a wink, and he gives me a grateful look—and guide her outside to the patio. I can see why he asked me to take her under my wing this morning. Harper was beastly on the boat. Telling Lauren I didn't want her here? And then that awful story about Zach and Mom. I wouldn't be surprised if she made it up, just to shock Lauren.

"When you're at a winery, you must keep drinking wine," I say as I hand her a generous glass of dry Riesling. "It's a rule." I've learned a lot about wine over the years just from being in this family. I'm nowhere near an expert, but I can note enough about the differences in oak and stainless-steel aging, or what foods pair best with what wines, to get by. And this bonding moment, surrounded by the beautiful, expansive outdoors, calls for a crisp, light Riesling.

We settle on two of the snow-white Adirondack chairs that overlook the vineyards. They've been hosed off and dried, so they look brand-new, no insects and dust and dirt in their crevices. I take a sip and swoosh the wine in my glass. "You don't believe anything Harper said about me not wanting you here, do you?" I ask, turning to Lauren.

"No, no." She bites her lip. She's lying.

"I really hope that's true. Like I said, I'm thrilled you're here. It's nice to have another woman around who's not..."—*Harper*—"...who didn't grow up here."

Lauren glances over at me. "It sounds like their childhood was—"

I sigh. "Don't mind Harper. Mom was perfectly lovely. You would've liked her."

"What's it like? Being part of the family, I mean. Do you find it...hard?" she asks, hesitant.

"Hard? No." I pause, remembering the first time I visited the estate with Harper, all her warnings and caveats. *Mother can be so horrid*, she'd said on our drive, her convertible top down, our hair whipping behind us in the breeze. *And the house is way too big, you'll see. We'll spend most of our time outside, on the boat, hiding from everyone. With gin.* I'd expected some grim gothic haunted house with a wart-nosed crone from the way she spoke, but when we pulled up to the estate, Mom had padded down the front stoop barefoot to welcome us, her shiny gray hair in a sleek bob, glass of wine in hand and a warm smile on her face. Sure, she loved nothing more than a good game, some competition, a little test or two—they all did—still do. But I'm a quick study. I was able to hold my own.

"I was an only child, so I love being part of a bigger family," I tell Lauren.

"I'm an only child, too," Lauren says, leaning toward me.

"So you get it," I say, and when Lauren gives a thumbs-up, I continue. "That's why I love coming here. Everyone all together. It just feels like a home. And this place is, well, it's got a long history. Lots of interesting stories."

"Like what?" she asks.

"Oh I don't even know half of them. But there are all kinds of secrets. Like, actual secret passages. You know that big book-case at the end of the hallway right near your bedroom? It opens like a door. Covers up an old servants' quarters, I think."

"That sounds kind of...creepy," Lauren says. "Have you ever been in them?"

I nod. "And there are underground tunnels. I think they were built for wine transport, rolling barrels and stuff? No one uses them anymore." Thinking about all the rooms and passageways on this property invokes a nagging worry, though. If there is something of value to find here, Mom's nest egg, it could take forever. And I don't have forever.

"That's so interesting. Zach didn't tell me any of this," Lauren says. The sun picks out flecks of green and yellow in her eyes. She's got the kind of face you want to confide in. "What else can you tell me?"

I realize I've already finished my glass of wine and reach over to pour more. I can see the journalist in Lauren now, sense she's trying to lead me for more information. I don't mind. It's nice to have someone who's actually interested in what I have to say. This is exactly how Mom and I would be when she'd tell me stories, only now I'm the one giving information instead of getting it. I tuck my legs up under me, settling in. "The Van Nesses have had this land for decades, but hardly anyone ever lived here full-time. It's gone through periods of neglect. I mean, Katrina's parents basically just abandoned it."

"Really? Why? It's such a beautiful place." Lauren tops off her glass.

"They sounded like horrible people, honestly. Dumped Mom off with her aunt and traveled a ton. They were killed when she was five, in a plane crash, and she lived abroad with her aunt for years because her grandmother wouldn't take her in— she was too selfish or something. And then Mom came back here in—I think it was 1975"—I flutter my arm toward the vineyards—"and the winery was all but done for. Like, no family left to care about it. I think only Bill worked here then as the groundskeeper, and the family lawyer managed all the bills and repairs and maintenance by mail and phone. Mom basically put it back on the map herself."

"She seems like a powerful woman."

"Oh, she was. She could be ruthless too. But she loved her kids. Make no mistake about that, no matter what Harper says. She spoiled them, really. I'm not sure they ever appreciated all she did for them." I take off my sunglasses, rub my eyes.

"I'm sure Zach did," Lauren says quickly. "I mean, he never mentioned anything about the swimming thing. But I know he really misses her."

Zach's a sweetheart, but even he didn't know how good he had it. None of her kids did enough for her.

Linnet comes out with a small tray of cheese and crackers and almonds, and we snack, pouring more wine, enjoying our buzz. Lauren asks me polite questions about wine, the vineyards.

"Seems like so much work," she says. "And tough to be so dependent on the weather."

"From what I understand, grapes are a fairly hearty plant if they're in the right place," I say. "Just don't ever bring a cut vine back to the house. It's terrible luck."

Lauren laughs.

"No, seriously. Mom used to say it all the time. *A cut vine means a severed line.* It means one of your relationships will turn sour. One of her superstitions. Even Richard won't do it, and he's not really one who buys into that sort of thing."

"How did you and Richard meet?" Lauren asks.

"Here, actually," I say. "Harper invited me. We were best friends once."

Lauren pulls back. "You're kidding."

"I know, I know. Hard to believe. But it's true. We worked

together. Had a lot of fun, too. Anyway, she invited me here for a long weekend. We went out on the boat, and on the way back, there was a handsome guy standing on the dock, waiting for us to come in. He made my heart race. I said to her, 'Is that your brother?' And the rest, I guess you can say, is history."

"How romantic," Lauren says with a smile.

I leave out the fact that the brother standing there on the dock was Zach. Crisp white shirt and khaki shorts, his hair getting tossed by the wind. Our brief flirtation feels like a million years ago and also just yesterday. But time is strange, life stranger.

Lauren settles back in her chair, kicks her feet out. She starts scratching her ankle, lifts her pant leg, and I see several red bumps.

"Did you get bit?"

"I don't know. I think it's some kind of rash. I might've picked it up this morning on our hike," she says.

"Looks like poison ivy. I've got a cream I made upstairs. I'll leave it in your room. It should help."

"You made it?" Lauren asks, still examining her leg.

I shrug. "Just a hobby of mine. It's hard to find all-natural products."

She looks up, surprised. "Thanks," she says, then sighs, admiring the view. "This is so nice. None of you are interested in moving here full-time? I'd be tempted."

"I am. But Richard would never go for it. He likes the city too much."

I stretch my legs, imagining how different life would be if we were out here all the time. I used to love living in New York, the wonder of having anything and everything you could ever want right there. It felt like you were walking on the pulse of the world, like all your dreams were possible. But lately it's felt oppressive. Richard works all the time now that he's taken over much of Mom's responsibilities, and the friends I do have are always shifting loyalties, keeping me off-balance, like I'm the marble on a tilt maze board, unsure where to head next. Life would be simpler here—a place to raise kids, make a family.

"I guess I can see that," she says. "And what about Harper? I imagine she could work from anywhere she wanted to."

I laugh. It sounds like a cackle. "Harper here full-time? Are you kidding? No way. She's so very *busy* with her company." I twirl an almond in my fingers before biting down on it. Lauren needs to know who she's dealing with when it comes to Harper. "She told me once that she's the only one of the Van Nesses who's self-made. That if everything crumpled, she's the only one who'd survive."

"Wow…"

"Because she thinks she's an *entrepreneur.*" I do air quotes, and Lauren laughs, then covers her mouth with her hand. "She's no more an entrepreneur than I am a brain surgeon. Everything she's done with VNity has been because of her family's connections and influence."

It feels good—no, feels bad in a good way—to vent. I've had no one to talk to about this, and Lauren is like a sponge, soaking it all up.

"Not that I can ever criticize her to Richard," I say. "He thinks the sun rises and sets with Harper. She can do no wrong in his eyes. It's exhausting. If only he knew about Todd." It slips out before I can help myself.

"What about Todd?"

I glance behind me to make sure no one's out here eavesdropping, and then lean in. Lauren twitches whenever Harper blinks. She won't rat me out to her. "Let's just say Harper has her fingers on a lot of things."

Lauren looks shocked, and it pleases me. She tries to smile, but it doesn't quite erase the discomfort in her face. "No! You're kidding me," she says, her eyes wide.

I shake my head. "I shouldn't have told you," I say, but Harper deserves it after the way she treated me on the boat.

After the way she always treats me.

"But seriously, oh my god. You can't say anything." I try my best to sound sincere. "She'd kill me!"

LAUREN

When Elle excuses herself to go check on Todd, I sit for a moment, thinking about everything she's just revealed. Secret passages. Katrina Van Ness's superstitions. Harper's affair.

I have access to information people would pay for. Pay a lot for.

But everything's different now. I'm on a big, beautiful terrace, paradise spread out before me, an expensive glass of wine in my hand. I've got the promise of all that being Mrs. Zach Van Ness affords.

The question is, is it enough?

I run my hand along the Adirondack chair, tip back my glass and finish my wine.

I bring up the *Van Nessity* blog on my phone. Gossip web sites like these thrive only when new content gets added daily, even hourly. It's all about maintaining the hype, feeding the hunger.

On the latest post about Harper's treatment of her employees, people are still commenting wildly.

What does her husband think of all this?

That dude is rolling in it. Not sure why he hasn't divorced her ugly ass yet.

Tempers run in the family! I saw Zach Van Ness nearly punch a hole
in the wall at Club MXII last year. He got pissed at the bartender
because his card wouldn't go through.

Zach would laugh if he saw that one. Because that's just
it—most of the juicy stuff out there is just rumor, speculation.

The truth is worth so much more. At least, that's what my
editor Diane would say.

I slip inside the back door and set my wineglass on the
kitchen counter. It's quiet, and I have no idea where the others
are. I push through the swinging doors into the hall and listen for movement—still nothing. There's something haunting
about such a large house. But also so much to explore.

I step into a bright room down the hall from the kitchen. If
he were here, my dad would call out the textured wallpaper,
the nine-foot drapes covering a windowsill so deep that a small
family could have a meal on it. My mother would scoff—*no
family needs all this*—and tell me I'm getting too posh for my
own good.

On a side table next to the doorway, a guest book lies open,
a pen in its crease, a record of all who've visited over the years.
I flip the pages backward and recognize names, politicians and
celebrities. I snap pictures of a few notable entries, but a different kind catches my eye, from more than two years before, a
note in purple ink—*We had such a great time! Thanks for the fun
and games—and the wine!*—Sara & Zach. Both of the lowercase
i's are dotted with hearts.

He buys things for all his ladies, Harper said on the boat. I wonder if they played tricks on Sara too, or if they liked her better
than me. I shut the book and head upstairs to find Zach. I hope
skeet shooting was fun, that shattering clay pigeons made him
forget all about pool. I don't know how to respond to this version of him. I tried to grab him after we met Todd, but he got
a call and rushed off, distracted, which usually means work.

Right before I reach our bedroom, I spot the bookcase just past it and recall what Elle said. Curiosity gets the better of me.

The hall is silent, all the doors closed, so I tug on the right side of the bookcase. It doesn't budge. Was Elle just messing with me like the others?

I try again, putting more of my weight into it, and this time it gives. The entire shelf swings out. Behind it is a small landing and a set of narrow stairs leading down. I think about all those people commenting on the blogs. I bet they'd kill to hear about the hidden rooms of the Van Ness mansion, be jealous of my access. I step inside and immediately feel claustrophobic. The ceiling is much lower here; Lucas would have to stoop down, maybe even Zach. It smells musty, like the deep stacks of a library.

I look back where the plush carpeted hallway stretches, the doorway to my safe, comfortable bedroom just a few feet away. It's like another world, like I've slipped behind the looking glass. I hesitate. Being too curious can get you in trouble, but a good journalist always investigates a story.

I leave the bookcase cracked open in case there's a dead end at the bottom and this is the only way back up, and slowly descend into the darkness, the wood creaking from my weight. It's like the night before in the wine cellar, only I'm not sure what I'm going to find when I get down here. There's no railing, so I press my hands on either side of the wall for balance as they curve.

At the bottom is a narrow hall that leads both ahead and behind me. I take the route behind the stairs first. The passageway is dim and stretches farther than expected. After fifty paces, the hall veers abruptly to the left, almost like it's wrapping around the edge of the house, and leads to an imposing wooden door with a dead bolt that looks like it hasn't been opened in several decades.

I grab the dead bolt with both hands and pull. It slides out easily. I turn the knob. Maybe there's something here Zach and his family don't even know about yet. Didn't Elle say this house had a lot of secrets? The heavy door protests with an angry creak as I shove it open and shine my phone's flashlight inside. Below is another staircase, swirls of dust and mist swishing in the bright light, darkness beyond. This has to lead to the servants' quarters Elle mentioned, hidden at the end of a wing in the back of the house, designed to make the employees invisible.

I shiver. The air drifting up is cooler, but also denser, and it's dead quiet. Even I'm not curious enough to venture down alone. I slam the door shut and head back the way I came.

At the stairs, I consider exploring the other end of the hall. Light from the floor above streams through vents in the ceiling, Linnet's voice drifting through. "You know how they are. None of them listen to reason…" Then Bill's deeper voice, too low to make out the words. I'm inside the walls of the house, like a mouse, scurrying unseen in places I shouldn't be.

I've had enough. I take the stairs quickly. But when I get to the top, the bookcase has closed and locked. Maybe someone came by. *Shit.* I slide my hands on the wall, trying to find a lever or handle, but there's nothing. I train my phone's flashlight along the wall, but that doesn't help either. I bang on the door. "Zach!" I call out, but my voice feels like it's bouncing back at me.

I head down the stairs again, this time going the other direction, praying there's a way out. I cannot imagine descending into the servants' quarters now. This way is shorter, and with relief, I note there's glass at the end of the hall that allows me to see into the formal sitting room I stumbled into last night.

The border around the glass is made of rough wood that scratches my palms, but my finger catches a gap along the left—a sort of door handle—and I tug. Something clicks, and the glass swings outward. Fresher air pours into my lungs as I step into the room.

I brush the dust off my clothes, look back and realize I entered through the frame of the full-length mirror. This was the room I was in last night. It had felt cozy and inviting then with the soft glow of the lamp, but now the grand piano in the middle is imposing, and the narrow, tall-backed velvet chairs stare at me in a fussy, uppity way. Two eagle statues perch on the hearth like they're ready to dart over and peck at me if I get too close.

As I cross the room to leave, I notice a box on a small table next to one of the chairs. There's a label affixed to the top that says *For Harper* in loopy handwriting.

I lift the lid. It seems to be a random collection of stuff. My dad used to have boxes like this in the back of his store, and I always loved dipping into them, never knowing what I might find. I claw through this one, and my hand lands on a dark green jewelry box that must be old because the material has turned a light brown near the gold hinges. Inside is a silver necklace with three large jade stones. I go to the mirror and hold it against my neck, feeling the smooth cool jade, wondering how long it's been like this, forgotten.

I put the necklace back and rummage deeper in the box. There are papers, old bills and receipts, newspaper clippings about the winery or Katrina's investments. A cheap key chain with an Ace playing card embedded inside it and *Monte Carlo* at the top, *1975* at the bottom. The year Katrina Van Ness returned from Europe, according to Elle—this must've been hers.

Diane's voice creeps into my mind before I can stop it. *Find out what you can about the family's history. Especially Katrina Van Ness.*

I pocket the key chain before I can think too hard about it.

At the bottom of the box is a hardcover poetry book. It looks well-loved, the sleeve torn in places and curling at the edges, pages earmarked, tiny notes and underlined phrases. There's an inscription at the front that reads, *For you, K. Monte Carlo forever. From your partner in crime, C.*

I start to put the book back and notice an envelope stuck upright against the side of the box. Inside is a packet of the family's birth certificates. Harper's and Richard's, signed by the same doctor with the same date—thirty-five years ago tomorrow. Zach's is next—his middle name is Benton, which I never knew. Katrina's is paper-clipped to another one. I try to remove the clip, but it's old and scratches the surface of the certificate, leaving a mark.

"Making yourself at home, I see."

I freeze, glance over my shoulder to find Zach hovering in the doorway. I quickly stuff the birth certificates inside the book and turn toward him. "Just looking for something fun to read," I say, waving my hand toward the shelves. "So many choices."

He crosses the room, studies the book, takes it from my hands.

My pulse races. I've been caught. He's going to see the birth certificates and think I was snooping.

But Zach just sets it down. "I missed you, *future wife*," he murmurs into my ear.

"Me too," I say, twisting and snaking my arms around him, relaxing into his body. "What was that call about before?"

"Just a frantic client making sure their wealth is still alive and kicking." He bops me on the nose. "I came to find you to see if you want to jump in the shower before me. Dinner's in an hour."

I nod, relieved that he's back to his normal self.

As we leave the room, he says, "I didn't even get a chance to ask. How did the boat ride go?"

"Good, for the most part. I don't think Harper likes me very much, though," I say, half joking, half not.

"Nonsense," Zach says, as we climb the staircase. "You're

being paranoid. In fact, she told me how smart she thinks you are. So there."

I force a smile. He's lying. I catch Zach in white lies sometimes, often about silly things that don't even matter, like claiming he canceled a gym membership or telling me one of his friends' wives really wanted to have lunch with me, only to find her completely unaware when I mentioned it. In most cases, it's because he doesn't want to hurt my feelings or because he wants me to feel like I fit in, but other times, I don't understand the purpose or why lying comes so easy for him.

"Did Elle grill you on antiques? I told her you were something of an expert," he says.

"An expert? Zach! You need to stop doing this." I stop at the top of the steps and twirl around.

"Doing what?"

This is another version of Zach's white lies. Talking me up, making me look good, all weekend, which is sweet. But it's a story he's scripting.

"You keep making me sound—more important than I am," I say.

He laughs. "You are important."

"I know, but it's just—it's almost lying."

He seems genuinely puzzled. "You know a ton about antiques, don't you? From your dad? And you're a great writer."

Here I am, accusing Zach of lying, and I told him my dad owned an antiques store, a stretch of the truth at best. He's never pressed for details on my family or career, which so far has worked in my favor, but it also means he fills in the details he wants to be true.

"Yes, but I was also a food server," I say. "And I do some freelance writing, but you make me sound like some award-winning international journalist."

"Lauren, you're not a waitress anymore. Now you let people serve you, not the other way around. *That's* how you need to act." He rubs my nose again, like he's summoning a genie, an alternate Lauren who will swirl out and become the girl he imagines me to be.

All weekend, he's been embellishing the truth. Perhaps he's just trying to help me fit in with his family, but we're keeping important things from them. The first night here, he cut me off when I was about to tell Harper we were moving in together. And now we're hiding our engagement. Is he embarrassed of me?

He kisses me again. "I was thinking…maybe there's a chance, depending on how things go, we might announce our good news at dinner tonight."

My stomach does a little flip at the thought—everyone around the table, Zach's beaming smile. How will they react? Surely Elle will be gracious, ushering a round of sparkling wine to toast. But what about Richard? Harper? Lucas? I swallow. What if they think I'm not good enough for Zach?

"It's going to be fine," Zach says, almost like he heard my thoughts. "Of course they'll love you as much as I do. You're going to be part of the family now. For better or worse."

HARPER

Cocktail hour has always been a sacred routine in this family. Mother swore by it the way others would practice a religion. She said it was a necessity to well-being, a gentle transition from daytime to nighttime, from working to playing. Of course, when you've got a winery, drinking is work and work is drinking, but a good ritual is a good ritual.

I'm more than ready for this ritual tonight. After a soak in a bergamot and jasmine muscle balm bath, I head downstairs, bumping into Richard in the hallway. He's wearing a crisp white shirt with dark blue buttons, no jacket, and those cigarettes tucked into his chest pocket.

"Isn't this Zach's shirt?" I say, tugging at one of the buttons.

He glances down, shrugs. "Elle picked it out for me."

"Very stylish," I say. "So unlike you."

He rolls his eyes in response.

"So did you get in touch with good ole Victor?" I ask casually. "Does he want my head on a platter, or a stake?"

That elicits a smile. "I did. He agrees the rest of the board is overreacting. Wants to discuss it tomorrow at the party."

"He's coming?" Every time I see Victor Hastings, he blows cigar smoke in my face, and I must endure his advice about how I need brick and mortar stores, that I'm missing out on all the "impulse buying" women like to do. But in this case, he happens to be right about the board overreacting.

"He is. And if you're just darling to him, maybe you can keep him on your side."

"*My* side?"

"Don't start, Harper. I don't need more problems."

It takes all my strength not to respond as we walk down the staircase. Richard loves acting like he's important, burdened with all our problems. It's his not-so-gentle reminder that he's the one who now handles all Van Ness Inc. matters, so we can all bow down to his sacrifices. I won't let him guilt trip me, though—it's not like he had much to do before he inherited the responsibility.

"Tell me you're not smoking in the house," I say as I catch a whiff of stale smoke. "I'd like to keep *my* lungs intact."

He points back up the stairs. "Office balcony."

Mother's office, with its French glass doors leading to the balcony she used to sit on to survey her kingdom, like some evil queen. When we were kids, we would sneak out there and dangle our legs through the railing, dreaming up items we could throw to the ground, what they would look like when they smashed. In our privileged world, the idea of destruction was intoxicating—things cracking, pulverizing, splattering, scattering into tiny pieces, never able to be made whole again.

A house built on lies will crumble like sand.

The words on the hourglass flit into my memory, and an unease settles in the pit of my stomach.

"Wait." I stop Richard at the bottom. "I need to talk to you about that gift."

"What about it?"

I chew my bottom lip. "I think someone's taunting me."

Lies. My heart starts beating faster. Why hadn't I made the connection before? Could someone know about my lie, about what I did? Was the hourglass a veiled threat that they will expose me?

"I think it's a threat," I say, and feel that same panic coming on, the intense fear that's been gripping me over the past few weeks. "Someone's trying to sabotage my company."

Richard cocks an eyebrow, then laughs. "An hourglass? *Harper.* Not everything's about you." But he's unwilling to meet my eye.

He's hiding something.

"What did the card say?" I demand.

He opens his mouth, but at that moment, Elle steps into the hall and spots us.

"There you are," she says, hands on her hips. "Come on, we're about to start."

Richard moves forward, but I grab his arm. "We'll be right there," I tell her.

He's got that tiny smirk, just a hint of one, that says he's getting irritated. "What's the matter? I thought you'd be eager to get in there and do wellness or whatever."

Todd's voice drifts down the hall from the library. I've always found it calming, sensual in his meditation videos, but hearing it in this house, right now, it feels as abrasive as a pumice stone.

I won't let him distract me. I pull out my phone, show Richard the text messages.

For once, Richard doesn't have anything snobbish to say. He drags me around the corner. "Okay, fine." He lowers his voice. "I don't want the others to know, but yes, there was a card. But it has nothing to do with VNity. Remember that person who was harassing me after Mom's death about money? Well, now she's claiming she's related to us."

That ends my spiraling thoughts. I was sure that hourglass's engraving was about VNity, some other threat from whoever released that video.

My brain regroups. "And you're worried why?" This kind

of thing has happened before, people approaching us with wild stories, empty threats, pleas for help. It all comes down to the fact that we have money, and they want it. No one wants to put in the work to get rich—they want it handed to them.

He shrugs. There seem to be gears turning in his brain, but this is how Richard is. He overthinks everything, keeps it inside. The key is to know how to draw him out.

He reaches into his back pocket and pulls out a small envelope. Inside is a birthday card with an hourglass on the front that says, Time Has a Way of Taking Care of Things. Inside is a photocopy of lab results with comparisons and segments and bar graphs. There are no identifying names, but the summary at the bottom says:

14.4 percent match, likely 1st cousins

It's circled, and scrawled below that, someone has written in pen: *Now I know why we were getting payments from your mother. Our family link is just the beginning of the story. I can tell you all about it soon.*

Richard is a fool if he's even thinking of believing one bit of this.

"It's a scam," I say, handing him back the card. "There aren't even any names on here. This is fake. Not even worth a response." These situations are best handled by doing nothing at all. Acknowledging it would just stoke the fire.

My twin frowns, tucks the card back in his pocket. Pushes up his glasses. "I don't know, Harper."

"Okay, fine. We'll look into it. Put your mind at ease. *After* this weekend. Can we just enjoy our birthday?"

Richard nods once, tucking the card back in his pocket, then disappears around the corner. But I know it's not over. My twin is incapable of ignoring things like this—he'll worry and analyze all angles, making everyone else miserable with him.

I follow him into the library, where a silver platter of finger foods has been set up on a table to the left of the doorway. Todd's standing next to it, greeting us with tumblers of ice and a thick light green liquid.

"Avocado margarita," Todd explains. "Superfood mocktail. Rich in heart-healthy fats and fiber." He brushes his fingers across the back of my hand as I accept my glass. I tip the drink into my mouth, wanting to hate it, but it's actually smooth and sweet.

"Come back if you want another," Todd whispers. "I'll be here."

Todd and I met at a wellness convention earlier this year, just after we'd buried Mother. Lucas's company was on the rise. The new luxe cosmetics line we'd launched was tanking. And there was Todd. He was presenting on happiness, about how we deprive ourselves of the smallest pleasures because we don't think we deserve them. *Eat the donut. Hit the snooze button. Buy the cool sunglasses. Get naked in the hot tub.* As he said the last one, he met my eye where I was sitting in the front row.

Todd was the embodiment of the small pleasures I'd been denying myself. His ideas resonated—where Mother had always preached willpower, resist impulses, be stern and strong, here was someone who told me to indulge, love, wallow. He was young, good-looking, well-liked. Along with our affair, we developed ideas for how to partner, to cross-promote our businesses, to make each other better. But over the last few months, our relationship started to become too complicated. He wanted to get more serious, even though he knew that wasn't possible, and I realized even small pleasures can begin to feel like big problems. So last week, I told Todd we needed to focus solely on our business relationship. Our emails since then have been purely professional, but now I'm wondering if my message sunk in.

Why is he here?

"Okay, everyone," Elle says, Todd next to her. "Now that we're all finally here, enjoying the delicious drinks and vegan canapés that Todd and Linnet have prepared for us, Todd's got an amazing short activity for us to do before dinner."

I look around the room. Richard has gravitated toward the food. Zach's on the couch with Lauren, who's wearing a one-shoulder black top, her hair pulled back to show off dangling silver earrings and cheekbones. Lucas hovers at the back of the room with a drink, notably not an avocado margarita.

"And remember," Elle continues, "there's a surprise after dinner. Get ready to play."

"Play what?" Richard asks, finishing off the last of the vegan cream cheese and pecan stuffed dates on the tray.

"You'll find out," she says playfully. "We shall meet again… in the dark."

Everything around me seems calm, but there's this restless nervousness fluttering inside me. Like I'm going to throw up a bunch of moths. I'm surrounded by family—my husband, my brothers, my sister-in-law. It's supposed to be my inner circle, people I can trust. But that's what Julius Caesar thought, too, right up until he got stabbed.

Todd is beaming, ready to show off his vast knowledge. This is when he's in his element, in front of an audience. He gets tons of views, likes, follows, on his YouTube channel, but I've always thought he was at his best like this, in person, eye to eye, where you can feel the energy.

Todd bows to all of us. "Friends, we're going to do an emotional balancing exercise. To get our chakras in order."

I lean back against the bookcases. The house creaks and groans from within the walls, as if protesting the company.

Lucas walks over, scotch and soda in hand. He sways his drink toward Todd. "How do you know this guy again?"

Todd picks up a dark leather box and carries it over to Elle.

"Work," I mutter, gripping my glass tight. "He's a business partner."

"I don't like the way he looks at you." Lucas sips his drink slowly.

Once Lucas gets an idea in his head, he's like a dog with a bone, not letting up until he's chewed all the marrow out of it. I'll have to get Todd alone, make him understand he cannot breathe a word of what happened between us. Make him understand this time that it's over.

"There are seven chakras, and they run down your spine. They are your energy centers," Todd says. "We must keep them open for mind and body harmony."

We should've gone on the ski trip. Even flying down a bitter cold mountain on two pieces of plastic would've been more enjoyable than being here in this miserable house.

"When we open ourselves, become vulnerable, we start to make connections. Start to see the world in a different way. We become transcendent."

Beside us, Richard uncaps a bottle of Mother's tequila and dumps it in his avocado drink, stares out the window at the vineyards and the woods and all that's beyond.

What else is hovering on the horizon? Maybe it's all Todd's talk about opening our energy, seeing things differently, but suspicion begins to poke inside me. What if someone really is related to us? And why would they go through all the trouble of the hourglass gift, the anonymous texts, the cryptic card? Why now, right when my business is blowing up?

Is it related, or just a coincidence?

And if it is related, what the hell does this asshole want?

I can tell you all about it soon, the note promised.

THE PARTY GUEST

Adjacent to the Van Ness mansion, just a few dozen yards from the back terrace, is a small workshop/storage shed. I open the door and step inside. There are useful things in here—wire cutters, hammers, containers of gasoline for the harvester—and useless things—broken gears, sharp staples, dirty newspaper. The wood floor is stained from years of smashed grapes and skins, and it smells like rot and oil.

There's a single window, grimy with dust and dirt, a smeared handprint near the bottom of the glass. It's interesting, I think, the traces of ourselves we leave behind wherever we go. Fingerprints, hair, skin, saliva—all this essential information we shed. It's why I was able to get my proof. Not so difficult, once I could get close enough to a Van Ness to secure the evidence I needed. A toothbrush, sealed up and sent off to Discreet DNA testing. It cost more than a normal cheek swab, but it'll be worth it in the end. An investment that will pay for itself and then some once this weekend is over.

I check the time, roll an empty wine bottle around and around on the work desk. I'm tired of all this waiting. Waiting, waiting, waiting. It makes me think too much, and then I get angry. I think about my dad, a handyman who could fix anything, who always knew the right tool for the problem. He'd work hard, do his best job, but there'd always be a client or two who found something wrong. Wealthy assholes who wanted some excuse not to pay him for his labor, who wanted to screw him out of what was rightfully his.

But justice will come for all those people. It will come for the Van Nesses, too. They won't be the first corrupt empire to fall.

We trust people to be good and decent. We trust our food, our drinks, to be safe. We trust our friends, our family, our partners, to have our backs and do the right thing. Honor their word.

And we should not.

People are selfish.

They will lie and cheat if they think they can get away with it, if they think it will gain them fortune and fame. These traits are inherited and taught, passed down from generation to generation, a family tree of deceit and lies.

So many tools here, some shiny and sharp, others dull and rusted. I make my selections carefully.

ELLE

Todd walks around the room with the leather box, and we drop our cell phones in.

"Friends!" His voice is powerful but soothing. "You are entering a healing space. It's time to clear your mind of distractions."

He sets the box in a corner and pulls out another. Inside are different colored pairs of glasses. "I want you to select a shade that sings to you. We are going to experiment with color therapy." He tells us that each color represents a different type of energy, and the colors can help to counterbalance any negative ones. "Pick one, but don't put them on yet."

I go first, to show a good example. After all, he's here because of me. And we all need this, don't we? The Van Nesses need time to reflect—all of us.

I choose the rose glasses, for grounding. Lauren plucks the aqua pair after Todd reveals that blue light will help you to express yourself clearly and be better understood. Zach, green for giving and receiving love. I almost think Richard isn't going to participate at all. He sighs and takes a glug of his drink before finally choosing the yellow, which Todd says is good for self-esteem, digestive issues, and power.

He will love tonight's game, though. They all will. A little nostalgia, a reminder of better times.

A little competition.

Todd stops in front of Harper. "These enact our sacral chakra." He doesn't wait for her to choose, just hands her an orange pair. "They release our sexual and creative energies, tapping into pleasure."

She hands them right back. "Which one counteracts rage?"

She says it calmly, but I can tell she's jittery, and a small part of me feels satisfied. Harper loves to make other people feel uncomfortable. Now maybe she'll understand how it feels.

After Harper selects a different pair, a darker blue than Lauren's for knowledge and authority, Todd bows slightly toward Lucas. "And you, my friend. I think you might find these useful." He offers him a pair of purple glasses.

"What are these for?"

Todd points to the middle of his forehead. "The third eye. Intuition. It allows you to be more aware of your surroundings. Of what's going on right under your nose."

Todd stays perfectly still, glasses extended, until Lucas gives in and accepts them. He swigs the rest of his drink, crunching the ice hard with his jaw, his eyes not leaving Todd.

"What a great idea this is," I say, trying to diffuse the tension. "A rainbow of energy!"

Todd shuts the box with a quiet snap and moves on from Lucas. He uses his phone to play soft music with ocean waves through a wireless speaker. There's a whoosh sound—a match catching fire—and an earthy incense fills the room.

"Now, everyone, close your eyes," Todd says. "Stand up as straight as you can. Imagine you have a string stretching from the top of your head to the ceiling, pulling you up."

I concentrate on my breathing. In and out. In and out. But I'm distracted by every noise—Lucas sighing, Zach shuffling, dull thumps and thuds in the walls as the house settles. My mind wanders, travels to all its shadowy corners, poking at the bits and pieces of trouble, bringing the wrong shaving cream, letting Harper embarrass me on the boat, not being able to solve Mom's riddle.

My parents were good at reminding me where I didn't measure up. I went to the prep school they wanted, I aced all my classes, I took etiquette lessons, learned ballroom dancing, got into Cornell. But I wasn't interested in med school or law school, and therefore whatever else I pursued was a failure in their eyes. In college, I put my all into my sorority but never felt pretty enough, thin enough, popular enough to be my best. I was always worried about not stacking up.

"Okay," Todd says, "now we are going to open our eyes and put on our glasses."

I slide the lenses on, and the room turns a shade of pink, like the horizon during a summer sunset.

Todd walks around barefoot. "Nice, nice," he says, stopping in front of Harper. Next to her, Lucas crosses his arms, glaring at Todd. As he passes, Lucas flicks his neck above his shirt collar, so hard it must sting, but Todd continues as if nothing happened.

"Loose thread," Lucas mutters.

Seems like his glasses are making him more aware, as Todd suggested.

And maybe mine are working, too.

I watch Harper through the pink haze. When I met her in my first job, she was refreshing. She was blunt instead of fake nice. She was confident and funny. I loved her. I would've done anything for her.

Now, through the pink lenses, she's suddenly delicate, crushable, like spun sugar. Her reputation and brand mean everything to her, and now it's dissolving.

The videos and screenshots I sent to the *Van Nessity* blog have long been purged and deleted from my laptop and email, but they are just starting to have their effect. It was pure luck that they posted this weekend, when we are all together.

When I could see Harper's reaction in person.

HARPER

It's soul-sucking dark outside.

After Todd's color therapy session, I find Bill and ask him to make sure the gates are locked, to not buzz in any unidentified cars without clearing it with one of us first. He reminds me about the storm. "Roads will flood," he intones, like some weathered sage from a fantasy novel. "You will get stuck."

It looks like Elle won't get the party she hoped for.

Because of my pleasant and uplifting run-in with Bill, I assume I'll be the last to arrive for dinner. But when I enter the dining room, Elle isn't there yet.

"Where's our hostess?" I ask. Everyone else is already seated. My husband and Richard on one side of the table, Zach at one head, Lauren next to him.

It's Linnet, filling the water glasses, who answers. "Miss Elle asked me to save her plate for later."

"Why?" It's not like Elle to miss out on *family time*. I start to sit at the other head, but Lucas waves me off.

"Assigned seats," he says, pointing to the place cards, and I take my spot across from Richard, beside Lauren.

"And we've got these." Zach twirls a deep purple envelope,

and it's then I notice we each have one, propped up against our wineglasses.

I pick up mine. In calligraphy it says OPEN AFTER DINNER.

"I guess we'll have to enjoy each other's company until then," Richard says with a smirk. He pulls out a toy and shows it to Lucas. "Seriously, you don't remember these?"

It's a motorcycle with a small stunt driver. "Oh god, not that Evel Knievel doll," I say.

"It's not a doll, it's an *action figure*." Richard rolls the motorcycle around the table like he's a five-year-old.

Linnet has prepared fresh salmon with couscous and grilled vegetables. I take a small bite—a little overdone, but that's Linnet's signature touch—and uncork a pinot noir that's light-bodied enough to pair well with the fish.

"Where the hell did you unearth that from?" I ask Richard about the toy. "I thought you'd long ago set fire to it with all the stunts."

"Elle found it in a box," Richard says proudly.

"I seriously have no memory of that toy," Zach says, squinting at it.

"Of course you don't." Richard pushes it toward me across the table. The driver's painted clothing is scratched and dirty, his helmet askew from all the rough stunt driving on the pavement. "By the time you were old enough, we'd moved on to archery and video games."

"You guys were always ten steps ahead." Zach gestures with his knife. "I was always playing catch-up."

I toss the toy back to Richard, who sets it on the sideboard and digs into his dinner.

The atmosphere is more relaxed without Elle trying desperately to force everyone to have fun. She plans so much that there's nothing spontaneous left, and we have to fight for freedom to stray from the rigid schedule. Which is why I insisted on the boat ride earlier, a little wrench in the machinery to remind her she can't control everything. Elle thinks she can design her life down to the smallest details and then gets upset when it doesn't go exactly right. Like her wedding. She and Mother treated it like it was their full-time job. As her maid of honor, I had to endure the weekly meetings, the constant texts, the dance lessons, the gown fittings, the destination bachelorette party. It was Elle's entire world, and she couldn't understand why I wasn't gushing over the lace samples for the edges of the tablecloths or upset that the yellow in the centerpieces wasn't an exact match of her bouquet.

It was the beginning of the erosion of our friendship.

But it was her conniving, model-daughter-in-law act that really drove the knife between us. After all the stories I told her about Mother and her tests, after Elle and I bonded over our parents' expectations and the way we felt when we failed them, she threw herself into this family anyway and left me behind.

I stab a zucchini with my fork. Above us, in the ceiling, a scurrying sound starts and just as quickly stops. Wonderful. We probably have a squirrel problem again.

Richard nods at Zach. "So, are you going to tell everyone your big news?"

Beside me Lauren watches Zach like a hawk. She's clutching her hands on top of the napkin in her lap.

"Oh, right," Zach says. He claps his hands together and rubs them. A sparkle of light in my peripheral vision draws my eye back to Lauren's lap. It's a ring, which she begins to slide on her finger just as Zach opens his mouth and says, "I got a promotion to partner."

"Oh, nice, man," Lucas says.

The ring slides back off and disappears into Lauren's fist as she takes a large gulp of wine.

But not before I spot the diamond.

Zach's accepting the congratulations, oblivious to Lauren's

discomfort. She manages a smile and a hug, though. "Such great news," she says.

So he was serious last night, all that talk about her being the one. What the hell is he thinking?

But that's just it—Zach often doesn't think things through. He chases the high, the good feelings, and when the confetti has settled, he gets bored. Mother babied him his whole life, but now that she's gone, it's time for him to realize we can't keep stepping into that role. We're not going to keep bailing him out of his mistakes.

I wonder if Lauren has any clue about Zach's spending habits, because that might make this whole affair a little less fairy-tale for her.

Everyone besides Lauren, though, seems to be in a good mood. Even Richard is lighter, sucking down a chocolate raspberry cupcake and asking for seconds. Maybe it's the alcohol, or Todd's glasses exercise.

We're polishing off the dessert wines when Zach points at the purple envelopes and says, "Should we open these now?" Without waiting for a response, he shoves a thumb under the flap of his and tugs out a stiff card. He glances at it, then picks up Lauren's and opens hers too. *"Play vines brings?"* he reads off her card.

Lauren shrugs, barely looking at the cards, and tugs on her hair. She's wadded up her napkin into a tight ball in her lap.

The men are too into the cards to notice. "Yeah, mine makes no sense either," Lucas says, and tilts his head at me. "Open yours."

I slide out the card. Nice stock, heavy, premium, no expenses spared when Elle's spending Van Ness money. Mine says: *Remember. See. Light.*

The candles in the middle of the table flick back, then forward, as Linnet clears plates, brings more wine.

"It's a riddle," Richard says. "We're supposed to figure it out."

I get up and walk around the room, studying everyone's cards over their shoulders. Elle can't be that clever. I can figure this out.

"Maybe it's a code," I say. "A message."

The words on each card don't say much, but they feel familiar in a way that makes my stomach turn.

"Elle's behind this?" I ask Richard, giving him the twin stare-down.

Is he getting the same vibe? The cards. The words—*vines, see, darkness*. I remember last time we played that game—running, hard breath, my palms scratched and bleeding, nothing but darkness and the smell of the trees.

"So are there words missing or something?" Zach nudges Lauren, gesturing for her card again. She passes it to him without a word. He brushes his hair out of his eyes, comparing it to his. He looks so much like Mother.

"I don't think so." It's Richard's turn to walk around the table. After one rotation, he snaps his finger. "I think we have to read a word at a time. Like, go around the room."

Of course. I should've thought of that.

"Starting with who?" Zach asks.

"Me," Richard says, as though he's won a prize. He points to himself and says, "Come."

Lucas snorts at that. We all ignore him.

Then he points to Lucas, who reluctantly says, "Outside."

"And," says Zach.

"Play," Lauren says.

We go around like this, Richard pointing at each of us like a conductor.

"Remember," I say.

"Without."

"Sight."

"The."

"Vines."

"See."

"Deeper."

"Darkness."

"Always."

"Brings."

"Light," I finish.

"Is that it?" Zach asks, looking at all of us for confirmation. Then he repeats it for our benefit. "Come outside and play. Remember, without sight the vines see deeper. Darkness always brings light."

"Well, that clears everything up," Lucas laughs, fiddling with his napkin.

Elle is good at details. I look over at Richard, and I know he knows, too.

But it's Zach who says it aloud.

"Mom's forest game?" he asks, puzzled.

We played it so many times over the years. Hands outstretched, exploring the woods, forging forward, racing to be first, to win Mother's approval.

I think about Elle's comment on the boat this afternoon. *Mom always loved this view.* All her talk about surprises, about reliving the good days here. Just like before Mother died, she's inserting herself where she has no business.

The drama. The staging. The memories.

She's trying to *be* Mother.

"Did you know about this?" I ask Richard. But I can tell from his face he did not.

"Know about what?" asks Lauren, but no one acknowledges her.

And that's when we all hear it ring.

The gong.

Let the games begin.

LAUREN

A low tone sounds as we head outside to the front yard. Elle stands there in a black poncho with a hood, holding a mallet next to a large gong.

"Hello, everyone," she says, waving her arms, a witch greeting her coven. "Linnet tells me you've figured out the riddle."

Todd is next to her, his hands clasped behind his back, wearing a short-sleeved T-shirt even though the temperature dropped when the sun did. I wouldn't have thought the younger, tattooed guy was Harper's type. Plus, he's so earnest, so unlike her. She's already got Lucas—why would she risk messing that up for Todd Christie?

"Todd has generously agreed to help us with this game," Elle says as we gather around her.

I avoid standing next to Zach, though I can feel him trying to catch my eye. I'm tired of him acting like he's ashamed of me, that he feels he has to lie about me and our relationship to others. It's cold, and I cross my arms to keep warm. I was only able to grab my light coat near the door on the way out.

"Got a chill, Delaware?" Lucas smiles down at me, suppressing a yawn.

"I know some of you will recognize it, but I do hope it will be fun for all…" Elle continues.

Lucas unravels his scarf from his neck and wraps it around mine, tucking in the edges. It smells freshly laundered.

"Aren't you such a gentleman," Harper murmurs on his other side.

"Some women appreciate a simple act of kindness," he says.

I bury my face in the scarf to hide my smile, not daring to look at Harper.

"I do hope I can recreate it the right way. Lauren, Todd, I know you've never played," Elle says, and my name snaps my attention back to her. "But as I understand, it's all about the power of your senses."

She holds up a thick purple envelope and slides out silky material. At first I think it's a necktie, but then I see: blindfolds.

Elle gestures across the sloping lawn to the dark woods. "This patch of woods leads to our Concord vines. When Richard, Harper, and Zach were kids, they used to dare each other to race through it in the dark. Who was brave enough? Who could get through to the other side the fastest?"

"Not just as kids—we've played it nearly every year. And it was Mom who dared us," Richard corrects her. "She waited on the other side, ringing the gong to guide us."

In response, Elle rings the gong. The sound seems to vibrate around us, disappear into the dense, hulking trees. "And tonight, we're going to bring that tradition back. We'll be one with the night. We will let the night determine our fate."

"I love this idea," Todd says, nodding at Elle. "To be in tune with nature. There's nothing better."

Lucas tosses me a look and then addresses Elle. "But they all know this place so well." He gestures to me. "Delaware doesn't. And I don't really either."

"I've already thought of that," Elle says dramatically.

Under her breath Harper says, "Of course you have."

"You will all pair up in teams, and the more experienced one will guide the newbie."

"*You* will all pair up?" asks Harper. "And what will you do, Elle?"

"I'm your guide."

Harper stares at her, and I can feel the tension like it's a live electric wire between them. "You mean you'll ring the gong. Like Mother used to."

"Exactly."

"I'm not playing," Harper declares. "This is ridiculous."

Elle lifts an eyebrow. "Scared, Harper?"

"No, Elle," she says condescendingly.

"I don't know. Sounds to me like you're chicken," Lucas says, chewing a fingernail.

"Oh, for fuck's sake," Harper says. "Fine. Let's get this stupid game over with."

Elle smiles—a victory—and raises a small envelope. She tells me to step forward and pick a scrap of paper to determine my partner. I close my eyes and choose a piece. "Zach."

Zach offers a high five. "Nice, we're a team. Don't worry, we've got this. It'll be fun. I promise."

I'm relieved it's not Harper or Richard who will be leading me around the dark woods, but I don't let Zach see it. I bury my face further into Lucas's scarf.

Lucas chooses Richard's name from the envelope, which means Harper is paired with Todd, who makes a murmur of pleasure at the outcome.

"Wait," Richard says before Elle can tie on his blindfold. "What are we playing for? We need a goal."

"No, we don't," Harper says, her tone clipped.

A burst of wind kicks up, rustling Elle's poncho like it's alive.

"Mom always had a goal," Richard protests, ignoring the daggers Harper's shooting his way. "Like a prediction. It can be whatever, but it has to be something. Like, whoever wins will always find happiness, or will find something they lost."

"She just did that to mess with our heads," Harper says, though her hands are fluttering nervously. "Superstition. If you cheat, you risk ruining your fortune. We aren't twelve anymore, Richard."

"No, no, I like this," Elle says. The lawn is dark, but the lights in the house illuminate Elle's eyes ominously. "Okay, whoever wins gets first pick at the reserve wines in Mom's cellar. And if you cheat—" she pauses, squaring her shoulders, "you will be forever haunted by your worst fear."

She rings the gong again to seal it, and I shiver as the low tone reverberates around us. It suddenly does feel like we've made some sort of pact. That we're in it now, no way out.

Elle ties a silk blindfold around Zach's eyes, and then another over mine.

"Remember, you are one with the night now," she says. "Feel your way, use your instincts. Have fun. I'll be waiting for you on the other side."

Zach touches my arm, slides his palm down it, grasps my hand and tugs. *This way.*

I take two steps and wobble. The ground's uneven, and we haven't even made it to the woods yet, where the tree roots lie in wait.

I've always been afraid of the woods, especially at night. Since I was a little girl walking with my mom through a nearby park to get home from a friend's house, worried about every crunch or hoot. All the worst stories are about what happens in the woods—kids disappearing, creatures attacking, creepy men lurking. Anything's possible in the darkness.

Did I ever tell Zach this? I have a vague memory of confessing it one night over drinks, but surely if I'd told him, he wouldn't put me through this kind of game. Would he?

The hairs rise on my arms as we enter the woods. The smell

in the air intensifies, soil, rotting leaves. It's colder here. Something brushes past my head, and I yelp.

"Just relax." Zach squeezes my hand reassuringly.

Relax. It's what he said to me last night right before he covered my eyes so Harper could hand me grape juice.

As we walk, I wave my free hand out in front of me so I don't smash into a tree trunk. I have no idea where we are. Each time I blink, my eyelashes brush noisily against the silk. My feet crunch twigs and leaves and god knows what else.

The gong sounds from somewhere far away. It feels impossible we'll ever get there.

But it sets off an urgency in Zach. "Hurry," he whispers. He tugs, grasping my fingers so hard I can feel the joints straining.

"Zach, you're hurting me. I—"

And then something snags my foot. I trip and go down hard. There's barely enough time to break my fall so I don't land on my face. The impact scrapes my palms. I roll to the side, my foot still caught. A rope. A snake. A vine. I imagine being pulled down into the earth, swallowing soil, never to be seen again.

I rip off the blindfold. It's so dark in the woods that it takes a minute for my eyes to adjust, but then I make out Zach, his blindfold still on, turning in a circle. "Lauren?"

"I'm here," I say. I walk over to him and he grabs my hand again, presses his mouth to my ear. "Are you okay?"

"Yeah. I'm fine. But we're going to hurt ourselves with these things on."

"That's the game. Just don't take it off, it's cheating."

"I already did."

He slides his up, blinking. "Then we've lost," he says, disappointed, "I can't believe it. That's the one thing we aren't supposed to do."

"Well, I guess that makes two of us who say they're going to do something and then don't," I say. I wasn't planning to do this tonight, but the dark woods have me extra on edge.

"You're mad about before," he says quietly. "I'm sorry, Lauren. I didn't want to announce it without Elle there."

"It's not just that. You didn't tell me about the promotion either. Richard knew? But not me? You've been waiting to hear about that for weeks."

I can hear the whine in my voice, and I don't like it. I was determined to go along with things this weekend, be the agreeable girlfriend, make everyone like me, but the role is wearing me down.

"He overheard me on the phone," Zach says. "I didn't know he was going to put me on the spot like that. I wanted to tell you first."

Everything he says is reasonable, understandable, but something still feels off. Is it me? Is it because a part of me craves confirmation that our engagement isn't a secret Zach's too embarrassed to share? My fear that at any moment, Zach's going to realize his mistake?

Just make sure you don't get too big of a head, Lauren Brady, my mother said when I finally told her I was moving to New York. *No one from Maurville ever makes much of themselves. What makes you think you're so special?*

"Look, we can tell them tonight, okay?" Zach says. I can tell he wants to drop it, smooth over the conflict, move on. "They'll be thrilled for us. They freaking love you."

He's got that dazzling grin on, so wide I can see it even here in the darkness of the woods.

"They don't, Zach," I snap. "They don't love me. I'm not sure they even like me."

The grin dies as fast as it came. "What's with you, anyway? It's not like you to be this negative." His tone is light, but there's an accusation behind it.

"It's not me being negative, Zach. It's the truth. My interactions with your siblings have been a bunch of polite nods at best and otherwise snarky comments."

A gust of wind works its way through the trees, rustling what's left of the leaves. They shake above us as if protesting in Zach's defense.

"That's not fair—"

I won't let him spin this away. "You can't just keep creating these alternate versions of life just because that's what you wish it was like. You talk like everyone's glad to be here, but your family doesn't even like this place. They're going to sell the estate right out from under you and you don't even know it." I stop, out of breath. I've gone too far.

Zach backs away. I can barely see him in the shadows now. "Is that really what you think of my family?"

"It's not what I think. It's what I heard. Last night, after you went to bed. Zach, they've been going behind your back. Making some kind of deal."

Elle's gong rings out once more. How much time has passed? It feels like we've been here for hours, and also barely any time at all.

"You want to talk about alternate versions?" There's a slow-burning anger in Zach's voice, something I've never heard from him before. We've never fought. Anytime there's been a slight disagreement, Zach's turned it around, made it go away. And I've let him. "You were worried my family wasn't going to like you, and now you're convinced they're villains. You keep saying you want to fit in, but you won't even try to play this game with me. Fine. Don't play. But don't stand there and tell me my family is turning against me. Find your own way back."

He whirls and marches off, his feet crunching the decaying leaves. By the time I realize I should follow him, he's long gone.

I tear up in frustration before I can stop myself. I'm alone in the woods. All I can make out are the dark outlines of the trees. But I need to get out of here. I start off in the direction I thought I heard Elle's gong ring from. An owl hoots in the distance. The varying shades of black before me begin to morph into shapes. Tentacled monsters, gargoyles, witches with long, wild hair. I try not to think about the coyote we saw last night from the terrace, those shining green eyes, the way it slinked off silently into the night.

Why hasn't Elle sounded the gong again? Did another team already win? What if the others have already returned, are in the warm house sipping wine and placing bets about when and if I'll ever make it back?

Maybe Zach is right. Maybe I do tend to jump to the worst conclusions. It's an old habit of mine, a way to set expectations so I wouldn't be upset when I got home to find my new bike sold or our summer vacation canceled.

There's a thrashing of leaves behind me. I stop, wait, hoping it's not a coyote looking for dinner. Then Lucas appears through the trees, walking quickly, his breath visible in bursts, and I recognize just how much the temperature has dropped.

"Delaware." He looks surprised to see me.

"Thank god," I say. "Where's Richard?"

He shrugs, points his thumb behind him. "We gave up, took off the blindfolds. Richard said he had too much wine and wasn't feeling it. He went to find Elle and call it off. I decided to head back. But I think I got lost. This is a stupid fucking game."

I laugh. It's a relief. But Lucas must hear the watery tone to my voice, because he peers into my eyes.

"Uh-oh. Trouble in paradise." He smells like his scarf—fresh laundry—and cedar.

"No, it's fine, it's not—"

He puts a finger to my lips, leans forward, mouth to my ear. "They're nothing like us. They've always had anything they want. *Anyone* they want."

Like Todd Christie? Or Sara with the heart-dotted i's? But I don't have to ask that. I know. Lucas knows about his wife's affair— maybe he's always known, or maybe he's just discovered it.

Maybe it wasn't even the first time, or the last. It doesn't matter. What matters is he's right. The Van Nesses are nothing like us.

He takes the blindfold from my fist, slowly unfolds it, his hand brushing my wrist. He holds it in the air between us, watching it dangle for a moment before meeting my eyes, then steps forward and ties it around my head. He puts his hands on my hips and walks me back against a tree. My heart thumps loudly in my chest, and time seems to have slowed, or stopped altogether.

And then Lucas kisses me.

His hands are in my hair. His beard prickling against my chin. His warm lips, our breath, the crisp air.

You're part of the family now. Zach's words echo in my ears, distorting and changing, first teasing, then angry, then mocking. *For better or worse.*

Just as suddenly as it starts, the kiss is over. There's a crushing of leaves, an animal or a person approaching. Lucas pulls away, and I hear him rush off.

I yank up my blindfold.

My stomach flips. The rustling stops, then gets farther away before disappearing completely.

And there's nothing, no one, at all.

HARPER

Mother first introduced us to the blindfold game when we were kids. Back then it was simple, sitting in the garden sniffing flowers or getting tickled with grass stems, or Pin the Tail on the Donkey. As we got older, the stakes got higher. Blindfolded trust walks, taking turns guiding one another through obstacle courses with just the sound of our voices.

She added the goals to make it more interesting, and to keep us honest. *Whoever wins will be lucky for a week* or *If you win, the monsters won't attack*. And then when we were older, we'd compete for bigger stakes—cash, a weekend getaway with friends, or once, a light gray Porsche Boxster convertible. Implying, though it was never said, that if we cheated, our luck would fail, the boogeyman would find us, we would be punished and stripped of privileges.

I was always the best at the races, fast, merciless, groping my way through the woods like an animal. I'd emerge on the other side bruised, dirty, pricked by thorns, rushing toward that gong to be the first to ring it, to be the one who pleased Mother most. Only I never was. She always found something to criticize—*You must've cheated. Go back. Start again.* Or if not, she'd rig the game so I'd be disadvantaged. She'd make me wait, give my brothers a head start, because *that's how it is in the real world, Harper—men always get an advantage, and you have to learn to win despite it.*

"Where are we going?" Todd asks. If Richard hadn't mentioned the goddamn goals, I'd abandon Todd right now and finish this bullshit on my own. He's an anchor holding me back.

But Mother's superstitions, as much as I despise them, still taunt me. Not worth the risk.

"Harp? Can we stop for just a sec—"

"No."

Once the gong has rung, Harper, you must continue on.

I zigzag through the trees, get low. I can't go as fast as I used to, but I still have the instinct. "Stay behind me," I tell Todd. "Don't trip either. You're too heavy for me to carry."

"I feel the negative energy radiating off you," Todd says. "Are you not doing your breathing exercises?"

How nice it must be to live a life where breathing deeply fixes all your problems. He doesn't have to worry about people judging his every move. There are no debates online about whether he's gotten plastic surgery done, or random strangers snapping unflattering photos of him on the street. He doesn't have Kat Fucking Sparks blogging about him every five seconds, squeezing the juice from every random bit of gossip she hears and blasting it out to the world.

The world will judge you if you're a woman. The world will eat you up and spit you out. That's why Mother avoided talking about her age, her past, her youth. She used to tell me I'd be able to open doors just because I was young, beautiful, but that only lasted so long. There comes a point, she'd say, where the world stops seeing you—and that's both a curse and a blessing.

My life began and ended when I turned twenty, Harper, she would say.

We're not getting very far. Todd is slow and clunky—all that muscle, he's like a goddamn bulldog. I imagine this is not what he signed up for when he agreed to entertain the Van

Ness family for the weekend, or maybe it is. Maybe when Elle told him we'd be running around in the dark, he thought it might be a chance to rekindle our affair, be one with nature in several *different* ways.

"I'm glad we're alone," Todd says. "I've been wanting to talk to you about something, Harp."

I pause, press my hand against bark. "Stop calling me that. I'm not an instrument."

He lets go of my hand, and then I feel his fingers in my hair. Somewhere far away, Elle rings the gong.

"Is it this game causing you stress, Harper? Being back here?"

The last time we played this game was right before Mother got diagnosed. A storm was brewing then, too, the sky heavy with moisture, threatening to spill over, and Mother with her black cloak beckoned us forward. *Humor me, just one more time.* It was just the four of us that spring—Lucas had been traveling for work and Elle had stayed in the city to supervise some work being done on her and Richard's house—but Mother seemed to enjoy the intimacy of it. We were all much too old for these games, but Mother hadn't been herself, tired, unwell, and we wanted to appease her.

The goal that night was especially morbid. *Whoever wins the game will live the longest,* she said. *And if you cheat or quit, it's me you'll curse.* Then she rang the gong, sealing it.

"This is not a therapy session, Todd," I say, pulling him hard now.

"I can see the worry lines on your forehead."

"What?" I tear off my blindfold. Todd is staring at me, a smile playing on his lips. "You cheated," I hiss. "You made us lose."

He tilts his head. "There are more important things to talk about than a game." He slides his hands in his pockets and lifts his face like he's baying at the moon. "You were right, by the way. About this place. It's magnificent. All this fresh air. So good for your lungs."

That last game, I'd done my best ever. It was like I had a shield and a compass guiding me, like the trees were bending to get out of my way, creating a path for me. I knew I was way ahead of my brothers. I was almost to the other side. I was going to win.

Todd interrupts my memory. "This stress, this bitterness. It's very unhealthy. Are you regretting the ending of our relationship?"

"We didn't have a *relationship*. We fucked a few times. It was *okay*."

He flinches at the "okay," like I hoped he would.

"Harper, you and I both know that's not how you feel. Why did you really end things so quickly?"

He stretches out an arm and draws me closer. I smell the essential oils evaporating off his body. Tea tree, silver fir. His white shirt is visible in the darkness like a surrender flag. *Sometimes it's okay to give in to your urges*, he lectured that day I first saw him. *Sometimes the best thing you can do for yourself is the one you think you shouldn't.*

"It was so sudden. I'm not ashamed to admit I was hurt," he whispers.

"I'm sorry you were hurt, but I'm married," I say, as gently as is possible for me. I need to keep him on my good side. "And you and I still have a good thing going with our cross-promotion, don't we? We should focus on that."

"Actually, Harper…" Todd steps back. I hear the hesitation in his voice. "That's what I wanted to talk to you about. I think we need to hold off on that for a while."

What?

"Image is everything." He's talking more quickly now. "You of all people know this. I have to be careful who I associate with. If this is going viral, now is not the time for us to partner."

"If what's going viral? Some unwarranted complaint about the way I manage my employees? It's nothing. It'll be gone by morning."

He's unnervingly quiet. He can't be serious. After all the work we put into the cross-promotion. The videos, the testimonials, the ad sales.

"What about the bruise, Harper?"

My hand flies to my chest. "What about it?"

"If the truth ever comes out…"

"The truth *won't* come out." I'm being too loud. Sound travels unpredictably out here, and we aren't that far from the others.

"I just can't have this hanging over me if someone finds out what you—"

I slap him. Hard. The sound of my palm on his cheek startles us both.

"I was attacked," I hiss, and then I run, my sneakers crunching the fallen leaves. I run out of these woods, away from Todd, away from all the bullshit.

You haven't won the game, Harper. You don't know how to play right. Mother's voice rings out in my mind, so clear I feel like I could whirl around and she'd be there with the mallet in her hand. Like that last time we played.

I'd cleared the woods. All I had to do was get across the yard to where she was standing. But just as I emerged, I felt something skittering across my face. Before I could brush it away, it crawled under my blindfold.

I screamed, pulled the mask off, pawed at my face. In the moonlight, I saw the spider, big as a quarter, on the back of my hand before I knocked it away into the grass.

And then I ran to Mother.

But she wasn't pleased. I wasn't supposed to remove my blindfold. I'd shown weakness, I'd failed. I cursed her.

Two weeks later, Mother was diagnosed with cancer.

You broke the rules, Harper. It's your fault Mother's dead.

ELLE

Once their silhouettes fade into the trees, I lift the gong into the back of the golf cart Bill brought around earlier and drive myself to the other side of the woods.

Mom told me about this game, how much she loved playing it with Richard, Harper, and Zach. It was not one of the ones I ever participated in, but Mom said it was a great test of character, of grit, and I knew that bringing it back would make this weekend even more special.

I park the golf cart and perch on top of a picnic table, leaning back on my elbows and staring up through the leafless trees. It's a shame it's so overcast, because out here there are so many stars visible at night. One time, when Richard and I were still dating, he spread out a blanket and we opened a bottle of wine and I'd never seen anything so beautiful in my life—hundreds of twinkling stars, revealing themselves in the night.

But tonight, there's nothing. Not even the moon can penetrate beyond a dim glow. The air feels heavier. I hope Bill and Linnet are wrong about the storm coming early.

I ring the gong. I like the power of it, the solemn ritual, but it's lonely out here in the dark. Maybe I should've put Todd in charge so I could play. I might've even won—Mom was always impressed with how quickly I picked up on her games, how eager I was to join. I could've beaten them all, proven once and for all that I am worthy of the Van Ness name.

But no. I couldn't trust Todd with such an important role, Mom's role. It had to be me.

I miss her. She and I had a connection, a bond. She would've wanted me to finish the work she started, to keep this family's traditions alive, maintain the house and the land. Spoil Zach, give Richard responsibility and purpose, teach Harper lessons. Mom told me once near the end that she feared she'd been too hard on Harper. That she tried to make her a strong person, to set her up for success, but instead she worried she'd driven her away.

But Mom could've gone easy on Harper, and it wouldn't have made a difference. Harper's too self-absorbed to see anyone else, to understand their intentions. She only pays attention when something affects her image. That's why I sent that video out to the world. She needed a mirror to look into. To see she's wrong.

It's taking longer than I thought for everyone to cross the woods. It's so quiet out here. I can almost imagine that everyone's disappeared. That the world has come to an end and I'm the only one left. Elle Diamond Van Ness—the sole survivor.

Then I see the beam. A flashlight, sweeping the vineyards behind me.

A flashlight isn't part of the game. It's probably Bill. Sometimes he does night checks, making sure deer aren't sneaking in to eat the fruit. But these are dormant vineyards—the fruit is gone. There's no need to check them this time of year, and whenever Bill does, he takes one of the small tractors. He wouldn't just trudge through the vineyards on foot.

The flashlight seems to be getting nearer, and my chest tightens. I slide off the picnic table and sprint over to the golf cart, hoping the beam won't catch me. I crouch behind the cart, waiting.

And then, just like that, it turns off.

I don't move, don't take my eyes off the spot where the light disappeared. The vineyards are a black sea, and beyond them, more darkness, endless places to hide.

I glance back to the woods. I could run for cover in there, conceal myself behind a tree trunk. Yell for the others.

When there's no other movement or sign of life, I begin to doubt myself. Am I overreacting? Maybe I imagined the whole thing.

But then, the gong rings. A harsh, loud sound.

Did someone emerge from the woods? Did someone win the game? I rise and walk back over to the picnic table. The gong's still resonating a faint sound, the mallet abandoned on the ground beside it. But there's no team here triumphantly claiming a win. There's no one at all.

Just a white box at the center of the table.

I open the lid. The inside is padded with white satin, and on top, tied with a gold bow, is a brittle, dried grapevine branch.

My pulse pounds in my ears. I immediately think of Mom's warning.

A cut vine means a severed line.

W-JKA BREAKING NEWS

"It was definitely a Van Ness." Two dead at popular winery.

SUNDAY, October 15—A WJLK news source confirms one of the Van Ness siblings has been killed at the Van Ness winery and estate early Sunday morning. "It was definitely a Van Ness," he says, though WJLK cannot yet confirm which of the three siblings has died. The second body remains unidentified.

Officers at the scene could be seen scouring the grounds for evidence, while others were posted at each of the security gate entrances of the family compound.

"No one gets in or out of here until we figure out what the hell happened," one officer was overheard saying.

Emergency responders were delayed because of the torrential thunderstorms that hit the area starting Saturday afternoon, flooding many roads. Lightning downed a tree, blocking a major artery leading up to the winery's main entrance.

As word got out about the deaths, fans of Harper Van Ness, CEO of the popular, though controversial, beauty company VNity, took to social media to show their support. "Harper, let us know you're alright!" one fan tweeted. The beauty mogul has been under the spotlight since Thursday for alleged mistreatment of employees.

Attempts to reach someone at VNity for a statement about the tragedy have gone unanswered.

SATURDAY

The Day of the Party

ELLE

Outdoor morning yoga sounded blissful when I'd planned it with Todd. I imagined us waking with the dawn, stretching arms to the blue sky, cold invigorating air expanding our lungs. I imagined striking a powerful warrior pose with the vineyards as a backdrop, unrolling our mats on the dewy grass for a satisfying downward dog.

But the sky is a flat, slate gray, and the chill in the air sinks deep to the bone. There's a light fog hovering just above the vineyards, giving them a haunted feel. I slept too late and rushed Richard out into this weather only to find the single sign of life in a lone cricket on a picnic table under a nearby pavilion, swishing its feelers like it's preparing to burrow under my skin.

"The others will be here soon," I tell Richard, scanning the landscape. Zach said they'd be walking, but it's not *that* far. What is taking so long?

A cut vine means a severed line—I keep thinking about the prank from last night. A broken vine signifies a betrayal, the end of a relationship, Mom always said. So which of them thought it would be funny to leave it for me? Who snuck away from the game to mess with me?

My money's on Harper.

I threw the box and the vine in the trash and acted like nothing happened. When Richard found me by the picnic table, I told him I'd seen a coyote and it spooked me. I'm not sure he believed me.

There Elle goes with her stories again. I hear my mother's voice in my head, my father's knowing chuckle.

I take a large swig from my portable insulated coffee mug.

I need to focus.

I unroll my yoga mat as Richard continues to pace behind me. "Let's just sit," I say, light, chipper. I kneel. The wet, cold grass seeps into my lilac yoga pants, but somehow it feels good—the painful shock grounds me.

I press my hands together, close to my chest. There are tiny scratches on my wrists, a few scabbed over. I must've given them to myself in my sleep.

As a kid, I had terrible nightmares. I spent so much time trying to be the perfect daughter—violin recitals, math lessons, Girl Scouts—that I hardly ever got to do the fun things, watch movies, eat too much candy, go to an amusement park with friends. I'd get angry at my parents for this and think bad thoughts about them as I fell asleep. Then I'd wake screaming, convinced they'd died in a fiery car crash or been crushed by a falling tree. Sometimes when my nanny would try to shake me out of it, I would claw at my face and my neck, leaving red welts that wouldn't disappear for days.

I rub the scratches now, shallow and thin like paper cuts.

Richard makes no move to sit. "Aren't you paying this guy a lot of money to be here?"

Yes, as if I really need the reminder, Richard. But he's right. Todd should already be here, set up, ready to begin class. I hired him because I wanted to give us something to do this weekend, activities that would keep our mind off Mom's absence. And yes, I'd be lying if I didn't admit I was swayed by the fact that he and Harper were making out like teenagers in one of her conference rooms one afternoon when I swung by VNity's offices to return the sunglasses Harper left at our house.

But where is he now?

Richard finally stops pacing and sits cross-legged beside me, frowning at his phone. "Dale and Ginny aren't going to make it tonight. They think the weather's going to be too bad."

I take a calming breath. I haven't told Richard yet that the fireworks people have canceled. If I do, he'll push me to call the whole thing off.

"It's not that far. People are seriously afraid of a little rain?" I ask.

But I had gotten attitude from others, even before the weather forecast. *Can't you just have it here? In the city?* they'd asked. They clearly don't understand the meaning of the word *tradition*.

Richard pokes at his phone. "Maybe we should cancel it, Elle."

"Absolutely not," I say, rising. "We haven't entertained since your mother—" I stop myself from saying *died.* "—in a long while. And you said yourself you need to schmooze the board."

I'd wanted to invite just our friends, make it more about the fun and less about business. But so many of Richard's "friends" are tied to the family's investments, it's hard to separate them out.

"The board members certainly won't approve the investment plan if they're stranded on the side of the road in a hailstorm," he says in that sarcastic tone he and Harper have perfected.

The wind shifts, and the scent of rotting grapes descends over us, a deep decaying smell that seems to be permanently etched into the soil. It's worse during the harvest season—it worms its way into your nose, and you can't escape it. At the end of the summer, I sometimes handpick grapes in the mornings with Richard. It's hard, tedious work. The leaves snag my hair, the gnats swarm in twirling spirals in front of my face. Some grapes fall easily into my palm, but some you have to twist and tug to get off the vine. But it's the smell I can never stand. That sweet, rotting flesh and juice. I can still be anywhere—at a cocktail party, in the middle of a desert—and conjure up that awful stink like a spirit.

Mom loved the ritual. She said it helped keep perspective on the product, helped keep it real and tangible. Richard agreed, of course—he'd do anything for the business—and Zach claimed he enjoyed the physical labor but really just wanted to make his mother happy. But I never saw Harper pluck a single grape off a vine in all these seasons. This year, Richard had too much on his plate and hired day workers to handpick the most delicate blocks.

A long, high whistle comes from the distance. I look up and spot Zach, Lauren, and Lucas trekking their way over the lawn.

Still no Todd.

I imagine him passed out on one of the lush quilts in the bedroom, empty wine bottles on the floor. Wouldn't that just be the icing on the cake of this weekend?

Richard stands as they approach. He'd wanted to drive, so we parked in the tasting room lot just across the field. As the three of them near, I notice Lauren and Zach aren't holding hands like they usually are. Maybe I'm not the only one having a less-than-stellar morning.

"Morning, kids." Zach's breath puffs in the air. "Are we rejuvenating?"

"More like regretting," Richard says. "It's cold as shit out here."

They brought yoga mats from the gym. Zach tosses his down but doesn't unroll it, and Lauren has hers under one arm, fiddling with the zipper of her jacket with her other hand. She's wearing a black knit cap, the ends of her hair curling out from under it.

"Harper's not with you?" Lucas asks me and Richard. "She

didn't show up in the kitchen, so we assumed she went ahead without us."

There's a long pause. I think back to the last time I saw her. She had seemed angry and irritated when she returned from the woods. She said she was retiring to the den with a bottle of wine and didn't want company.

Lucas frowns. "I can't remember now when she came to bed last night. I conked right away, and she wasn't there when I got up." He scratches his head. "So none of you saw her?"

Heads shake.

"I haven't seen her or Todd since last night," I say. Had Todd found Harper in the den after we all went upstairs? Would she really be that reckless to rekindle something when everyone is here, watching?

"Jesus Christ," Lucas mutters, stabbing at his phone.

"She might've fallen asleep in the den," I offer. *Or Todd's room.* "Or just decided to skip yoga."

"That's possible," Zach says, kicking at his mat. "Harper's not always a joiner."

Lucas steps away from the group, phone to his ear. Maybe Harper's phone is buzzing on the floor of Todd Christie's bedroom. It wouldn't be her first *mistake*. Years ago, when she and I were out in the city, before I met Richard, and Lucas was still living in California, Harper was upset because she didn't think their relationship had a future. She hit it off with some hot Italian guy with dark hair, and we ended up at a penthouse party, me sitting in the living room listening to someone play bad acoustic guitar while Harper hooked up with the guy in a back bedroom. She'd given me her phone to hold, and I remember staring down at it as it buzzed, over and over, with calls from Lucas. I wasn't about to rat her out—she was my best friend, and one thing that was ingrained in me by my sorority sisters is that you never rat out a friend—but I couldn't answer and lie to him, either.

She felt so terrible about it the next day. Made me promise never to say anything. She loved Lucas and had screwed up. Of course, I never did tell. And I wouldn't tell Lucas now, either—that's for Harper to fess up.

"Maybe she was mad she lost the game," Richard says when Lucas returns.

"Lost? None of you *won*," I point out. "I don't think any of you even *tried* to play."

"Oh, we tried," Lucas says. "But it's very confusing out there in the dark."

Lauren scratches at her ankle, and her yoga mat falls to the ground. I notice the red rash is much better, thanks to my cream.

"Do we have to stand out here in the cold?" Richard asks.

"I think we should go back," Lucas says. "I need to find my wife."

It's then, as if summoned, we hear the crunch of gravel under car tires, and Harper's gray Mercedes enters the tasting room parking lot.

"Speak of the devil," says Richard.

She gets out and slams the door behind her. Her coat is folded over her arm, sunglasses perched atop her head even though there's zero chance the sun's going to come out today.

"Where the hell were you?" Lucas asks her as she approaches.

Her hair is still damp from the shower, but she manages to look camera-worthy as always in dark, slim-cut jeans and an oversized sweater.

She frisks her hand through her hair. "Good morning to you, too," she says.

Zach clasps his hands together and takes a deep breath. "Well, now that we're all here—"

"We're not. Yoga boy is still MIA," Lucas says, his eyes on Harper.

"—I've got something to tell all of you," Zach finishes. He seems almost giddy, like a little kid bursting with a secret.

"Another announcement?" Richard asks wryly.

Zach glances over at Lauren, then back at the group. And I know. I know before the words come out of his mouth.

"I've asked Lauren to marry me, and she said yes."

A range of emotions floods through me—shock that he finally proposed to someone; anxiety over planning a wedding; fear over what this might change. Zach and I never dated, but there's always been something between us. It started with our first kiss, right here on the estate. That night after I spotted Zach (not Richard, like I told Lauren) on the dock for the first time, Harper and I made ourselves comfortable in the boat, while Zach sat on the edge of the dock next to us. We'd all been drinking too much gin mixed with too little Sprite, and we were telling Zach stories about our coworkers back in the city. When Harper left to go pee, Zach waved me out of the boat, told me he was an expert at constellations, but we only got to the Big Dipper before he made his move. We flirted all weekend, made out, snuck into the tasting room after hours and sipped all of Mom's best wines at the big mahogany bar. I thought he was really into me, that we shared a connection. I'd never felt that with anyone before. But the next time I came to the estate, one of his female friends was with him, and the way he teased and charmed her made me realize if I dated him, I'd always be worried that someone better would come along and turn his head.

Still, sometimes when we're here at the estate for holidays or family events, when he compliments my outfit, appreciates the time I take to make things special, gives me that Zach wink, I wonder how my life would have been different had I taken that risk.

Thankfully the sensible part of me steps in. I swallow the suffocating feeling that keeps expanding at the back of my throat and squeal, covering my mouth with my hand. "Oh my god! You're engaged?"

"As of yesterday, yes," Zach says.

"First the promotion, now a wedding," Harper says. "It's been quite a weekend for you, Zach."

"I wanted to tell you all right away, but Lauren insisted we wait. She didn't want to overshadow the birthday celebration." Zach beams down at her.

Lauren pulls the ring out of her pocket, slides it onto her finger self-consciously, and shows it off. I leap forward to examine it. It is, of course, only the best, a brilliant-cut pear diamond with a platinum band, a rock that seems weighty on Lauren's thin finger.

I throw my arms around Lauren, but her back tenses at my touch. As I pull away, she won't meet my eye, as if my emotions are written all over my face.

Richard and Lucas are congratulating Zach, Richard with a formal handshake, Lucas with a half hug and a low, "Dude!" He turns to Lauren and holds his arm out for a fist bump. "Welcome to the family, Delaware." And at that, she blushes.

Once the celebration is over, Harper clears her throat. "This is all very sweet and heartwarming, but I came to tell you this weekend's over. Lucas and I are going home."

LAUREN

Everyone's attention shifts, just like that.

It seems to be part of Harper's power, this ability to command attention at the snap of a finger. That slightly superior attitude that makes you feel like you need to earn her approval and be thankful if you get it. I have to admire it. I'm not like her or Maisie, who can work a room. Not that I mind. I prefer when the spotlight swivels elsewhere. People like them are plants; they thrive and bloom when all the light is on them.

But they also wither and die without it.

"What's this crazy talk? You can't leave," Zach says, shoving his hands in his coat pocket.

"You've seen the weather predictions?" Harper says. "Thunder, lightning, hail, terrible winds. I don't think any of us should stay."

I look up. The sky is menacing in the distance, an army of gray clouds gathering for battle. She may be right. Maybe we *should* leave. Sweep our toiletries off the counter, stuff the dirty clothes in a laundry bag, zip shut the suitcases and retreat. Maybe that wouldn't be a bad idea at all.

Enough has already gone wrong this weekend.

I glance over at Lucas. He's been ignoring me all morning, except for the "welcome to the family" comment.

I lay awake for a long time last night, replaying our kiss, my stomach twisting. *We were drunk is all. It doesn't mean anything. Zach up and left you in the woods.* Eventually I got out of bed and worked early into the morning, responding to the emails piling up in my inbox.

But in the light of day, it seems unreal. I can almost pretend it was my imagination, that it never happened at all.

Except that my chin still feels tender where Lucas's beard rubbed against it.

Elle and Richard offer to give us a ride back to the house, but I decline. "I think I might walk back and spend some time in the sauna," I say, hugging myself. "Warm up."

I want the time alone, but Zach jumps in quickly. "I'll walk with you," he says, grasping my hand in his.

It takes willpower not to snatch it back. I wasn't prepared for Zach to spring our news on everyone like that, tossing it into the crowd like a badly thrown Frisbee. Especially after our fight last night. He's putting on a show for everyone, playing the part of the happy couple. But underneath the act I sense that same tension lingering from last night. We both went to bed angry, barely spoke a word, Zach turning away from me and facing the windows. Which was fine by me. He didn't even ask if I was alright when I finally got back to the house.

But then this morning, he rolled over, kissed me, his tone as cool and calm as an ocean breeze. "Morning, sunshine! Are you showering before yoga?"

I was so stunned I just shook my head, stayed in bed while

he walked around getting dressed, humming, like he had not a care in the world.

I've always known Zach has a talent for defusing drama, for making everyone feel comfortable and welcome. But now I see his behavior for what it is, the tendency to avoid conflict by pretending it doesn't exist, like the other person must be misunderstanding the situation.

"I'll walk, too. It'll give us time to talk about wedding plans," Elle says to me in a singsong voice.

The last thing I want to talk about is wedding plans. Especially with Elle. She's been so intense about this simple birthday weekend—I can't even imagine how she'd be about a wedding. But I can't think of a reason for her not to come, so she sends Richard off to drive his car back to the estate and tags along with us.

The grounds are less charming today. I don't know if it's my mood or the weather, or Elle's nervous energy, but the landscape feels bleak. Even the trees seem sapped of color. I pull my hat lower on my head to cover my ears.

"Do you think you'll get married in the spring? Or fall?" Elle asks, taking a breather from her rant about the challenge of finding venues that are big enough for everyone to have dinner in the same room. "I've always loved a good winter wedding—you can do so much with faux fur."

"Haven't thought that far ahead," Zach answers, turning to look back at us. "But I think it'll definitely be here at the estate, don't you agree, babe?"

My emotions are tangled in a messy knot I don't know how to unravel. And there's no one to talk it through with. No one from home—even if I had kept up with any of my friends there—would even begin to understand. Maisie would adamantly insist I go with the flow, let them all plan whatever elaborate affair they wanted. And Diane would think I was a fool to marry Zach at all.

What do you *want, Brady?*

"I don't know," I say, wanting to disagree with him, to regain some control. "I actually thought a city wedding would be nice."

"Oh god, no." Elle swipes her hand like she's waving away an annoying gnat. "You totally have to have it here. Our wedding was just marvelous—like a fairy tale. The estate is prettiest in spring. You could do light greens, maybe? Or purple and silver is always a favorite with me." She's rattling on a mile a minute.

Everything's moving too fast. It was just two days ago that I arrived here with the man of my dreams by my side. But now I feel like I'm being molded and shaped—Zach presenting whatever perfect image of me he thinks I should be, Elle hiring herself as my wedding planner. Plus, there's the matter of Diane breathing down my neck. I want to take off in a sprint across the field and find a hole to hide in.

"Well, we'll see," Zach says. I feel his eyes on me. "Don't have to decide everything now. If Lauren wants to get married in a donut shop, I'll be there with Boston cream filling." He winks.

Elle grabs his arm and hugs it. "Zach, you are just the sweetest. Lauren, you've got yourself a keeper." She smiles, but there's a flicker of something else in her expression that I can't make out.

One more day. I just have to get through one more day, and then we'll go back to the city, talk, make decisions about our future, regroup. I'm not going to go into this marriage—if I go into it at all—with a blindfold on like some Van Ness game.

Until then, I need to avoid getting pulled too deeply into this family's undertow.

THE PARTY GUEST

The Van Nesses' generator is on the left side of the house, behind landscaped bushes, tucked away so not to ruin the illusion of perfection. It's not too far from the entrance to the old servants' quarters, but that, too, is hard to spot unless you know what you're looking for.

I examine the generator. It's a compact device, fueled by a propane tank. Very useful for times like these, when a vicious storm is coming in and the surrounding power lines are oh so delicate.

Crunch.

I jerk my head around, sure I heard a noise. Crouch behind the bushes. Watch. Listen. There's nothing but a distant rumbling in the sky. An ominous warning.

So many things swirl in my head, thoughts, emotions, calculations. Doubt begins to creep in—can I go through with this? Will it even matter?

Yes, it matters. I steel myself against the doubts. I can't let the Van Nesses get away with what they did. I've come this far, haven't I? I'd never forgive myself if I walked away now.

The lid of the generator has a lock with a small keyhole. I'm not sure if I have the key for it. But when I try to lift the lid, I realize it's not locked anyway. Security around here is so lax.

Inside, the generator battery looks similar to a car battery. My father taught me a lot of basic car maintenance, including how to jump-start a dead vehicle. I tug on the connecting cables, loosening them, grab the wire cutters I found in the shed, and snip off the ends.

With a little luck, tonight the Van Nesses will be powerless.

HARPER

Lucas and I don't talk much on the drive back to the house. I have to explain where I was, since he was apparently so very concerned about me disappearing into thin air. I didn't sleep well, got up early, and escaped for a long walk. Everything seems piled on top of me, like I can't get out from under the weight of it. I'm tired of worrying about VNity. Someone tweeted today that all my employees should strike until I apologize, and it's gaining traction. And I didn't like what Todd said last night about dropping our partnership. Who does he think he is to decide that? He's a wild card, and I can't be here any longer if he's here, too.

I wish we'd listened to the damn weather reports and left last night. What Bill said about the roads flooding, about getting stuck, now makes me want to scream. I can't get trapped here while Zach is making major life decisions on a whim, with a woman he barely knows, with money he doesn't have. I can't handle Elle pretending everything's great while Richard frets about someone trying to scam us out of money. I don't want to think about the fact that whoever sent those text messages and that gift knows we're here.

But mostly, I just need to get away from the games, the estate, the ghost of Mother hovering everywhere. Being in those woods last night was too much.

Lucas heads upstairs to pack, and I linger in the kitchen. A pale pink pristine cake box sits on the counter. I flip it open. It's a two-tier monstrosity with a vineyard theme—how original. In the center of the top tier, royal purple icing spells out *Happy birthday, Richard & Harper!*

There's a cake knife next to the box. Long and shiny, with a heavy marble handle. I don't even know where Elle found it. I pick it up, run my finger along the blade. Might've been from our parents' wedding. We hardly ever used it.

I set the teakettle on the stove and scroll through my phone. It's the email from Frances McMillen that makes my blood hot. Frances McMillen, queen of vitamin face masks, who recently agreed to partner with VNity on a sponsored campaign, is pulling out of the agreement in light of the "unfortunate" publicity that's come my way. I stare at the words, not believing them. After that dinner at Carbone? The spa pass I'd given her to try out our hot stone massage? First Todd Fucking Christie and now her. All the rats are jumping ship. The cowards.

The teakettle hisses and whines. I shut off the gas and pour scalding water over a black tea bag in my travel mug. Fuck fuck fuck.

I dial Penny.

"Harper?" Penny's voice echoes, like she's in a subway station.

"What the fuck is wrong with people?" I say.

"What? What do you mean?"

"We have a situation. I just forwarded you the email. But don't worry. I'll be on the road soon and back in the city this afternoon. Frances is not going to get away with this. She already signed the agreement. As soon as I get back we'll—"

"Harper, hang on."

It's then I remember again she's out of town. "Where are you?" I prefer to do my damage control in person, in the office.

"Family reunion, remember?" she says. "But did you say you were leaving to go back to the city?"

"Right. As soon as Lucas gets packed." I fish the tea bag out of my mug with a spoon and toss it in the trash.

"You can't," she says.

"What are you talking about?"

"You need to stay there."

"What? Why?" I take a small sip of the tea, let the hot bitterness activate the taste buds on the back of my tongue.

"There are...well, there are people outside of your house. Protesters? And reporters. Looking for a story."

"How the hell do you know that?"

A white-hot panic unfurls inside me. Are they there because of the video? Or is it more than that now? Todd's words last night come back: *What about the bruise, Harper? If the truth comes out...*

Did he tell someone? Could he really be that desperate? Or use it as his own attention-grabber? Was it revenge?

Penny sighs. "One of the reporters called me. So I had a friend go—" her voice blips out, then returns "—she saw them all there."

"What's their angle?" I ask. "What is going on, Penny?"

There's a pause. I imagine her weighing her words, trying to decide how to frame it. The white-hot panic is a full-out fire now. "Must still be about the video. Maybe they think you'll scream at them all with a megaphone and they can get it on camera... I don't know."

"For fuck's sake, that was a joke. Taken out of context—"

"I know, Harper, but they don't, do they? Lay low there for a few more days at least. Until we get our messaging straight." Penny's voice is urgent—it's unlike her to give me orders.

I look outside at the back lawn. Lauren, Zach, and Elle are just returning from their walk.

"I need to get out of here, Penny. Like, stat."

"You can't, Harper. It won't be good. Trust me. Also, the weather reports? It's not looking good for driving."

I feel it boiling over. My anger. I'm trapped, and everything is collapsing around me, snapping right into pieces.

That's how it felt backstage at the ambassadors event last month. I was supposed to go out there and energize them. Give my speech. Pretend everything was fine, that online engagement wasn't down. Convince them all that they should buy our new cosmetics line even though the items were over-priced because I'd spent too much money on the primary packaging. Even the event, which was usually packed, only had about half the members it usually did.

They hate you. Mother's voice popped into my head. All her criticisms of VNity, the reasons she refused to fund it. *You really think the world needs another beauty company, Harper? After all I've taught you, and you want to be a lipstick CEO?*

The walls were crowding in. How was I supposed to face those people?

I fled. I ran up to my office and my throat clenched up and—

You're so weak, Mother had whispered again. *They're going to turn against you.*

I touch my bruise now. If I press it, I can still conjure up the pain.

The sharp pain that took my breath away when I created it. One of Todd's hand weights, held above me and dropped. The pain blossomed into the physical manifestation of everything I felt inside.

It also silenced Mother's voice.

So, I tweaked the story a little. There might not have been an attacker, but with all the bullshit and double standards I have to deal with as a woman leader in a world that dismisses us, there might as well have been.

I showed the world my vulnerability. It *resonated* with them. My followers rallied behind me.

For a time, anyway.

I pick up the knife and poke slightly at one of the sugar grapes. It cracks, then shatters in a satisfying way. I press the tip into another grape, watch the veins form like spiderwebs before it, too, shatters into a million pieces.

"Harper? You still there? Please say you'll stay."

They love you for such a small time—that rush of sympathy, the posts and well-wishes, the burst of support. And then the tide shifts, and you're a monster that everyone loves to hate.

Suddenly I want it to storm. I want the sky to open, thunder to burst our eardrums, lightning to pierce the darkness, rain to flood this place. I squeeze my fingers tighter around the handle, feel the cold of the marble, and stab right into the center of the cake.

"You didn't even wish me a happy birthday," I tell Penny, and then I hang up the call.

ELLE

My phone rings just as we approach the gardens behind the house. Natasha's photo appears on the screen, pink flower tucked behind one ear, snapped during her trip to Hawaii last year.

I motion for Zach and Lauren to go inside and step away to take the call.

"Elle. Hon. I haven't heard from you, but the party's off, I assume." Just like Natasha, to state her opinion, or what she wants to happen, instead of asking.

"No?" I say and hate that my voice rises in a question. "We're still planning on it. And we'd love for you to stay over."

I wander past the garden fountain, follow a path to a wrought-iron bench. The sky is darkening. It's not raining yet, but there's an invisible weight pressing down on every-thing, a forceful wind kicking up.

"Well, I don't think we're willing to risk it. That drive is…" She trails off. I hear voices in the background. Natasha answers low, as if she's pulled the phone away. "No, they're still having it!… I know!" And then she's back. "Elle? Yeah. We're gonna have to pass."

"Oh, I hate that, Tasha. We'll move it inside if—"

Click. She's gone. Three seconds later, I get a weather alert from W-JKA, a local TV station. The link brings me to a short video, where a weatherman waves his hands across the map bursting with reds and oranges and yellows, the worst of the storm heading right toward us. "...Right now we're advising everyone to stay inside and stay safe..." he says as I increase the volume on the phone. "If you have a garage, park your car inside because we could see hailstones the size of golf balls—"

I close out the browser, cutting him off midsentence.

I have a caterer coming to drop off food for thirty people and no one will be here to eat it. There's a tent outside. For no one. There won't be any fireworks.

Good. The thought comes suddenly, my own relief a surprise. Maybe the storm is a blessing. I won't have to spend all my energy worrying about details, stressed if people are having a good time, making small talk. I can focus my time elsewhere. On more urgent matters.

A growl of thunder in the distance gets me off the bench and into the house. If this storm is going to be as bad as it sounds, preparations are in order. No one else will think about emergency supplies until it's too late. The worst will hit tonight, and we want to be ready when it does.

And Harper won't be here.

That thought is a relief, too.

I find Linnet vacuuming in the sitting room and ask her to call the caterer to cancel and craft an official email to the guests who haven't already backed out, following up with a text message in case some of them are already on their way. It's possible someone will show up anyway, having left early to avoid the storm, but at least we won't run out of wine.

We store emergency supplies in the employee offices at the warehouse. I could ask Bill to bring them, but now that the party's off, I can focus on locating Mom's nest egg, and I haven't searched the tunnel yet. The video of Harper did the job I needed it to, and it's time for me to settle things up. Fair is fair.

Hidden in plain sight. This house has many secrets. Let that lead your way.

Since I told Lauren about all the secret passages yesterday, I've been wondering if Mom might've hidden something in the tunnel—inside one of the house's best secrets?

If this nest egg even exists. It's possible this is just one last game. That I'm being made a fool.

But Mom and I got so close those last few months of her life, and I think she wanted me to have something of hers, something all to myself.

It's for you, Elle.

I'd asked what she meant, where it was, but she shook her head.

You know me. Everything in riddles, riddles in everything. You have to find it. Rewards come to those who work for them.

I open the dead bolt on the wine cellar door and stick in a jamb to make sure it doesn't close and someone accidentally—or purposely—locks me in. It would be just like Harper to follow up her prank by trapping me in the cellar.

"You can't think about this now," I say to myself as I start down the cellar stairs. I put any thoughts of Harper out of my mind and focus instead on the treasure hunt.

It was Mom, after all, who showed me this shortcut one Christmas, when it was too cold to venture outside to get wine from the warehouse. *Let me fill you in on a little secret*, she'd said, leading me past all the racks to a door. She was delighted by my astonishment at the tunnel that appeared beyond the door—Mom always loved shocking people, bringing them in on secrets.

I tap the code into the keypad now—C-R-S-1-9-7-5—and there's a loud beep. The door slides open, revealing a narrow tunnel stretching straight ahead. To the right is an old steel door that used to lead to the old servants' wing I told Lauren about, but it's been locked for years. I step forward, and the beep sounds again before the motion sensors cause the door to slide shut, and I am sealed in the tunnel.

Soft orange recessed lights in the ceiling provide enough visibility to watch my steps, but I use my phone's flashlight to illuminate the walls, looking for a message in the stone or any other clue. The walls are damp beneath my palms, and there's the odor of a freshly watered garden, as if beyond the walls, flora is sprouting up, twisting around itself, threatening to strangle the tunnel.

Halfway down, it's evident that there's no place to hide anything of value, no real reason why Katrina would choose this location. I turn off my phone light. My footsteps echo in the cavernous space. At one point I swear I hear music, a tinny beat, but when I stop, there's nothing but the drip of water from a crack in the stone.

Your mind plays tricks on you in the dark. In boarding school one year, we took a field trip to a cave. Our tour guide took us deep down, hundreds of feet underground, and then shut off all the cave lights and flashlights. *You are now experiencing total darkness*, she said, and I remember the eerie sensation of my eyes being completely open but not able to see a thing, not even my hand waving directly in front of my face. She told us if we stayed there long enough, our brains would start to create images; we'd see and hear things that weren't there.

It's not that dark in here, but the silence is unnerving, and I'm relieved when I reach the end of the passage, climb up the short staircase, and insert my key in the door to the warehouse. But it's already unlocked. The winery employees don't have access to this passage, so did Bill forget to lock it? Harper would throw a fit—she's been hyper-concerned about security since she arrived.

The wine warehouse has always felt sacred to me, quiet and

cool, like walking into a church. We store all the aging barrels here, rows and rows, stamped and labeled with the grape and date. In each barrel, a large cork covers a hole where our winemaker can sample the wine with a long plunger, a wine thief, to test how it's aging. People pay a lot of money for the privilege to come down here for barrel tastings.

But right now, it's just me and hundreds of thousands of pounds of fermented grapes, the low hum of machinery. Occasionally our employees will stop by to check on processes, but it's off-season. Even so, I make sure to walk each aisle, peering into the shadows and crevices, lest one of them steps out of a barrel rack and gives me a heart attack.

The office is at the back, a combination workspace and employee break room. Cold air whooshes toward me as I step inside, and I quickly spot the culprit—an open window behind the desk. Who left this open? And how long has it been like this? With a storm coming too. I lean over the desk to shove it closed, and that's when I notice a grapevine on the ground outside the window. There's no way the wind would have blown it all the way over here.

Someone had to have dragged it here. To break off a piece.

Harper's always had a sick sense of humor.

I shut the window and turn the lock.

The emergency supplies are in a waterproof tote bag above the microwave oven—rain ponchos, candles, matches and lighters, a few flares. As I'm pulling it onto my shoulder and pivoting to leave, something thuds deep in the warehouse. I turn, listening hard, but it's just the fans whirring, machinery clunking.

Still, I cross the warehouse, secure the tunnel door behind me, and head back.

The tunnel feels colder and damper. I walk fast. I think of the warm fires in the house, the gleaming kitchen and a hot cup of tea. As the passageway stretches on, the bag with the supplies bounces at my side; something metal rattles with each stride. Is the tunnel getting longer? My perception feels off. Instead of the earthy smell, there's a scent of something cloyingly perfumed. Like incense or essential oils.

Finally, I see the light over the door ahead.

But my breath catches in my throat when the light moves.

It bobs, flicking off the walls, like someone is holding a flashlight. I can see a silhouette, warping and reshaping against the stone walls like a disturbing shadow puppet play.

It's just one of the family looking for you, Elle.

"Hello? Richard?" I call out.

The light stops moving and then goes out.

Just like it did last night in the vineyards.

"Harper, I know it's you," I call.

Silence for a few seconds, then I hear a low, chilling laugh.

I can't help the goose bumps that ripple up my skin. How dare she do this to me? This is exactly why Mom was always trying to make her grow up, be more mature.

I pat myself, looking for my phone to flash in her eyes. But when I tug it out of my back pocket, I lose grip and it clatters to the ground.

Shit.

I reach down to pick it up. At the end of the tunnel, I hear footsteps. Clamoring and scraping. Then silence once more.

I hold my breath, waiting for what seems like an eternity.

Then I rush to the end of the passageway. The door is closed, the keypad's light blinking slowly. Harper didn't go through it—I would've heard the beep as the door unlocked, slid open.

From the doorway, I turn on my phone's flashlight and sweep it around the tunnel, but the only other way out is the door to the old servants' wing. I tug, but it's locked.

Harper has disappeared into thin air.

HARPER

Penny told me to stay put, which means I want to leave even more. Nothing irks me more than being told what to do. Lucas suggests I cut back my leadership role, hire people to manage things for me like he does, and instead I go all-in with my responsibilities at VNity. My hairstylist said she loved the natural highlights in my hair, so I made her dye it dark. I even defy my daily horoscope when it tells me I should be extra social one day, or to go to sleep early the next. No one knows me better than I know myself.

But a mob of reporters screaming questions and pointing video cameras in my face is unappealing, to say the least, and I still feel safer here on the estate, with the gates locked tight, than in the city.

On my way upstairs to tell Lucas about the change in plans, I spot my brothers through the window. I step out onto the side porch, the wood planks making their familiar creak. Mother always wanted to tear this porch out and build a new one. She thought it was too dark and buggy with the bushes and the overhang. But Richard and I loved it. It's secluded out here, our own private clubhouse, a place to hide our secrets.

"What's going on?" I ask them.

They both look up at me.

"I thought you were packing up, running off?" Zach says. He's leaning against the railing, arms crossed. I've walked right into the middle of something.

I raise an eyebrow at Richard, but he just shrugs, a cigarette hanging out the side of his mouth. Cobwebs span the bottom of the railing, dried leaves in the corners. A planter that once held flowers has a jagged crack along its side, a sign that something has rooted in the soil.

"So you're not leaving?" Zach asks. "Because Elle just sent an email. The party's canceled."

"Not a surprise," I say, motioning toward the sky. Moisture thickens the air. We're on the cusp of the storm, right before the sky opens and all holy hell rains down. I reach out and snap off a branch from a massive bush growing on the other side of the railing. Its leaves are small and rounded, and I pluck them one by one like we did when we were kids. "You know I love our birthday tradition. All the games. How can I leave?"

A soft pattering drumbeat starts, the opening act of the storm.

I break another branch off the shrub. "Come on, boys. Play with me." I hold up the branch, twirl it in my fingers.

"Harper, not now," Zach says, swatting my arm away.

What's his problem?

"You remember how it goes," I persist. I rip off a leaf. "I will eat."

Richard shoots me a look—*watch it*—but I ignore him. The call with Penny left me unsettled, out of control, and I need someone to do as I ask.

"Play," I say. "We need to discover our birthday fortunes."

Richard blows smoke slowly out the side of his mouth, flicks ash into the manicured bushes.

"Smoking is so blue-collar," I tell him, though it'd been my idea to buy a pack of clove cigarettes when we were in middle school. My idea to see who could smoke it down to the filter the fastest.

"I ignore your questionable habits, so why don't you do the same for me?" he says.

Thunder echoes in the distance. I think of something Linnet used to say—*God's angry, he's throwing boulders.*

This house brings it out in all of us. Superstitions, omens. Like we can somehow predict the future, twist fate, if we just say the right thing, avoid bad luck, win a game. I pull off another leaf. "I will cheat." Work my way down the stem. Each leaf produces a tiny bit of liquid from the stem. It smells bitter, acidic. "I will swill. I will kill."

We'd made up the rhymes ourselves. The last leaf picked is the fortune, a darker version of the *she loves me, she loves me not* game other kids played.

Zach grabs the stem from my hand and tosses it to the ground. Against the swiftly darkening sky, he reminds me of Zeus, ready to toss lightning bolts, start a war. "You really thought you could sell this place out from under my feet?"

So that's it.

Richard smashes the remainder of his cigarette into the brick pillar, cursing quietly.

The rain picks up, hitting the porch roof more steadily now. Thunder rumbles again, a warning.

"Under your feet?" I laugh. "That's very cute."

Richard flashes me another look.

"This place is a money and time suck," I continue. Which is true, though more pressing is that I won't have to feel haunted by our mother everywhere I turn, relive her lessons and conditions and realize all the places I fall short. And it's not like Zach's going to step up and take care of this place. I kick the planter next to me, but it doesn't budge. "Mother knew that."

"Bullshit. Mom *loved* it here. She would've never wanted it out of the family." He crosses his arms again, and it's all very Brontë-esque, his angry jaw and the darkening clouds in the sky.

"Do you even hear yourself?" I say. "You sound like a spoiled little child."

The wind begins to howl, causing the rain to shift direction. I back up, closer to the house.

Zach doesn't seem to notice or care he's getting wet. "Lauren said you were leaving me out of things, but I didn't believe it."

"Lauren?" I tip my head slightly. "How the hell does she fit into any of this?"

"She's going to be my wife." Zach raises a finger. "At least *she's* honest with me."

"Honest? How do you know? You met her three minutes ago. She could be a—"

"I don't want to hear another word about Lauren!" He's clenching and unclenching his fists. "Do any of you even care that I'm in this family? I've never gotten a vote, ever."

"Oh, right," I say, losing my patience. "You've had it *so* hard." Mother coddled him, and now we're paying for that mistake. He has no sense of responsibility. He's the charming, loveable, sociable Zach Van Ness to most people—his friends adore him—but to family, he can be bitter when we don't give him what he wants. There's always some reason it's someone else's fault. It used to work on Mother, and now he thinks he can work us as well. That if he pouts and yells enough, we'll cave.

It's the one thing I left out of the story I told Lauren. After we got him back in the boat, Zach turned on Mother, pummeled his fists into her, angry and crying, and she let him. Maybe she deserved it—she certainly thought she did. She let him walk all over her after that day, always relenting to his wishes.

"Harper's right," Richard says. "You're not exactly the one to turn to for financial decisions."

Zach seems like he's going to explode. "My money has nothing to do with—"

Richard holds up a hand. "We'll still keep our name on the winery. Still get money from the business. But we won't have to deal with operations."

"And what about the house? And Bill? And Linnet? Do either of you care about anyone but yourselves?"

When we don't respond right away, he flings open the sliding glass door and stomps off.

Richard sighs. "That went well."

"He'll get over it." I pick up the stem Zach wrenched from me. There are only a few leaves left.

"I knew we should've told him sooner."

"It's not really his business anymore. He made that choice," I say, twirling the stem in my fingers. There are too many other fires to worry about the house right now. "We never finished our game. It's bad luck not to." I stare into Richard's eyes, pluck off another couple of leaves. "I will lie. I will cry."

Mother said when Richard was born, he was quiet. They had to slap him to get him to cry. Me? I came out three minutes later wailing. Red in the face, fists up, ready to fight.

"I will fly." I tear off the last leaf and hold it out for my twin. "I will die."

Richard gives it a quick huff, blowing it from my fingers.

It floats like a feather to the floor between us.

THE PARTY GUEST

The near run-in in the tunnel has me on edge. I need to be more careful.

The rain is cold, but I don't dare move. From where I am below the side porch, I can hear everything Richard, Zach, and Harper are saying. I'm so close to them right now, I could reach up and touch Richard's foot. Anywhere else, there are a lot of barriers in place to keep people like me from interacting with people like them. My letters, calls, emails in the months after their mother died were all basically ignored. It was like I was thrown to the ground and stepped on.

It's not easy to realize how expendable you are, how little you matter in this world.

By the time I got solid evidence to prove my suspicions about the family tree, I noticed the birthday weekend was coming up—the perfect time for me to share my story with all of them at once. They are never together in the city—and it would be too hard for me to get to them there even if they were. No, out here, where their guards are down, I can force them to see me. To listen. It's my best shot. I've got nothing to lose, anyway.

The canceled party throws a wrench in my plan—with a crowd full of people milling about, it would have been good incentive for the Van Nesses to do as I ask. But I've come this far. There are other audiences. If the Van Nesses are stupid enough to try to deny me what I want—what I deserve—then they will discover just how publicly I can air their dirty laundry. Zach has just stomped inside. He seems angry. A little conflict between the siblings won't hurt.

I hope, however this turns out in the end, people can understand that I didn't want to have to do it this way.

I hope they understand that the Van Nesses brought it upon themselves.

LAUREN

I set the sauna to the highest temperature, undress in the changing area, and grab one of the oversized plush white towels to wrap myself in. As I come out of the stall, Linnet appears with a fresh stack of towels. Her hair is pulled back into a tight bun, and the lines in the skin around her eyes make me think of cracked, dried mud.

She hands me one of the towels. "Seems like a good idea to warm up on a chilly day like today," she says.

"It does, doesn't it?"

She surveys me, head slightly tilted, like I'm a picture askew on the wall. "Do you need me to bring you anything? Harper always prefers some cucumber water while she's in there."

I shake my head. "Oh, no, thank you. I'm fine. Please don't go to any trouble on my behalf."

"No trouble. It's my job. Cucumber water for Harper, lime seltzer for Richard, and let's see, for Zachary, he enjoys a cold microbrew straight from the bottle."

"You must know everyone's quirks by now," I say with a smile.

"After all these years? Yes, ma'am." She smiles back, but it's a polite nothing smile. She's used to dealing with rich people, to being agreeable, helpful, but as invisible as possible. When I was a waitress, our manager used to tell us to make the customer happy no matter what. A private party snorting cocaine in the back room? Discreetly show yourself out until they are done. The point was to take care of it quietly and efficiently, accept the tip with a smile, and never discuss what you saw.

I'm sure she's seen a lot in her years here.

"It's like you're part of the family," I say.

Linnet's smile dies for a second. "I like to think so," she says briskly, pressing the piles of towels onto the racks outside the sauna.

Great, I've offended her.

"I mean, I know how much Zach values you and Bill and all you do," I say, trying to win her back. I'm sure she has valuable insight into this family, and I suspect it's better to be friends with Linnet than enemies.

"Congratulations, by the way," Linnet says, her tone still a little pinched as she turns from the racks and smooths back her hair. She nods at the ring on my finger. "I heard a wedding is in the works."

For some reason, those words make me blush. "Thank you. Word travels fast around here."

"The walls have ears…" she says slowly, then laughs. "Elle mentioned it."

The sauna's temperature gauge lets out a little *ding* to let me know it's heated up, like I'm a meal ready to go in the oven.

"She said you may have it here? On the estate?" Linnet looks at me oddly. I can't tell if she's annoyed at the prospect or wouldn't have it any other way.

"Nothing's been set yet," I say. "But I know how much Zach loves it here."

"Does he now?" Her eyebrow lifts. "Could've fooled me."

"Why do you say that?" I ask.

She sighs. "Oh, don't mind me. I'm talking out of turn."

I wait, knowing she'll come around. People always open up if I give them a little time, let them fill the silence. And sure enough, she glances over at me again, and then away, before lowering her voice. "He was a fool to give up the house. He will come to regret it."

Give up the house? I keep my face as neutral as possible so Linnet doesn't realize what she's revealed. "I know," I say. "But Zach had his reasons."

She flutters her hand. "It's none of my business."

"What is?" I ask innocently, winking at her.

She points at the sauna behind me. "Go, go. Don't let me keep you. There's a buzzer if you change your mind and need anything."

Inside, the wood bench creaks and groans as I lean against the wall. The warmth is incredible after being outside in the damp weather.

I close my eyes, breathe in the dry, hot air. My body feels worn out, my limbs heavy, from a combination of too much alcohol and too little sleep. At least the cream Elle gave me for my poison ivy rash worked—the red bumps remain, but the itchiness is mostly gone.

But I feel itchy, anxious, inside. What did Linnet mean about Zach giving up the house? If that's true, why was he so upset last night when I brought up selling the estate? And what is with his mood swings? I want back the version of Zach I thought I knew, the Zach who doesn't anger easily and abandon his fiancée in the dark woods. I'm beginning to question which version of him is real.

"Lauren!"

It's Zach.

I open my eyes, squeeze my fingers into the thick cotton of the towel wrapped around me.

The sauna door flies open. Zach steps in, fully dressed. He seems distressed. The door stays open, letting in cold air.

"I had a little talk with Harper and Richard. You were right. They *are* going behind my back."

So now he believes me? I re-tuck my towel.

"I can't understand it." He paces the tiny room. "This was Mom's favorite place. She grew up here. How could they just throw it away?"

"But don't you have a say?" I ask carefully. "I mean, isn't your name on the deed, too?"

But Zach isn't listening to me. He's deep in thought. He stops, holds up a finger. "I can stall them. Now that we're getting married."

"What do you mean?"

"The estate." He's excited now, having found a solution. "We'll have the wedding here. They'd have to be total jerks to sell it if we're planning a wedding here." He kisses my cheek, grabs my hands. "This is the perfect place."

"But I don't understand, Zach. They can't sell without you, right?" I say, trying to pull the truth from him.

He waves my question off like it's an annoying fly buzzing around his head. "Well, it's a little complicated, Lauren."

I feel dread creeping up in me.

"Some of my investments lately didn't go as well as I thought, that's all." He pushes his hand through my hair, tucking it behind my ear. "I needed some money after Mom's death, but I can always buy back my share later. Look, don't worry about it. It all works out in the end."

It all works out, don't worry, honey. Just like my father used to say, rubbing my chin, sticking a five-dollar bill in my pocket. One month, new clothes and spending sprees, the next deciding which bill to ignore. Always with the reassurances, the breezy blow-offs, those charming smiles designed to hide the truth beneath—that there was no money. That it doesn't always work out.

Isn't that why I left? I saw how all those empty promises destroyed my mother. She fooled herself into believing that my dad would take care of her, that she didn't need a career, that she should rely on "the breadwinner," just like many of the other women of her generation in Maurville. By the time she figured out it wasn't going to be happily-ever-after like the movies and books she consumed, she was too resigned to care. I don't want to end up like her. I don't want to be dependent on anyone like that.

I also don't want to keep telling my own lies. But money and love, they're complicated subjects, so many gray areas, so many hard choices. It feels like no matter what you decide, you lose.

The sauna's heat feels oppressive now. I can't take a good breath.

"You're doing it again, I can tell," Zach says in a teasing voice at my silence. "Going right to worst-case scenario." He takes my hands in his. "Lauren, this is you and me. We're in this together, right? There will be storms worse than what's heading our way that we'll have to get through. This weekend has been a little stressful, and I'm sorry I snapped at you last night. I really am. But just because we had a disagreement doesn't mean that everything is doomed. Right?"

There's that twinkle in Zach's eye. It used to calm me down, reassure me, but now I see all of this for what it is.

Zach Van Ness is gaslighting me.

ELLE

When I get back from the tunnel, I'm angry. I'm furious at myself for getting scared, pissed at Harper for always poking. I don't understand what I did to make her act this way. We were so close once. We shared clothes, stayed over at each other's apartments. I was there when her period was late and she had to take a pregnancy test. We threw each other engagement parties and were in each other's weddings.

Now she's made a sport of giving me a hard time.

After I drop off the emergency supplies in the front hall, I head upstairs to see if another source of my anger—Todd Christie—has surfaced yet. I gave him one of the rooms in the other wing of the house for privacy.

I bang on his door with my fist.

No response.

"Todd!" I've lost my patience. Miss Phyllis, my etiquette teacher, would be displeased. *To lose patience is to lose the battle*, she always said.

I push the door open. The room is dark. The bed unmade. A set of small weights lies on the floor. There's a suitcase in the corner, and everything inside is folded neatly like it's ready to be zipped up and carried off.

The room smells like incense. I call his phone again, and again, it goes straight to voice mail. I can barely keep the irritation out of my voice. "Todd? It's Elle again. What kind of game are you playing here? Where are you? This is unacceptable. Call me back as soon as you get this."

I catch sight of myself in the mirror above the dresser, where Todd's deodorant stick sits, uncapped, a bottle of hand cream on its side. I right it before it leaks on the oak and leaves a stain, when I notice something next to Todd's bed.

There's a crumpled pamphlet, half under the bed. I tug it out, open it. It's a map of the estate—the ones they print over at the tasting room for visitors, to show them the walking trails and directions for driving in and out of the property. Someone, presumably Todd, has circled several of the more remote areas of the estate, highlighting paths in and around the house.

I get a heavy feeling in my stomach. Why *didn't* Harper announce herself in the tunnel? Wouldn't she have been proud to show she "got me"? What if it wasn't her? Todd's been conspicuously absent since last night. He's got a map of the estate. And didn't I smell something like incense down in the tunnel?

Shit.

Is he trying to steal from us? To dig up our secrets? A panicked, irrational thought propels through me before I can stop it—what if he finds Mom's nest egg before I do?

I fold up the map, stuff it under my arm, and rush downstairs to find Richard. I storm through the swinging doors to the kitchen. No one's there, but I hear muffled voices. Richard and Harper are on the side porch in intense conversation. The storm is picking up, but Harper doesn't seem in a hurry to leave.

Before I can interrupt them to tell them my discovery, I notice the cake box open on the counter. I draw closer and cry out.

My beautiful cake has a giant knife stuck in the middle. The delicate sugar flowers are crushed, the blown grapes have been destroyed, their purple coloring leaking across the butter creme frosting. The happy birthday greeting is a swirled mess, like a child has melted crayons all over the cake.

The porch door opens, and I hear Harper say angrily, "Well, he'll just have to deal with it." She sees me and stops.

Richard bumps into her from behind. "What's wrong?" he asks me.

I ignore him, my eyes fixated on Harper. I pull the knife out, sticky with the raspberry filling. "What did you do?"

"I don't know what you're talking about." Harper looks down at the cake, and then up at me.

"You ruined it." My voice rises, the knife slippery in my hand.

"I think that's a little unfair, Elle." Harper crosses her arms in front of her chest.

"Are you kidding me? Do you know how much I paid for this cake?"

"You paid a lot for *Todd*, too, and he's spent most of the time here hungover," Richard says.

I came to find Richard so he could help me figure out what's going on with Todd, but here he is, defending his sister over me once again.

"You're seriously taking her side here?" I throw the knife into the sink, where it clatters harshly. "Unbelievable. I've worked so hard to make this a nice weekend for everyone, to do something nice for you two. To honor Mom's traditions. And instead of thanks, I get stabbed in the back."

Richard runs his fingers furiously through his hair. "Elle, please don't do this now. We've got a lot going on. I can't worry about you blowing up over the smallest details."

My mouth opens, but no words come out. My cheeks are burning hot, but the anger is building inside me. "Small details? Did you notice we have food this weekend? That the mail's been sorted? Was it a small detail to take Mom to all her doctor's appointments? To make sure she took her prescriptions on time? Or how about when I planned her funeral so that none of you had to worry about that on top of grieving? You…neither of you have the foggiest clue about all I do for you. For this family."

There's a short silence. Neither of them will meet my gaze. Then Harper speaks up. "We actually do, Elle, because you won't shut up about it."

"Harper…" Richard warns, but she cuts him off.

"No one asked you to do any of those things. I thought you did it because you wanted to, but maybe you did it so you could hold it over our heads for the rest of our lives, rub it in our faces that Mother loved you *oh so much*."

"I did not… How dare you," I say. "Is that how you feel, too, Richard?"

Richard looks trapped behind the lenses of his glasses, torn between us when it shouldn't even be a question. I turn on my heel and shove the doors open, leaving them swinging violently behind me.

HARPER

Lucas and I take lunch in our room. Linnet brings us a tray of fruits, vegetables, nuts, cold meats, and two protein shakes. She also informs us that a big tree has fallen across the main road out of here. "I tried to warn you all," she says, barely keeping the righteousness out of her tone. "No telling what other damage will happen before this thing has passed."

She fusses a bit more before leaving. Maybe it would've been cathartic to be smashed by a twenty-thousand-pound tree after Zach's rampage and Elle's tantrum.

"The problem with both of them?" I say to Lucas after we eat. "They are entitled. They want all the things to come their way, but they don't actually want to put in the work to make it happen. No one wants to put in the work. They want the house, they want their parties, they want everyone to adore them." I flounce down into the desk chair.

"I thought Elle did a lot of work to plan this weekend," Lucas mutters from the bed, where he's trying to nap.

"What else does she have to do?" I ask, my voice rising. "She has no job, no responsibilities, nothing to do all day but paint her nails and rearrange her throw pillows. Five minutes in my world and they'd eat her alive. She acts like she has these ideas and ambitions, but she has never lifted a finger to make them a reality. Then she points fingers when the world passes her by."

The only goal she actually accomplished was becoming the perfect daughter-in-law. I'll never forget the year Lucas and I drove up here after Thanksgiving to find Elle and Mother in the sitting room, putting up the Christmas tree without us. She wanted to replace me, be better than me. She knew how Mother treated me, the hoops I had to jump through, but she pretended not to see it. That I was exaggerating. *Your mom is so lovely, Harper! Stop it!* And Mother never tried to toughen Elle up. She liked her just the way she was. Maybe because she knew she could control her.

Meanwhile, I'm managing several crises, and no one seems to care how I'm doing. I twirl in the chair, open my computer, and do a quick search, but no new articles about me as far as I can see, no images of our town house show up in news feeds. There's another story on Lucas, though, this time from *Businessweek*, who calls him "the tech whiz following the yellow brick road" and claims his software will "change the way start-ups communicate forever." I glance over at him, but he's flung his arm over his eyes, so he'll have to see it later.

I skip the social feeds, but there's a message from the same troll who told me I was going to die: Happy birthday, bitch.

I click on the profile, and it brings up a photo of an older white guy from Indiana who, from scrolling his feed briefly, seems to like superhero movies, trucks, and harassing random women. Before I can think better of it, I respond, Go fuck yourself, and then block the account. This guy will probably screenshot it and blast it all over the internet as proof of what a rotten person I am, but I don't care.

"Stop looking at that shit," Lucas calls, evidently not asleep.

"How do you know what I'm looking at?" I ask him.

"You're mumbling to yourself."

I didn't tell Lucas about the paparazzi outside our house. I'm hoping they'll give up, be gone by the time we get home tomorrow, and he'll never have to know. We've been cold-shouldering each other for most of the year—it started after Mother died. I said Lucas was too busy prepping to sell his company to support me emotionally, and he said I was taking everything out on him. Then my product line plummeted, and he didn't have my back, instead criticized me for caring too much about image, for being too personal, sharing too much. He's mad that I sometimes twist the truth—as if not *every single other influencer out there* doesn't do the same? As if he's some saint?

"I'm sorry. We can't all be media darlings like you are."

He sits up. "What is that supposed to mean?"

"It means you sell a company and get a prominent flattering feature placement in the biggest newspaper in the country, and I'm getting death threats for playing an active role in my business."

"You could try being happy for me—or anyone else—for once."

He's aware of the shit I'm going through right now and he blames me, the victim? "You know how hard I work to make VNity successful, how much time I put into this business, how much I've sacrificed."

"Yes, I do," Lucas says. He gets out of bed, crosses the room to his suitcase, starts digging around for clothes. "And I think it's killing you."

I put my hands on my hips. "It's not a terrible thing to be driven."

He shrugs off his shirt and changes into his gym attire. "It is if it means you lose your soul. I remember the Harper Van Ness I met in Vegas eight years ago, the one who was excited about an idea, about making something people would enjoy. That Harper was creative and fun and wanted to experiment. You had a spark. Now?" He stops, gets that disapproving look on his face that I can't bear. And I know what he's going to say. "Now you make up fake stories so people feel sorry for you?"

I narrow my eyes. "You don't understand, Lucas."

"I do, actually. You accidentally dropped a hand weight on your chest and then you lied to the public and said you were attacked. Do you even know how fucked up that is?"

I never wanted Lucas to know. It was bad enough that I told Todd, but we'd been talking about the relationship between pain and happiness and it slipped out before I could think better of it. I wanted Lucas to believe it was a stranger, too, like the rest of the world. But my husband has always been good at sensing my lies. He pressed and pressed until he got it out of me.

"All you care about is showing everybody how successful you are, and manipulating things when they don't go your way." He finishes dressing, fishes out his sneakers. "It's unhealthy. It's making you mean."

"At least I stick with something," I say. "You play around for a while and then get rid of it when you get bored. And the world loves you for it."

He shakes his head. "Right. It has nothing to do with my actual, I don't know…success? Hard work?" He straightens. "I'm going to the gym. Maybe you can go find your buddy Todd and ask him to give you a personal massage to calm that stress."

He leaves, slamming the door behind him.

I walk over to the window. Our garden flags are whipping around in the wind, and sheets of water cascade across the paths, pooling into muddy puddles. A blur of purple and silver flies by—Elle's precious balloon arch dissolving in the storm. In the far distance, tiny fissures of lightning crackle into small veins.

I unhook the window latch, swing it out. The rain's like a greedy animal, pressing in. I let the cold shock my arms, my face.

It's making you mean.

The rain is freezing, tiny little pellets of ice popping along my skin.

I know where you live.

I can tell you all about it soon.

Happy birthday, bitch.

Dear old Mother always taught me to keep people at a distance. Don't show vulnerability, or you'll regret it. Every single time. No one wants to see your fear. No one wants even a peek inside the darkest void.

That's what all her tests were about. Willpower—setting out an entire meal of my favorite foods on the table that I wasn't allowed to eat. *You have to learn to give up the things you crave, have the strength to walk away. If you show any sign of weakness, they'll walk all over you.* Survival—bedtime stories that were worst-case-scenarios: what would you do if you were walking alone on a dark street and a man was following behind you? If you got in a taxi and the driver started taking you somewhere different than you asked to go, how would you get out? If you were broke and scared in a foreign country and a woman befriended you and offered you a place to stay, would you trust her? Her brain whirred in a million, vicious directions.

I slam shut the window. Wipe the water from my face.

Maybe I should go down to the gym, too. Ten miles on the bike might make me feel less like a tense cat ready to pounce.

I throw on my workout clothes and head into the hall. As I pass Zach and Lauren's bedroom, I notice the door is open. I stop, hear the shower running, Lauren humming.

I peer around the doorframe. Zach's not there. Even with all the windows, the room feels gloomy, and it's in chaos. The bed's unmade. Half-empty glasses of water on the nightstands. Zach's clothes bunched in a pile in one corner. Lauren's suitcase sits open in another—she wears pink bikini briefs, how cute. She's laid out her outfit, dark jeans, a maroon blouse, and another of those cardigan sweaters.

I should leave, but something in Lauren's tote grabs my attention. It's slumped sideways on the bed, its contents spilling out, a flash of purple and green in the pile.

I walk over and pluck out a VNity Ambassadors badge, the ones we hand out at our fan events. Our marketing director paid some college intern two hundred dollars to design it for us. I had been skeptical, but the ambassadors seem to love them.

This one's a VIP pass, though, which means she gets into my exclusive events at headquarters. I frown, turning it over in my hand. Lauren doesn't seem like the type. She's hardly mentioned anything about makeup and self-care while we've been here. I can't imagine her spreading the brand loyalty, cheering at our events like a teenager waiting for a terrible boy band, going gaga about hand lotion or red-light therapy. And why wouldn't she have said something? Was she too embarrassed? Does Zach know?

I toss it back among the mess on the bed when Lauren's laptop makes a dinging noise. It's sitting open on the desk like an invitation, piles of papers scattered around it.

Lauren's important work, no doubt. Her big freelance career.

The computer hasn't gone to sleep yet, her email browser pulled up on the screen, and the shower water is still going strong. I maybe have five minutes.

If Lauren was worried about security, she'd have locked her laptop.

I select an email, but immediately get a time-out message. *Logged out due to inactivity. Log back in to continue.*

I click through tabs half-heartedly, but there's nothing interesting. A clothing store, the weather report for the Finger Lakes tracking the storm's path. The wretched *Van Nessity* website.

I minimize the browser. Lauren's desktop image appears to be a woman walking a tightrope between two tall buildings, but it's littered with files so I can barely make it out. One folder's title stops me cold.

K SPARKS.

Kat Sparks. The name of the blogger at *Van Nessity* who's been posting lies about me.

The shower turns off.

I click on the folder. Inside is a series of more folders.

Zach.

Harper.

Richard.

Katrina.

What the actual fuck? I select my name, and it brings up a bunch of documents and photos: *Product line fail, Ambassador spring event, megaphone, HVN gala*. The gala photo is of me a few months ago at a charity event. I'm walking into the museum, Mother's emerald necklace around my throat.

I hear Lauren moving around in the bathroom, running the sink water, closing cabinet drawers. At any minute, she'll open the door and find me. I whip out my phone, take a picture of the files, then toggle back to her email.

I slide out of the bedroom and return to my room, panting. I didn't get a chance to see much, but what I did see changes everything.

LAUREN

My ring glints, and I stare at it with guilt. Was I being too hard on Zach earlier? Maybe gaslighting is too strong of a word. Everything has been good these last six months. When we return to New York, away from the eyes and ears of his family, we'll sort it all out.

After my shower, I decide to retreat to what I do best—work. I grab my laptop, my bag, and slip over to the office. I'm sure Diane is pissed she hasn't heard from me yet. Whenever she wants information, she becomes as intense and suffocating as a needy ex, multiple calls and texts.

I met Diane Foster about a month and a half after I moved to the city, at one of the parties Maisie dragged me to. Diane is the editor of Newlicious, a brand of gossip sites focused on elite families and celebrities. Maisie and I had been at the bar when a group of well-dressed men started talking to us. One of them took a liking to me, bought me another gin and tonic, asked me to dance. When he excused himself to use the bathroom, I turned, nearly bumping into a woman with a severe black bob.

"Excuse me," I said, attempting to move past her, but she stepped in the way.

"Do you know who that is?" she asked, indicating the man.

"How much he's worth? He could buy this entire building right here, right now, and it wouldn't even put a dent in his bank account."

"I'm sorry. Is he your—I didn't mean…"

She laughed. It was abrupt, blunt. "No. But he's very private. Hardly ever talks to strangers." She cocked her head. "He must like you."

I smiled. "It was probably my friend he liked, actually."

She shook her head. "No, you. You're that kind of person. People talk to you."

"Okay…?"

She whipped out her phone, punched some buttons. "Are you Lauren?"

"What?"

Seconds later, my phone buzzed in my bag. "Just sent you my digital business card. I want to hire you."

The man was making his way across the dance floor, back to me. "Call me," she said. She tugged at my handbag. "You'll need a designer one of these to fit in more. Maybe a haircut."

And then she was gone.

It was March—a dreary spring, cold and damp—and my prospects were bleak. I made good tips waiting tables, but the work was hard and the shifts long. I'd saved some money from my admin job back in Maurville, but I was tapping into it too fast, too soon, despite sharing a Queens apartment with three other women. Most of the writing gigs I applied for wanted more experience than a part-time role writing obituaries and laying out community pages at a local newspaper. It seemed you couldn't catch a break unless you knew someone, had an "in."

A few days later, after yet another rejection, I saw Diane's digital business card floating in my text messages and gave her a call. That's when she told me she wanted to hire me to talk to people. That was all. Flirt a little, strike up a friendship. Make connections. She would handle the invites, get me into the clubs, pay the covers, and I would get information for her blog. "It's a win-win. You get to party, go to amazing events. And I get to write juicy stories. There's a lot of money in it, Lauren."

I hadn't realized it myself, but Diane was right. People wanted to talk to me. Growing up, I was the quiet one in school—studious, well-liked. I had friends, but never a best friend. I knew everyone's crushes, their petty crimes, their worst fears. They confessed things to me.

I never understood that that was special; I'd always just felt alone.

Until I met Diane and my eyes were opened to the power I had unknowingly held all this time. All I had to do was be nice, friendly, open, and it was amazing the things people would tell me. They were all eager to impress, or shock. The daughter of a prominent CEO told me her father was sleeping with a young up-and-coming artist. Two old-money brothers competing for Maisie's attention each told me about the other's drug habits. I took photos of minor celebrities grinding against one another on the dance floor. Everywhere there were stories to tell, and Diane paid me well for them. I hoped she'd trust me soon enough to write some too.

But the night Zach stepped out of the shadows, it was different. There was an immediate mutual attraction. He found a way to the rooftop of the building, even though it was off-limits, hitching us a ride in the service elevator and sneaking up a flight of stairs. I was sure we were going to get locked up there. I *wanted* to get locked up there with him. He wasn't like the other people I met at these things, who only wanted to talk about themselves. He was interested in what I liked, what I read, where I wanted to travel.

But things got complicated when I told Diane about it.

"My god, you've struck gold," she said with glee. "I'll give you your own blog."

I liked Zach. He was one of the first people I'd met in New

York who viewed me as more than an ear to listen. But I had to be realistic. This thing between us wouldn't go anywhere. He had a reputation for being *friendly* with lots of models, actresses, socialites. Meanwhile Diane was offering me enough money that I could stop waitressing and rent a better apartment, where I didn't have to share a bedroom. She was offering me a writing gig.

So I did it. As my relationship with Zach seemed to persist, I told myself the job was just for a little while longer, a security blanket until I could get a different one, and there was still the likelihood Zach would move on any day now. Plus, it was just fun, harmless gossip. I even wrote a few posts about Zach and me, amazed (and a little creeped out) anyone cared when we went for a gourmet burger or saw the latest hit on Broadway. None of it was substantial information. None of it was hurting anyone.

I tried to ignore just how much I liked the feeling all the site traffic and comments gave me.

I sit down at Katrina's massive mahogany desk, open my laptop, feel the lush Persian carpet at my feet. My father would love it here. He'd want all of it, this one and this one and this one, plucking something from the shelf and handing it to me. "Here you go, honey." And then later, my mother would find it, take it away from me. "Your father doesn't understand the value of money," she'd say. "Would you rather have this or food on the table?" And I'd hear them fighting all night between the thin walls, torn about who was right, who to listen to, whose side to take. An impossible choice.

It was an impossible choice whether to post about Harper, too. Zach had already invited me to the birthday weekend when the anonymous email with the video came in a few weeks ago. I knew it would spread immediately—people love video evidence of others behaving badly. Diane would foam at the mouth. But

I also knew it had the potential to cross that line from harmless gossip to something more destructive.

I almost didn't do it. I had already decided I was going to quit after this weekend anyway. I'd come back, tell Diane I was pursuing this thing with Zach seriously, and shut down the blog. Diane would be upset, but she'd find some other shiny thing to take my place, I'd be free, and Zach would never know a thing.

But then Harper played that grape juice blind tasting trick on me.

Diane's pleased with how the post has performed, and she wants more. More, more, more. *Capitalize on the hype. Give them what they want.* I've been dodging her, hoping to find something harmless to appease her before giving my notice.

But now, with the way this weekend's gone, I'm not so sure I should quit. If I think about the situation too hard, I worry I will dig too deep into ugly parts of myself that I don't want to unearth.

I text Zach: Just working for a bit! Will catch up with you soon! XO and then focus back on my laptop. I search for Todd Christie and Harper Van Ness, but there are no relevant links. Only endless YouTube videos of Toddwell, his mind and body wellness channel. Whatever they worked on together has apparently not been released yet.

There are, however, tons of tweets and other articles around Harper's leadership troubles. I draft a quick follow-up post recapping them for the blog. When I've finished, I rummage through my bag for my phone in case Zach has tried to text me and find the Beat poetry collection I took from the box of old stuff yesterday. I pull it out and flip through it. The poems consist of scattered lines and breaks, like someone shook the words in a Yahtzee cup and tossed them out to fall where they may. Stanzas slide to one side or the other, long and rambling. One poem is a series of one-word punches, stark and harsh, surrounded by white space.

I try to imagine a younger Katrina Van Ness reading this. What she was like. When I started dating Zach, I looked up interviews she gave, and she always seemed imposing and reserved in a power suit, no hint of color except for bright pink lipstick. How did she transform from a teenager reading free verse to a slick, razor-sharp businesswoman?

I slip out the envelope with the birth certificates and examine them again. In the paper-clipped pile, there's one for Katrina Van Ness, and underneath that one is a birth certificate for someone named Celeste Robin Sonoma, born in Los Angeles in 1956.

Curious, I type "Celeste Robin Sonoma AND Katrina Van Ness" into Google. Most hits are Katrina Van Ness as one of the top women winemakers in the country, an article speculating whether the Van Ness winery might expand west to Sonoma County, others about her death.

I search again with just Celeste Robin Sonoma in quotes, and Google wants to know if I meant Robin Cellest, a physician in California. I scroll down anyway, and an excerpt of a news article from a library archive in Los Angeles jumps out at me.

…and missing persons in California… **Celeste Robin Sonoma**, 18…

I click the link, which pulls up a preview of a newspaper article from 1974. Without library access, I can only read the beginning. It seems to be a recap of a police town hall meeting about safety on the streets, but the paragraph right before the piece gets cut off reads:

Other business was discussed, including cold cases and community concerns. Ms. Talia Sonoma filed a missing person's report for her daughter, Celeste Robin Sonoma, 18, who she believes might've possibly left the country with an older man she met at her place of employment.

I try several other searches, but nothing useful turns up. A Celeste Sonoma also appears in a long list of names on a nonprofit website for missing and exploited children, but no further details about her or her case. *More than one million youth run away each year. Tragically, many of them disappear without a trace, never to be heard from again.*

I look down at the papers in my hand. Why would Katrina Van Ness have the birth certificate of a runaway teenager from Los Angeles?

I flip to the beginning of the poetry book. Read the inscription again:

For you, K. Monte Carlo forever. From your partner in crime, C.

I feel a twitch in my gut. A prickling along the back of my neck.

There's a story here.

ELLE

The sky rips in half with a violent streak of lightning. The rain is coming down hard, pelting the windows, sending giant water trails down the kitchen doors, like the house is weeping.

"Someone has made God angry," Linnet says ominously as she wraps the huge salad bowl in nearly an entire roll of plastic wrap. She scowls at me as if I'm the culprit. "I hope you are all prepared."

I open the refrigerator door for her, and she tries to find a place for the bowl. It's like a game of *Tetris* in there, but Linnet's a pro and makes it fit.

"We aren't helpless, right, Zach?" I ask him as he mulls over the remaining vegetables on the counter.

"Guess it depends on who you ask." He pops a baby carrot into his mouth, crunching it loudly. His raincoat is on and his car is pulled up out front. "But yeah, I think we'll survive."

"Okay," Linnet says in a disbelieving tone. "I have a few things to finish. I'll meet you up front."

Since Harper won't do it, I asked Zach to drive Linnet home. She and Bill live in a house across the property, and she'd made it very clear she'd rather wait out the storm with him there than with us.

I walk with Zach to the door, biting the inside of my lip. "Zach…" I hesitate, even though I know I can trust him. He's more understanding than Richard, more trusting. "You haven't seen Todd today, have you?"

He looks surprised. "No… Why?"

I tell him about the person in the tunnel, how they disappeared, the map in Todd's room. "Plus, there was someone in the vineyard last night." I mention the grapevine in the box.

Zach's brow furrows. "Wait, what? A vine?"

"Yes. Broken off at the end."

"I don't get it."

Is he lying? I assumed Mom had repeated that mantra to all the siblings. She loved her sayings and superstitions. "Because…" I stumble. "Well, like Mom used to say—it's bad luck. An omen."

He stares at me like I've sprouted an extra head. "I have no memory of that. But that's weird. Why would Todd leave something like that, though? Seems like something Richard or Harper would do, to screw with you."

My mood blackens at the thought of those two, ganging up on me earlier in the kitchen. I'm still avoiding Richard. He needs to know he fucked up.

"Exactly, that's what I thought at first. The vine sounds like Harper," I try to agree. "But what if it was Todd in the tunnel? He's been gone all morning, so what if he's been snooping around the house?"

I recognize how it sounds, but to his credit, Zach doesn't burst out laughing. "Hm." He rests his fingers on his chin and squints. "Are you sure it was a person down there? That tunnel can mess with your head."

I'm sure, but I also know how implausible it must seem. "I guess. Maybe," I say quietly.

"Hey." He throws an arm around me. "It's okay. If you're that worried, I can pop down there? Ease your mind? But really, I think it's more likely that Todd's just blowing off his work, using the storm as an excuse."

I nod, even though it doesn't add up. Why would he blow off work to sneak around a tunnel?

Linnet interrupts, noisily shrugging on her raincoat. She's not happy we didn't listen to her and Bill about leaving before the storm hit. As she takes the umbrella I hand her, she glances at the scratches on my wrist, her lips twisting in a slight smirk.

The door flings open, cold, wet gusts of wind plowing inside, and then she and Zach rush out to the car. I press my palm to the glass next to it and watch until the taillights disappear into the fog and mist.

Back in the kitchen, I make myself a seltzer water with a squeeze of lime and a few drops of CBD oil to try to calm my nerves. Linnet must have found icing in the pantry and did her best to fix the top of the cake. I position birthday candles carefully in it. It's a good distraction, soothing the way the wax forms slide in, creating tunnels.

Before I place the last candle, I hold it up and light it, observe the wick catch, the flame grow into a white-hot bulb of light. I stare into the flame, making my wish. Blue wax drips onto one of my riddle cards from last night that someone left on the counter. It lands on the word *sight*.

Without sight, the vines see deeper.

I blow out the candle. Mom would've been proud of my riddle. Not that it was especially elaborate or clever, but it caused everyone to think differently, a little outside the box. Mom enjoyed logic puzzles, brain teasers, anything that tested the way you viewed the world. She told me once that I should try sitting in a new chair in my favorite room, or turning it around, to view things from a new perspective. *There's always something new to see when you take the time to look.* One time we went for a ride in her plane, soaring high above the estate, and she showed me the wine warehouse from above, the giant purple VN painted smack in the center of the roof that I never knew was there, that no one standing on the ground would ever be able to see.

Hidden in plain sight. Something clicks in my brain. Barely there, but I dig, not wanting to let it go.

I dash back upstairs to the office, my mind on Mom's last riddle, her last game for me. I look up. The Cessna model, Mom's first plane, suspended from the ceiling where it has a different perspective, an alternate viewpoint.

Hidden in plane sight.

A play on words.

I follow the line of sight from the nose of the plane. It's pointing at the bottom of the massive bookcase that takes up one wall of the office, lined with storage cabinets. I kneel in front of them.

They all open easily except for one.

My heart starts racing. It must be some kind of secret panel. But there's no catch, no sign of hinges or anything that would suggest a hiding spot. I knock on the wood, but it sounds solid, not hollow.

I run my hand along the side of the bookcase where it meets the corner of the wall. I sweep up and down, as high as I can reach, feeling smooth, cool wood. But as I'm drawing back down the second time, something snags my sleeve.

It's a small lever.

I tug at it, and it snaps forward. There's the whirring of a motor, and then the entire front of the panel pushes out and to the side.

My excitement is short-lived. Inside is a black safe with a push pad combination lock.

Dammit.

I punch in the same combination for the lock that leads to the tunnel, but I get an angry buzz from the keypad and a blinking red light. I try Richard and Harper's birthday, Zach's, even mine, but get the same angry buzz each time.

I sit next to the safe, resting my head against the bookcase, thinking furiously. What else could it be? What else was important to her?

I look up again at the plane, pointing directly at me. *My fourth baby*, Katrina said once, fondly. Painted on the side of it is the registration number of the actual plane she owned. An *N* plus five digits.

Could it be...?

I type it in, using the 6 as *N* like you would on a telephone landline and wait, holding my breath. The light on the combination pad beeps and blinks twice, then turns green, and the door releases.

I stuff my hand inside.

There's no cash, no bonds.

Only a small blue velvet box.

It's encased in blue velvet, Katrina had said.

I crack the lid.

What's inside takes my breath away.

It's an egg. A jade egg with gold and jeweled flowers, diamonds and rubies. There's a delicate gold clasp, and I lift the lid of the egg, revealing a diamond-encrusted portrait inside.

Katrina's nest egg. A literal egg. A Fabergé.

I cup it carefully in my hands, cradle it like a baby. This. This is what Katrina Van Ness wanted me to have. This is what she gave me in case of an emergency.

I unlock my phone, take a photo, and send a text. I've got the money.

There's a cost to everything, even silence.

Now no one will ever have to know what I did.

THE PARTY GUEST

The text lights up my dark room.

I've got the money.

Everything's going to be just fine.

I have to laugh at the earnestness, at that unflinching belief that it's all going to work out. That money can buy anything. She's been saying that—*Everything's going to be just fine*—for weeks now, acting as though it's no big deal, that we have all the time in the world for her to pay off her debts. What would the credit card companies say if I tried something like that with my bills? Or a landlord—*just tear up that eviction notice, please. It's coming—I promise! Trust me.* She has not one fucking clue how reality works, wrapped up in her own desperate, petty revenge.

I check my watch—party time is getting closer. My party, that is. I must get ready.

I grip my necklace until the grooves and creases make an imprint on my skin. The feeling grounds me. My dad gave me this necklace before he died. It belonged to my aunt, his sister. He thought I'd want to have it. He said I reminded him of her—we were both big dreamers.

Now that the party's off, I hope the Van Nesses can still have some together time. Family is important, after all. Blood is thicker than water or wine. I hope when I arrive, they'll have had time to uncork some wine, get their drinks in early. That they are good and dulled when I show up.

I smile as I picture their faces when I tell them why I'm here. When I hand them the final, and most important, birthday gift.

Won't they be surprised.

HARPER

I pound down the stairs. The house seems deserted.

In the sitting room, I sit down at the piano and start playing mindlessly. I never liked taking lessons when I was younger, mostly because Mother forced me, but now that I'm an adult I find the stroke of the keys soothing. The storm outside rages and howls, but the music, the movement, helps me think.

Lauren has files on all of us on her computer. Or should I call her Kat Sparks? The woman who's been writing about us for months now—about as long as Lauren and Zach have been dating. Zach's really outdone himself this time, bringing an enemy into the family, oblivious to the fact that she's using him to destroy us.

I slam my fingers hard on the piano keys, making a dissonant noise, and get up.

This room is the gaudiest in the house. Gold brocade, velvet, thin, hard arms on the furniture. An old globe in the corner, useless as wars have since been waged, new country lines drawn.

I walk over to the full-length mirror. This weekend was supposed to be a getaway, but I look tired, the skin under my eyes the color of my bruise when it was still fresh. I imagine a half-dozen ways to ruin Lauren—out her in front of Zach, go public on social media, beat her with her laptop—and like a good meditation, it calms the nerves.

I dislike this room, but I love this mirror. The thick frame looks like a heavy metal, imposing and solid, but it's actually hollow, lightweight, swings out easily. Mother mounted it here to block off the old, dreary servants' quarters.

When visitors came to the house, Mother loved to settle them in this formal sitting room, pour them her best wine, and then excuse herself. She'd sneak upstairs, slip through the passageway behind the bookcase, and listen from the mirror to see if they talked badly about her.

Another of her games.

But that was Mother. Always testing. Slipping into the walls, pushing levers, manipulating from behind the scenes. She loved the control, the power.

A plan begins to emerge. I take Mother's gun from my purse. My gun now. It's heavy in my hand, small, with a white pearl handle. *A lady's gun*, Mother told me once, *but it'll get the job done.*

The weapon gleams as I stare into the mirror as if Mother is on the other side staring back.

I will myself not to blink.

Wait, wait, wait…

Hold my gaze, Harper, I can hear Mother say.

Don't blink.

LAUREN

A missing woman. The daughter of a powerful family. What's the link? There's a story here, a prize to be had.

All these powerful families have secrets, things they don't want anyone to know, Diane says. I know she's cynical, sees the worst in everyone.

She's also usually right.

Celeste might've been an old friend of Katrina's. Maybe they met up in Europe. Or maybe they first became friends there and Katrina helped her get a job, establish a life, like Maisie did for me. There could be an easy explanation, something mundane.

Or it could be something more sinister.

I type a quick email: Maybe look into a Celeste Robin Sonoma, missing in the mid-70s?

Right after I hit send, there's a boom so loud it sounds like the house has collapsed.

And the light above me goes dark.

HARPER

I blink.

Mother's voice runs through my head. *I always win, Harper.*

I feel her presence, so intense that I dig my fingernails under the mirror's frame, feel the latch.

Click, like a whisper.

I tug on the mirror, pull it open like a door.

The passageway appears empty. No Mother, fingering the jewels around her neck, disappointed in me for blinking first. Not a spider or cobweb or speck of dust in sight, as if someone has been in here recently and all the dirt latched onto them.

I step one foot inside. Richard and Zach and I never played back here, something about standing in that small, cramped space where someone used to walk, live, was enough of a deterrent, even for us.

As I swing my other leg inside, a roar of thunder shakes the house.

And all goes black.

ELLE

"I'm sorry, Elle." Richard walks into the bedroom, wraps his arms around me, murmurs into my hair.

He's come to me, like he always does. In the reflection in the bedroom mirror, we are a painting, a husband and wife in an intimate embrace. Mom always said we are a *handsome couple*, that we fit together so well. And it is true. We are good-looking, powerful, gracious. We make things happen, together. Richard realizes this. He understands that I am important to this equation. This is why, when we fight, he always comes to make up.

He says he's stressed, there's a lot going on, he didn't mean to snap at me about the cake, knows how hard I've worked. He tells me I'm beautiful, that he's the luckiest man in the world. And I believe him, I forgive him, like I always do. It's like the tide of the sea, a rhythm that ebbs and flows, predictable and soothing.

I kiss him, push him down on the bed. I'm beautiful to him now, but I might not always be. And what happens when beauty fades? Mom always said it's good to have a backup plan, that women had to be twice as tough and twice as smart to gain half as much as men. Maybe that's why she gifted me the egg.

It's tucked away, safe, where no one will find it. I'll sell it, and whatever money is left once I pay for the video, I'll keep for me. Just in case.

"I love you, Elle," Richard whispers.

When his face is so close to mine like this, I'm reminded how much the two brothers look alike. At just the right angle, you could almost exchange one for the other.

An immense tremble of thunder explodes outside.

Our bedroom is plunged into darkness.

LAUREN

The house is dark. The grandness of it, the spectacle, feels terrifying now, like it's turned against us. Every time it stormed with abandon like this when I was a kid, I'd imagine a tree was going to smash through a window and snatch me up, like in *Poltergeist*. Here, it's the vines. So many of them, being called in by the house, twisting up the walls, under the sills, worming their way up the stairs and under the doorframe.

Out of nowhere, the door to Harper and Lucas's room flings open, and Lucas steps out into the hallway. "What the hell's going on?" he says, squinting at me, his eyes still adjusting to the darkness.

"The storm," I say, but it comes out as a whisper.

We keep finding ourselves like this—alone together in the dark. I think about the night before. The blindfold. The woods. The kiss. Pressed up against the tree. What it must be like in the woods now, the rain beating down, the mud pooling.

"Scared?" he asks, eyebrows raised.

"No, but I might need a glass of wine," I say.

"No rule against starting early." Lucas winks. "Especially if the power's out. What happens in the dark stays in the dark, right?"

We hear someone coming up the stairs, and Harper appears at the top of the landing. She stares at us for a moment, her eyes jumping between us, her jaw tightening. "Where's Richard? Bill called. He says there's a substation down—whatever the hell that is—and there's no telling when we'll get power back."

"Isn't there a generator?" Lucas asks.

"Bill says it should've turned on automatically. He's going to check on it once the storm lets up."

She strides between us and cups her hands. "Richard? You up here?" She moves farther down the hall toward his bedroom.

"It might get cold." Lucas looks me up and down, taking in my blouse and dark jeans. I follow his eyes, realize I didn't fasten the top two buttons. "You may want to put on something warmer."

There's the click of a door, and a few seconds later, Richard emerges from his bedroom, adjusting his glasses and buttoning his shirt. Elle is behind him. She's changed into a sweatshirt and dark yoga pants.

"For fuck's sake," Harper says, crossing her arms. "Sorry to *interrupt*, but in case you didn't notice, we have no power. And no heat. And, since no one thought to cover the outside woodpile last night, we have no wood for the fireplaces."

Richard sticks his hands in his pockets. "We could go to the sitting room. It has gas logs."

I grab my sweater from our room and join them in the sitting room. Harper is in the chair closest to the fire, and Lucas stands in front of her, warming his hands over the flames. Elle and Richard fix drinks in the corner, talking low. But Zach is missing. I haven't seen him since he told me he was going to take Linnet home an hour ago.

I find a spot on a couch. Zach's been acting strangely this weekend, but if I'm being honest with myself, I've not exactly been an angel. And then there's the kiss with Lucas last night that sends a little jolt through me every time I think of it.

If Zach and I really have a future ahead of us, we need to start being honest with one another. Or part ways.

Outside, thunder booms like a warning. For tonight, I just need to get through this storm.

Richard looks over, asks if I want a drink, and to be easy, I tell him anything is fine. He hands me a very full martini. It's strong. I take a sip, try not to cringe.

Elle lights a few pillar candles and sets them on surfaces around us, but they don't do much to improve the lighting. She eases into a chair next to Harper's, Richard hovering behind her with his own martini.

With the flickering fire and candlelight, the objects in the room are foreboding. Have the eagle statues on the fireplace shifted since last I saw them? Moved closer, like they're flocking together, preparing to hunt? Behind me, the long room disappears into shadow, including the full-length mirror that conceals the passageway. I wouldn't want to be inside it during this storm, that narrow hallway, the cold stone walls.

Lucas turns from the fire, cracks his knuckles, the loud pops reminding me of bursting bubble wrap. He kneels down next to the large coffee table in the middle of the room, pulls out an envelope and a packet of papers, and starts rolling a joint. He's fast and efficient, and when he's done, he walks back over to the fire and lights it, taking a long hit, holding it deep in his lungs.

Harper stretches out her arm toward him, her face stone. She still hasn't said a word since I entered the room.

He takes another hit before handing it to her, then sprawls out on the carpet in front of the fire, like a giant lion, his T-shirt tugging up to reveal a strip of hair.

Harper passes the joint back. "Elle?" Lucas waves it her way.

To my surprise she snatches it up. When she offers it to me next, I shake my head. I'm already feeling the effects of the martini.

"Hey, Elle, where's *Todd*? Shouldn't he be here with some

storm therapy exercises to help improve our mood?" Lucas snatches a circular glass paperweight from a table next to his head, tossing and catching it like it's a tennis ball.

"I have no idea where he is," she says, sipping her drink.

"Maybe he's dead," Richard says, dragging another chair over to sit beside Elle.

"Not that lucky," Lucas says. "But hey, maybe Harper can lead us in a wellness activity then. If she knows of one. If not, I'm sure she can make one up. She's good at that. Improv. Her specialty." He's tossing the paperweight higher and higher. Each time, it disappears into the shadows the fire and candlelight can't quite reach, and then descends again into his hand with a hard thwonk.

The tension is so thick it feels like the storm has found its way inside. I sink deeper into the couch. If Lucas is this angry at Harper, what if he tells her about our kiss to get even? What if that's why he did it in the first place?

"I'd hate to take all the attention away from you, dear. You so love the spotlight." Harper finally breaks her silence.

The paperweight narrowly misses a vase on the table next to Lucas's head, and he finally sets it down on the floor next to him.

"You break it, you buy it," Richard says dryly, fiddling with the olive in his martini.

Zach finally shows his face, balancing a birthday cake precariously in one hand, a giant steak knife in the other. The flames of the candles sway, threatening to go out with each step he takes. He scans the room, smiling, but avoids my eye.

"Someone told me there's a birthday happening," he says, setting the cake down on the coffee table. It's one tier of the larger one I saw earlier, and it's a mess.

There's a loud thud above us. A large branch must've hit the house.

"It's the apocalypse out there, but sure, let's have processed sugar," Harper says, swinging her feet up over the arm of her chair.

The candles are burning fast. Little pools of wax drip onto the icing like tears. My mother used to bake a chocolate caramel cake every year for my birthday, covered in waxy sprinkles. I suddenly have a fierce longing to be there in our kitchen, listening to my family singing out of tune. Something familiar and safe.

I haven't talked to my parents in weeks. They don't even know I'm here.

Zach hauls Harper up from her seat, pulls her toward the cake. "You have to make a wish. You, too, Richard."

The flames dance like fireflies in Richard's glasses. Harper whispers in her twin's ear.

I close my eyes, too, see the candlelight behind my eyelids, like fireworks. *I wish for this weekend to end.*

Harper and Richard lean over and blow. The candles snuff out all at once, trails of smoke rising above them like an omen.

ELLE

The storm has taken over, seeped into our bodies, made everyone tense and unhappy. I'm trying to shake it off, to focus on the positives—Richard and I are okay, I've got the egg, I can pay what I owe and no one will ever have to know that I released the video of Harper. She can have her petty prank with the broken vine and whatever she and Todd are up to in the tunnel. Or maybe Zach was right and I let my imagination get the better of me down there. Everything is fine. It's all going to be fine. We'll look back on this weekend someday and laugh at how much we let this storm push us to the edge.

"We need music," I say as people finish the cake.

"In case you haven't noticed, we have no electricity," Harper answers testily, right on cue. "We can't do anything without power."

Lucas laughs from the floor, where he fiddles with a sand timer now, watching the grains fall. "Now there's the most apt thing anyone's said today."

"We can drink," Richard points out, downing the rest of his martini, the metal olive pick clanging off the side of the glass.

"Zach?" I ask. "Do you have music on your phone you could play? You always have good playlists."

Zach's zoned out, as if he's listening to the storm. After a minute, he nods, pulls out his phone, and starts playing a tinny pop song. He ups the volume as loud as it will go and sets it on the fireplace mantel.

"Let's dance." I tug at Richard, but he waves me off. I try Zach. "Come on. We need to turn these frowns upside down."

I don't really care all that much. I'm doing it more to goad Harper, kill her with kindness. Maybe she figured out I brought Todd here on purpose and tried to get even by scaring me. And when I didn't seem affected by it, she decided to stab the cake. Well, I'm going to show her that her sour attitude won't ruin everything.

Zach lets me pull him up. "What the lady wants, the lady gets," he says. We sway, twirling around the room. Richard and I took ballroom dance lessons once—we can work a floor when and if needed—but Zach is out of sync, bashing into me as we shift, too fast for the beat.

He draws me in to his chest, arm wrapped around me, and I get a stirring in my belly. Then I realize we are close to the fire. Too close. But before I can protest, he flings me out. I whirl, our arms stretched—

And then his fingers slip. I lose my grip and fall backward toward the fire. My calf hits the edge of Harper's chair. I stumble, nearly crash into Lucas on the floor, but he reaches up, breaks my fall so I can ungracefully skid to the ground. Inches away from the brick hearth.

"Shit! You okay?" I hear Zach ask, horrified.

"Elle!"

"My god, you two are a mess."

I pick myself up, wave Zach off as he approaches to help. "I'm fine. I'm fine."

I sink back to the floor next to Lucas, who sets the hourglass down, sand side up, so it starts sifting.

Richard points at my leg. "Elle, you're bleeding."

There's a small cut where I hit a sharp edge of the chair. Everyone's staring at me. "I'm fine," I say, and dab at it with a tissue.

"Maybe we should do something that doesn't involve bodily injury," Harper says.

Outside, a particularly vicious streak of lightning flashes, followed by a boom so loud it sounds like we've been hit by a bomb. For a moment, we all stare out the window.

I get up from the floor and join Zach and Lauren on the couch, as if the proximity will somehow protect me from it.

"How about a game?" Richard asks, trying to bring the room back to an equilibrium.

I gather my hair, swish it to one side of my neck, and begin braiding it. It's starting to get hot now that the fire's been on long enough.

Harper suddenly smiles. "Elle's picked a lot of the activities this weekend, so it's my turn. I say truth or dare."

She knows I hate that game.

"Sure you wouldn't rather play more cruel tricks on everyone?" I glance over at her, needing her to know I'm not intimidated. "Send Todd down into the tunnel to scare someone. Or maybe Richard would like a broken grapevine in his bed."

"What the hell are you talking about?" Harper says.

"The message you left me last night," I say defiantly. "You're the one severing relationships, Harper. Not me."

"I didn't leave you any message. I have no idea what the fuck you mean."

"Please, let's stop," Richard interrupts. "Can we just play the game? Please?"

"Exactly what I was trying to do," Harper says. She points to Zach, turning away from me. "Truth or dare."

He looks surprised. "Why me?"

"Why not?"

"Truth," he finally says.

"Great." Harper presses her palms together, thinking. "Tell us what you love most about Elle and what you hate about her."

He studies me, thinking. I'm aware of how close we are on the couch, Lauren just on the other side of him.

"I love how Elle always thinks of other people and their happiness," he says, patting my knee.

I feel myself blush.

Harper laughs softly. "And hate?" she says eagerly.

"Oh, come on, Harper. Don't be so childish." Richard sets his glass down, rocks back on his heels. He's fidgety—I'm sure it's the awful smoking habit and the weather outside is too terrible to go out in. But at least this time he's defending me over Harper.

"I don't hate anything about Elle," Zach says. "Although she's kind of a terrible dancer." He smiles at me and squeezes my thigh.

"Me?" I hit him with a pillow. "You're the one that nearly flung me into the fire."

"That's a softball answer," Harper says, killing the mood like always. "You have to tell the truth."

"That is the truth." Zach sets his jaw. "Not everyone is full of hate, you know. Elle's beautiful, kind, generous."

Lauren shifts, studies me subtly as she bends forward to pick up her drink. Is she jealous of Zach's compliments? The thought pleases me. I hope she doesn't start to get competitive with me. That never boded very well for the other women Zach has brought around in the past. They get possessive—and then, somehow, they never make it. I would hate for that to happen to Lauren.

"Your turn, Zach." Richard nods at him.

Zach focuses on Lauren. "Lauren, truth or dare."

Thunder grumbles in response. The shadows in the corner of the room seem to grow, as if they're pressing in around us.

Lauren pauses, and then says, "Dare?" She carefully sets her martini glass down on the table.

Harper smirks. "Right. 'Cause the truth is too much for you."

"Look who's talking," Lucas mutters from the floor.

"Okay," Zach says slowly, tapping his finger to his lips. "Dump out your purse so we can all see the contents."

She pauses, as if waiting for the punchline, but when no one says a word, she picks up her bag and unloads it on the coffee table.

Zach rifles through it, but there's nothing important. A bunch of makeup, a wallet, keys, tissues, random slips of paper and receipts, a book of poetry she must've borrowed from the library.

"God, you people suck at this game," Harper says. "So boring."

"Okay, I'll go next." Lucas sits up cross-legged on the carpet. He points at Harper. "Truth. Or dare."

She looks smug. "Truth."

He threads his fingers together and cracks his knuckles like he's getting ready for a fight. "How many times have you seen Todd Christie naked?"

Harper recoils, her smile vanishing. "That's disgusting."

"Is it? How many?"

"What is wrong with you?" She stands, and for a second I think she's going to pour the rest of her drink on his head.

A log falls in the fireplace, sputtering.

"Do you deny it?" Lucas asks casually, like they're discussing driving directions. "Like you deny giving yourself that bruise?"

I knew it. I knew she was lying. That's why it's been so hard for me to conjure up any sympathy all these weeks. Something about her story didn't add up. She didn't want to call the police, didn't want anyone to make a fuss about finding her supposed attacker. Because there was no attacker. It was just another ploy to get her followers rallying behind her.

"Okay, okay," Richard says, holding up his hands. "Maybe we should—"

"I cannot believe you," Lucas says when Harper doesn't respond. He shakes his head.

"Fuck you. Fuck all of you." She finishes her drink and slams it on the table before rushing out of the room.

Lucas looks at us all, claps his hands together and rubs them. "Okay, who's next?"

Richard glances at me, then away, and I wonder if he somehow blames me. If he thinks I'm at fault for bringing Todd here. And if he thinks that, what would he say if he knew I leaked the video?

"Game's over," he finally says and leaves the room after her.

THE PARTY GUEST

The wind rustles the vineyards in the distance as I skirt around the edge of the house. I'm glad I'm not closer to the vines, lest they sweep me up with their rough bark fingers and squeeze.

With the wind howling like this, it's hard not to imagine the worst. It's hard not to become animal-like, prepared to fight for sheer survival.

Because when we become animals, we are ruled by our emotions. When we get scared, we panic. Make mistakes.

And when we fall, that's when we become prey.

I approach the front of the house, stop behind one of the stone pillars holding up the portico over the driveway. The mansion is such a grand, imposing structure. The Van Nesses didn't build it, but it definitely fits them. It has an arrogance about it, cold and haughty, enhanced by the way the pounding rain bounces off it harmlessly, like slugs off bulletproof glass.

It's nothing like the house I grew up in, a snug little bungalow my parents bought when they moved to Maryland from California. Modest, but cozy. Even after my mom left us, my dad and I made the house ours. I miss that place. It hurt to lose it. But we had no other choice when my dad needed full-time care.

People like Richard, Harper, and Zach never have to worry about those hard choices, about making ends meet. They live in a bubble of comfort and luxury, while the rest of us shiver out in the rain.

But after tonight, they'll understand what it's like to lose everything.

I slide around the pillar and nearly trip over something heavy. I train my flashlight on it.

A stone statue set in the bushes. Two fighting foxes, their paws raised, ready to draw blood.

If the Van Nesses sensed any danger, they would peer outside right now. It's so dark without power, only the solar lights lining the landscaping provide any illumination at all. And yet, if they looked through the glossy, rain-beaten window, they might see my silhouette, cast long and low across the driveway.

I slip under the overhang at the front door, behind the bushes, walk to one of the windows. I press my palm against the glass, watch the water pool and drip down. The room is empty, but I like the house from this point of view. How small the barrier is, less than an inch, nothing a quick, violent smash couldn't change.

We feel so secure inside our spaces. The twist of a lock, the pull of a drape, brings an illusion of security. And yet, there's not much dividing us from them. Me from you.

Not much at all.

A delicious shiver runs through me.

I'm on the outside, for now, but not much longer.

It's finally time for the party to begin.

HARPER

Lucas is an asshole.

He broke a solid rule of our marriage—no airing grievances in public—and he will pay for it. How dare he ask about Todd like that, in front of my family? And in front of traitor Lauren. I could kill him.

I stumble through the dark house. Why did I convince myself to come here? I knew this was going to be a terrible weekend, but I have to admit, I underestimated it. I should be home by now, under my cashmere weighted blanket, detoxing with a lavender eye mask and purifying oils and forgetting the past three days ever happened.

Instead, I'm in the kitchen. Someone, probably Elle, has lit a pillar candle in the middle of the island, a flickering light that gives the room a séance vibe. Next to it are empty bottles of wine, a can of pistachios, a cake knife, and a full glass of ice water sweating on the granite counter. The other tier of the birthday cake sits frumpy in its box next to the oven.

I run the tap and gulp down a glass of water. Whatever stuff Lucas rolled in that joint is making me dizzy and dry-mouthed. Coupled with the pinot noir, I might as well have swallowed a bag of cotton balls.

I'm refilling my glass when a shadow passes across the fogged window above the sink.

Someone is on the terrace.

I step back. I think of the text message and the gift.

I know where you live.

I'd told Richard it was fine, that we could deal with everything after this weekend. But what if I was wrong?

I take another step back, bump up against the kitchen island. A bolt of lightning strikes, and I make out the figure standing in the doorway. It's a man in a bulky jacket and hat. The rain rolls off him in sheets, but he seems serene, unaffected.

I bite the inside of my cheek and feel a sting, followed by the metallic taste of blood.

When I ran out of the sitting room, I didn't bring anything with me.

I don't have my purse.

I don't have my gun.

The back door handle rattles.

I look around frantically and pick up the cake knife, which gleams dangerously in the candle's flame, and slide around the island so it's between me and the door. My hand grips the knife down by my side as I try to slow my breathing.

The door opens, ushering in the howling wind.

And I scream.

"Ma'am?" The lightning illuminates Bill. He frowns as he enters, stomping the water off his massive black boots.

I nearly drop the knife. "Jesus fucking Christ, Bill. You scared the living shit out of me."

Bill takes off his hat, shakes the water off, and places it on the counter. If he's fazed at all by my reaction, he doesn't show it. He seems calm, actually, too calm.

"Mighty terrible out there right now."

Bill has been with us so long he basically came with the place, but I've never understood how Mother put up with him or his moody wife. How can you trust people who choose to live their lives on someone else's land?

"I told you all you should've left," he continues, tugging off one of his gloves with his teeth and setting it on the counter next to his hat. It sits there like an amputated limb, and I suddenly remember Mother once telling us that Bill used to be a grave digger. "Told you it was going to get bad." He chuckles. "Linnet even tried the broken vine, but I guess you kids don't care about superstitions anymore."

I clutch the knife tighter. "You tried to scare us?" That would explain Elle's accusations.

"Not scare. Just nudge." Is he trying to hide a smile? "Your mother could be so superstitious. Believed in omens. Must be this house that does it."

Everything feels heavy, but I manage to get out, "What are you doing here?"

He squints, blinks, trying to focus on me. "Richard asked me to come help with the generator. You okay, Miss Harper? You seem a little on edge."

"There you are."

I jump at Richard's voice. This time I do drop the knife and it clatters to the floor, landing just in front of my brother's toes. He picks it up and puts it on the breakfast nook, then raises an eyebrow at me.

"Everything okay?" he asks.

On the other side of the house, the doorbell rings.

LAUREN

The loud chime startles the room.

Elle, who'd been staring into the fire, braiding and loosening and rebraiding her hair, whirls around. "Who in the world could be here now?"

"And how is the doorbell working without power?" I ask no one.

Lucas doesn't bother to look up from the joint he's rolling, entirely unfazed that he just accused his wife of having an affair in front of all of us. "Maybe someone didn't get the message the party's off."

It's clearly a joke, but Elle doesn't seem to take it that way. "I hope not. I'll get it." She rushes out of the room. There's the creak of the hardwood floors in the entryway and then the door cracking open.

"Doorbell works because the security system I picked out for this place is backed up by battery," Lucas answers my question. "And if anyone ever finds the generator, we could have electricity back, too."

"I didn't even know we had a generator." Zach leans against me on the couch, our hips touching.

Lucas finishes the joint and reaches toward the fire to light it. "God help any of you guys if there ever was a true emergency. You wouldn't last five minutes."

A prick of unease pokes at me. What *do* any of them know about emergency situations? Basic needs? I could use my friends from Maurville—guys from high school who could shoot, skin, and cook a deer, fix any rattle in my car, climb up on a roof to nail down a loose plank. If you don't need to learn how to fix things for yourself, you never learn to. I stand up, sick of the pressure of Zach's leg against mine, and walk over to the window in the darkest part of the room. It's fogged up, and I draw circles with my palm on the glass. I can barely see out. The rain has become hail, tiny peppercorn-sized snow pellets battering down.

"You guys like your weird blindfold games in the woods," Lucas says. "Sometime, we should play a true survival game. Every man—or woman—for themselves."

I shiver. I could barely find my way out of the trees last night—I wouldn't want to be outside trying to outsmart Lucas while he's hunting me.

I turn back to the room. "Not sure I'm cut out for something like that," I say.

"You could do it, Delaware. If you really had to." Lucas releases smoke, slow and long, then nods toward Zach. "This one, though. Done for."

"Screw you, man." Zach shifts forward for the joint. "You need to apologize to Harper."

Lucas laughs. His eyes are bloodshot from the weed. "Your sister needs to understand there are consequences for her actions."

And what about your actions, Lucas? Our actions? I swallow the hypocrisy just like everyone else.

The room is quiet, and it's then we realize that so is the front hall.

"I'll go check on Elle," Zach says. "It was probably Bill about the generator."

"I'll come with you," Lucas says.

I follow, not wanting to be alone in the dark room. The three of us slip into the shadows of the house. It's cold in the hallway, away from the fire, and there's a draft.

As we get to the front, I understand why the draft is so strong.

The front door is wide open.

Elle is nowhere in sight.

THE PARTY GUEST

"What are you doing here?"

Elle's eyes are furious. She doesn't even seem affected by the weather. When she answered the door, she grabbed my arm, dragged me off the porch to the edge of the driveway, behind one of the massive stone pillars. I'm curious what she thinks is about to happen.

She presses her back against the stone now, trying to avoid the streams of water cascading off the overhang that covers this part of the driveway. She doesn't care about me, though.

When we met for tea at The Plaza, after I caught her snooping and she wanted to bribe me to stay quiet, I was struck by her hair, long and dark, falling down her back in perfect waves. Now, though, she looks like a child, her hair in a loose side braid, makeup smearing.

"You can't be here," she says. "I texted you. I'm getting you your money. They can't find out about this."

Never mind she's been putting me off for weeks now about getting money, sob stories about how her husband reviews all their accounts, as if I care. But it doesn't matter now. Elle's petty little revenge is small potatoes compared to what I'm about to reveal.

"It's time to party, no?" I ask with a smirk.

There are footsteps then, voices, and a man calls out from the front door. "Elle? Are you out there?"

Elle puts her finger to her lips like we're kids playing hide-and-seek. She's worried about getting caught. Worried her husband will find out what a rat she is. Scandalizing her sister-in-law and former friend. Elle can pretend she's high and mighty all she wants, but in the end, she's just as selfish as the rest of them.

The door slams. It's only a matter of time before they'll be back.

I can end this right now. Step out from behind the pillar and ring that doorbell again. Give them their real birthday gift, the one they so richly deserve. The hourglass was just a teaser.

"You need to go," Elle says. "We had a deal."

I laugh, low, like I did in the tunnel when I heard the fear and uncertainty in her voice. "You never held up your end of it, as far as I remember. I'm tired of waiting."

"That egg I sent you a picture of? It's worth a lot of money. I'll sell it, and you'll have everything you've ever wanted." She removes her earrings with shaking hands, opens her fist to show them to me. They are diamonds the size of walnuts. "In the meantime, take these," she says.

I swallow hard. Try not to think about how that jewelry would've helped Dad, the longer he might've lived. For her, they're just one pair of dozens lying around the house.

I slap her hand away, watch with satisfaction as the gems go flying into the darkness and disappear into the muddy lawn. She lets out a cry, and for a second, I imagine she might crawl on her hands and knees to find them.

But instead, she grabs my arm again. "You can't go in there. Look, I know I seem awful to you, trying to ruin Harper's reputation. I know you probably think I'm terrible, but I didn't tell you the whole story. You don't know what she's capable of."

She's pleading now, hoping I might take pity on her. Understand from the heart about all her struggles. That day at tea? She gave me all the sob stories about her hard life, the way she was neglected by her parents, misunderstood, as she chewed up handmade pastries and tea sandwiches served on a sterling silver platter. Not once did she ask about me, about my life, my worries.

But I agreed to help her. Why not? It was one more way to turn the Van Ness family against one another, more proof how corrupt they are, how little they care about anyone but themselves. One more way to take a share of the fortune they have and don't deserve. One more chance for revenge.

"You think I care about what you and Harper did or didn't do to each other? I care about that about as much as you all care about this estate."

"Of course we care about this place."

"If this place is so dear to your hearts, why are you selling it?" I ask.

Her face changes from pleading to confusion.

"Oh my god. You didn't know." I shake my head. "No, that makes sense. Of course. They didn't tell you."

"Tell me what?" There's water dripping off the end of her nose. "You're lying."

"You know I'm not," I say. "But you want proof? I've got proof. Come with me."

I stride down the front steps with purpose. Elle's only wearing a sweatshirt and yoga pants, but she follows me into the storm.

Maybe she thinks she can keep me from exposing her secret, but she won't be able to do that. She follows me around to the side of the house. The slushy hail pelts off our shoulders and melts, creating muddy pools in the lawn. My boots suction in and out with each step.

It's a big house, and it takes a while. When we finally reach the covered porch, Elle's hair is plastered to her head like a helmet. Her sweatshirt is soaked, her teeth chatter. Her shoes must be waterlogged, squishing against the dirt. She looks like a shipwreck survivor.

"Where are you going?" she asks as I push through the manicured bushes lining the base of the porch. Behind them are wood panels, and one of them is actually a gate. I open it, shuttling us under the porch, sheltered from the rain.

A short staircase leads down to a small metal door. The one I've been using all weekend. The one I'm pretty sure Elle never even knew existed.

"What the hell is this?" Elle asks.

"This house has so many secrets," I say as I slide the bolt aside and swing open the door. "Just like this family."

LAUREN

Zach slams the front door, cutting off the wind. Lucas is already moving purposefully back to the sitting room, where he searches under the couch, behind the chairs. For a moment I think he's looking for Elle there, but then he fishes out his sneakers and starts shoving his feet into them.

"I'm going out to look for her." Lucas's face is grim, and the seriousness of the situation suddenly hits. *Don't go*, I want to say, grab his arm and make him stay after his comment about the Van Nesses' lack of survival skills.

"What should I do?" Zach asks him.

"Get your shoes on. Where are the flashlights and umbrellas?" Lucas asks, and when Zach tells him, Lucas rushes off. Maybe it was all that earlier talk of survival, but it feels like they're preparing for battle.

There's no way Elle would've run out in this weather, in that clothing, without telling us. I remember what Harper said the first night at dinner, about everyone "wanting a piece" of the Van Nesses, and my mind leads down a dark path of possibilities—robbers, kidnappers, an angry investor. I try to remember what I heard when she went to answer the door. Did I only hear her voice? Was there someone else who spoke? Several someones? But I'd been too focused on Lucas and what he was thinking about Harper, what he might've told and to whom about the woods last night. I'd been too worried about myself.

Harper appears in the doorway. "Zach," she says. She notices his hurried shoe-tying and stops whatever she was going to say to him.

"Elle's missing," he says. "She went to answer the door and disappeared. The door was left wide open. We're going to look for her."

I'm expecting Harper to be afraid—she had warned Elle to make sure the gates were locked. But instead she throws back her head and laughs.

"What?" Zach asks, his jaw twitching.

"Don't you get it? This is another one of her games. Her surprises. It's something Mother would do—disappear in the middle of a storm and make us find her."

"I don't think so." Zach shakes his head.

"Of course it is. Are you sure there's no riddle card on the porch? Muddy footprints to follow?" She advances farther into the room and fixes her stare on me. "Don't worry, I'm sure *Lauren* can figure it out. She's a journalist and has gotten to know this family *so* well this weekend."

There's venom in her voice that turns me cold. *Did* Lucas tell her about the kiss?

But before she can elaborate, Lucas returns with rain ponchos, umbrellas, and flashlights. He hands one of each to Zach, making a show of ignoring Harper.

Zach stands. "You two stay here," he says, and gestures to me and Harper.

"Maybe we should go, too? Help?" I ask, alarmed at the idea of being stuck with Harper right now.

"No, Lauren, you and I can team up," Harper says. "Use your *investigative skills* to find clues. Maybe Elle's playing hide-and-seek."

Zach nods. "Sure, that's a good idea," he says without conviction. He's too distracted to pick up on her tone.

He and Lucas leave. The door slams, and it's quiet except for the crackling fire.

"How nice we're alone," Harper says. She walks over to the bar and pours herself a glass of whiskey. "I've been meaning to talk to you."

"About what?" I don't like her tone.

"About your job," she says slowly. "You said you're a freelancer?" She collects her purse from a side table and sits, tucking it next to her. Gestures toward the couch.

"Right," I say, surprised this is not about Lucas. I sit, keeping the coffee table between us.

She drinks the glass of whiskey like it's a shot. She's been drinking a lot tonight, mixing wine and liquor with pot. I'm glad I stopped at one martini.

"And you had to work this weekend?"

"Just a little," I say. Why does she care about my job? "I had a deadline."

"I bet you did." She unclasps her bag, pulls out something small and metallic that she tosses on the coffee table. It skitters, sliding off the edge at my feet.

I don't need to pick it up to know what it is, the VNity Ambassador badge Diane got me for Harper's event a few weeks ago. I talked to a few of her followers who didn't seem too thrilled about the latest VNity products, but otherwise it had been a dull occasion until it was time for Harper's speech and she didn't show. Her assistant ended up parroting some excuse about her not feeling well, but everyone there knew it was a cover. A few days later, Harper posted on Instagram that she'd been attacked, shared the nasty bruise on her chest. We reported it on the blog, nothing negative, just the facts, and most readers were sympathetic. But others emailed me to speculate that something didn't seem right. I could've written something claiming Harper was lying, but there was something raw and vulnerable in her story, and it felt too much like pulling the bandage off a deep wound and probing to the bone. I couldn't go there.

"So tell me again what you're writing about, Lauren?" She swigs from an open wine bottle. "Or should I say *Kat*?"

I freeze. Heat cracks and spreads inside me. She knows. She knows. She knows.

"Kat Sparks. Where in hell did you come up with such a stupid name, anyway?"

My favorite animal, combined with a last name that represented the start of something—a flame, an idea. An alternate me.

"Well?" Harper asks.

"It's—it's not—" *What you think.* I struggle to form the words, though we both know they're a lie anyway.

"It's not?" One eyebrow rises. "Oh, do tell me then. Because from here, it looks like my brother is engaged to this blogging bitch who likes to gossip about our family."

I take a deep breath. There's no pulling a fast one with Harper, so I start with the truth. "It was just a temporary thing. I was going to stop. I *am* stopping."

"I saw your computer. You left your laptop open, *Kat*. Rookie move."

She gets up and begins to pace, mumbling to herself. Where the hell is Elle? Richard? His wife is missing, but so is he.

"You've been writing trash about all of us?" I hear her say. "Do you even give one shit about Zach, or is that all fake, too?" She spins around and hovers over me. "You're here, accepting our hospitality this weekend without a second thought, and then you go upstairs and hit 'publish' and try to ruin my life?"

"Someone sent that video in," I try to explain quietly, worried Zach could come back and overhear us. "I didn't know—"

"Who sent it?" she yells, slamming her palm on the arm rest.

I flinch back. "I don't know. I really don't. It was sent in through anonymous—"

"And you have *files* on all of us? Neat little labeled folders on your desktop? Do you know how fucked up that is? You think Zach's really going to marry you when he finds out what you've been up to? I can tell him right now and it's over for you. All this"—she sweeps her arm out—"gone."

I stare at her, silent, and a sudden calmness overtakes me, a relief to have the secret out, that this moment will force a choice, force my life in one direction. Of course someone would find out. I'd been deluded to think I could have it both ways: The sense of power that came with getting the right information and wielding it, though anonymously, the ability to make money and be independent. And then the recognition, the prestige of being a Van Ness, and the way Zach had made me feel important and loved. I should've realized that people like me will never have it all.

"So what are you going to do?" I say, meeting her eyes.

"No, no, Kat. It's not about what *I'm* going to do." She sits back down and smiles. "It's about what *you're* going to do."

THE PARTY GUEST

I flick on my flashlight, throw the beam around the room. Give Elle the grand tour.

Her eyes sweep the small, dirty window at the top of the wall, my sleeping bag and suitcase on the floor, a plain wooden built-in desk, then back at me. "You've been…staying here?"

"Only since yesterday," I say.

The thought of someone sleeping anywhere else than a king-sized mattress must be abhorrent to her. "It's like a prison."

"Not a prison," I say. "A gateway."

I train my flashlight on the doorframe on the other side of the room. "That opening led to another room just like this one, the rest of the old servants' wing. There's the door to the tunnel there, too." I walk over to my suitcase on the floor, fish out the rolled-up blueprints, and spread them out on the desk. "Have you ever seen the original blueprints of this house?"

I was fascinated myself when I first saw them. The perfect straight lines, the way all the rooms align and connect, the complexity of having to envision the way people will move and live in a space and render it all with just strokes of ink. The secret passages, underground tunnels, hidden rooms.

I point to the top right of the first page, written in the architect's lean handwriting. "Did you know, for example, that this house has a name? The original owner named it Secret's Edge."

"Why do you have these?" Elle asks, though she's keeping her distance from me.

I ignore her question, shuffling the pages, finding the plans for the basement. "And Secret's Edge was really about hiding the unpleasant things. For example, the servants. When this house was built, the owners had full-time staff, and this was where they stayed. Lovely, isn't it? Could you imagine spending all your hours cooking dinners, changing linens, answering the ringing of bells to meet the needs of every whim, and then coming down *here*?" I tap on the map. "Of course, it's all been shut up, locked tight, walled in. Lucky for me, I know my way around now. So when you spotted me in the tunnel, for example, I was able to slip back in here and lock the door."

"It was you in the tunnel?" she asks.

"See how it works? Here's the wine cellar. And we are behind it. You can only get to this room via the door under the porch that you and I just came through, or the door I used in the tunnel when you almost caught me earlier today. The servants used to have a second staircase that went right to the main level, but you walled all that up to create your secret passageway. It was really an odd change, honestly. Bricking off all these forgotten rooms." I look up at her and frown. "It's almost like they were trying to seal off ghosts, isn't it?"

"Ghosts?" Elle says faintly. She swallows hard.

"Don't worry. I haven't seen any. Just me down here, poking around. Following the passages." I smile at her. "Anyway, it's a shame your family's just going to sell it off."

"They can't sell this place. They wouldn't do that," she says.

"Does it really surprise you, Elle?" I inch slowly toward the door, still open. The rain is blowing in, harder now. Another wave of the storm must be arriving. "This family is toxic. Lies.

Greed. You know this. You told me so yourself, Elle. Isn't that why you did what you did?"

She flinches.

I know what she's thinking. She wonders what kind of person would come here like this, hide out in an old, barren basement room. She can't understand it because she's never wanted for anything. She was born into wealth and married into more of it.

I read all about Katrina Van Ness's funeral, the big gothic church the service was held in, the snakes of people lined up to pay their respects. News coverage, tributes, profiles of her contributions to business, of her family's long legacy. My dad's service was held in a small funeral home in Maryland, no press or cameras, just me and a handful of friends and family and my mother, dressed in all black and hovering awkwardly by the doorway with her new husband, avoiding eye contact with me. I'm still paying off the bill.

"But don't worry. This is not about you, Elle," I say now, resisting my urge to slap her. "This is about far more. And now you need to stay out of my way." I place my hand on the door, step outside. I see Elle's eyes widen as I move fast out into the night.

"No!" She lunges toward me, but it's too late. I slam the door shut, throw all my weight against it and turn the lock, trapping her inside.

HARPER

Lauren slinks off to her bedroom after our little chat, claiming a headache. But that's not why she left.

I check the time—just past 8:00 p.m. Lucas and Zach must still be out looking for Princess Elle. It's just like Zach to drop everything and rush after her, buy into her drama. And Lucas, he prefers a hailstorm and lightning to being in the same room with me. We've always been competitive, Lucas and me. Each of us loves to win, and we're good at it. It's part of our attraction to one another. But this past year, all I've been doing is losing, while Lucas wins. When Todd started flirting with me, part of me just wanted to prove to myself I could win again. But maybe I took it too far.

My phone buzzes on the coffee table. I pick it up. "Hello?"

There's a crunch of static, and then it cuts to silence.

"Hello?" I say again.

"Harp?" Todd's voice skitters through. "You still at the house? I need—"

The line goes dead. Call disconnected.

I throw my phone and sink into the couch. Todd better not try to show his face in here. If he does, I'll kick him out myself.

I pick up the hourglass on the side table. The sand has almost finished falling, only a few black grains left.

Three, two, one...

"Harper?"

I look up. With the dim light of the fire, it takes me a moment to make out the person standing in the doorway. She's wearing all black—a dripping raincoat and pants—and carrying a bright white box with a gold ribbon.

She lowers the hood as she enters the room.

"Penny?"

"Happy birthday, Harper." She smiles, sets the box down on the coffee table, and lets the computer bag she always carries with her fall to the floor. She shrugs off her coat and hangs it on the back of a chair. "I remembered to tell you this time." Her dark eyes focus intently on me.

"What are you doing here?" I ask, still processing her presence.

Penny cocks her head. "I needed to give you your present." She shakes the box in her hands. "And we need to talk."

Of course. Penny's nothing if not reliable. In the middle of a crisis, she's the calm head. She's here to forge a plan, create messaging, motivate our fans to turn this all around. I didn't even have to ask her. She just knew. She'll take care of shit.

Penny walks over to the bar. She pours two glasses of wine and passes one to me. "Let's have a drink, shall we?"

"You work too hard," I tell her, feeling a flood of gratitude rush over me. "This is supposed to be your day off."

She laughs. It's a small, quiet laugh, like someone just whispered an inside joke in her ear. She sits down in the chair across from me. "This isn't work." She leans forward, and I spot the gold locket always dangling from her neck. A present from her father, she'd told me, surprisingly sentimental for a woman who has zero personal effects at her desk, not even a mug.

She sets the gift box on the coffee table. It looks familiar, and then I realize it's wrapped the same way the hourglass was—shiny white paper, simple gold ribbon. Almost as if reading my mind, Penny picks up the hourglass from the side table next to her and runs her finger along the etched message.

"I contemplated what message to engrave. But this one seemed fitting. What did you think? You never answered my text."

I'm starting to think you aren't very grateful.

That was from Penny? My brow furrows. Why would she deliver the gift to our house? What number was she texting from?

A prick of unease settles between my shoulder blades as Penny swipes a finger over the cake, scooping up some of the icing, and licks it off. "You know me, how I like to be thorough. I wanted to make sure you opened it, had time to process it before I arrived, without spoiling the surprise."

I've seen Penny rip into our vendors on the phone. I've seen her handle employee meltdowns. Once, I saw her actually yank a man out of a taxi she had hailed first and he tried to steal. I've always appreciated her no-nonsense attitude, but the hint of darkness in her voice now suddenly feels threatening.

"Penny, what the hell is going on?" I stand.

"All alone on your birthday?" she asks, looking around the dim room.

"Zach and Richard and Lucas will be back any minute now."

Penny nods, chewing a nail. "Right. They're looking for Elle, aren't they? That might take a while. Elle's…down in the dumps, shall we say?"

I thought Elle had been playing another of her little games, but staring into Penny's eyes now, I know I was wrong.

"The roads are flooded out, Penny. How did you get here?" I ask. I back up, pretending to fiddle with a vase on a side table. There's a storm. A tree fell. The power's out. And yet, here's

Penny, who said she had other plans this weekend. "I thought you were attending a family reunion?"

She laughs, turns her palms up. "Oh, but I am."

ELLE

I bash on the door until my hands ache.

"Penny!"

It's useless. She's gone. It was a trap, and I fell right for it.

I'm locked in the basement, in the dark, and no one knows where I am. My clothes are soaked and heavy. And Penny is heading to the house to say god knows what, to *do* only god knows what.

The thought makes me ill.

It was supposed to be simple. Penny would get money, more than she'd ever need, and I would teach Harper a lesson about what happens when you treat people badly. Justice served, we both win.

But it wasn't just about teaching Harper a lesson. It was my revenge for her turning her back on me and our friendship. For taking away my dream and rubbing it in my face. I couldn't stand hearing about VNity anymore. How everyone just adored Harper. When all she is is a thief.

It was my idea to start an online beauty business. All female employees, natural ingredients. *That's a great idea, Elle*, Harper had said, encouraging me. I even considered asking her to partner with me at one point.

And then, three years ago, she announced she was launching VNity. When I confronted her about it, she laughed in my face. *Oh, Elle. Don't be so dramatic. It's not like a company like this is proprietary. We worked for a beauty magazine, for Christ's sake. Everyone there has ideas about starting their own product line. But ideas are nothing without action.*

Since then, she's refused to acknowledge the betrayal, refused to admit she stole my idea. I've never talked to Richard about it—he wouldn't believe me, he'd downplay it, take her side, tell me I was overreacting. "You can't copyright an idea like that," he'd say, or something equally unhelpful.

I almost went to Mom so many times, but she hated weakness. She would've been disappointed I didn't do anything about it. After all, I *was* weak, as mad at myself for not even attempting to start the business as I was at Harper for stealing it. I'd been too scared to fail, too scared my parents would be proven right.

At first I tried to ignore the loss, throwing myself instead into decorating our house, maintaining our social calendar, attending events, and then, when Mom was diagnosed, helping her with her medical needs. I thought I was over it finally, but then a few weeks ago on Mom's birthday, Harper started posting about her, pretending she had some wonderful, loving relationship with her just for likes and comments. It was the final straw for me. I couldn't take all her lies anymore. I wanted her to suffer, be humiliated. I knew she didn't treat her employees well either, that the way she presented herself online to her adoring followers was very different from reality, and I wanted them to know it.

After she'd posted about being attacked, I stopped by her office one evening when I knew she wouldn't be there. I had bought a tiny camera on Amazon, and I was going to plant it in her office, just to see if I could get any information to use against her. Any proof. It was time to knock her off her pedestal.

I was sitting at Harper's desk, trying to hide the camera in her desk lamp, when Penny walked in. I tried to make up an excuse, but I've never been a great liar. Never learned *that* talent from Harper. Penny figured out I shouldn't be there, what I was up to.

And wasn't I surprised when she offered to *help* me. Even Harper's own employees hated her. I made a deal with Penny— she wouldn't tell Harper I'd been sneaking into her office. She'd even send me some evidence I needed to prove to the world that Harper wasn't the feminist role model she claimed to be. All I had to do was pay up.

It was a risk. It was possible I had promised a lot of money to Penny for nothing, that media outlets wouldn't want it. I sent the video to the *Van Nessity* blog weeks ago and heard nothing. I followed up with Kat Sparks a few days before we arrived, and she finally responded and said she would let me know if she would be running a story by next week, asked me not to send it anywhere else in the meantime. Then, out of nowhere, the story posted Thursday night.

Penny wasn't happy when I couldn't immediately get the money to her. She didn't seem to understand that Richard had his eyes on all our finances, that he would notice if tens of thousands of dollars were suddenly missing. I told her I had to do it in installments, and she didn't like that.

This weekend was the cutoff. She'd waited long enough, she said. If I didn't get the money to her by the end of it, she was not only going to tell Harper, but Richard and Zach, too. But I did it. I found the egg, and now I'm able to pay. So why is Penny here? Why would she expose me now, when we're both getting what we wanted?

I clench my fists, take the deepest breath, and release a belly scream. Expelling the demons, my hot yoga teacher calls it. Letting out the steam. I was always too self-conscious to do it in class, to really belt it out. But now, I have nothing to lose. I yell, digging into my lungs and pushing out the air. I yell again and again, until I feel lighter, until I can think again. I need to get out of here.

My eyes have adjusted to the darkness. Penny's suitcase is open next to her sleeping bag. I kneel beside it and pull out each article of clothing one by one, tossing them to the ground until I land on a T-shirt and a black sweater to replace my cold, wet sweatshirt.

Then I circle the room, searching for another way out. It's still so dark I can barely see. That smell of incense from the tunnel is strong in here—Penny must've been burning it, maybe to get rid of the damp, musty air. And it's so quiet. My breath sounds loud and harsh, echoing off the stone walls. I'm reminded of Mom's game. *Without sight, our senses deepen.*

There are three exits out of this awful place. Penny locked the door we came through—the one that leads outside under the porch. The door to the tunnel is also locked tight when I try it. And a third exit—that once opened to another servant's room, which led to the main house—is completely boarded up.

I'm trapped.

And time is running out.

I have to get out before she tells them what I did. Richard would never forgive me. Zach would think I was a terrible person.

The thought chills me.

I throw myself against the door. Pain shoots down my shoulder.

I slam the wall with my palm and slide to the floor.

LAUREN

I draw the drapes to block out the storm, light the two emergency candles Elle left here, and curl up on the armchair in our bedroom. The first night we were here, this room seemed so spacious and luxurious. I'd been excited for all the possibility of the weekend ahead. Now I feel trapped, trapped inside this massive house, trapped in a mess of my own making.

If Harper tells Zach about the blog, will he think I was using him all these months? I can't stand the thought. I've witnessed some of Zach's faults this weekend, but I still care about him. I'd never want him to believe I dated him just for gossip.

I didn't think I was a bad person. But the way Harper glared at me, the things she thinks about me, maybe I am. I tried to pretend it was all just frivolous, harmless, but then why did I hide that part of my life? I convinced myself I was making my own way, carving a path that took me away from my parents and my shitty hometown and all the traps and snares people get stuck in there, but I was doing it because I enjoyed it. Because I liked the power.

Because the more I wrote, the more I couldn't stop.

Harper's words come back to me, so matter-of-fact. *Here's what you're going to do. You're going to write some blogs. They're going to downplay this scandal. You can talk to my ambassadors, or employees who will tell you what a good place VNity is to work. You're going to find out who sent you that video and those screenshots—if you don't already know—and you're going to get dirt on her. Ruin her. Give her a taste of her own medicine.*

And in return? Happy life for you and Zach. Assuming you still want that and you're not a total lying bitch. I'll make sure you're both taken care of. Hell, I'll even grant you an exclusive interview. I was the beauty editor at Beauty Plus *for years, and I still know lots of people in the business. I can open doors, or I can slam them in your pretty little face. So what's it going to be?*

I pace back and forth.

What do you want, Brady?

If I accept Harper's offer, then I'm forever under her thumb. I can marry Zach if we work things out, have the career I've always wanted—I don't doubt her when she says she has connections—but I'll also have to write stories for her, create spin. And still, she could ruin me whenever she wants, no matter how hard I work to stay in her favor.

Or I could give Zach back the ring. Walk away. Take my chances on my own. But then what? What if I can't make it as a writer without connections, without a powerful family behind me? Diane only employs people for a few years, and then it's off to the next friendly, fresh face.

I never want to go back to Maurville, to the house with dripping ceilings and worn-out carpet. I never want to become my dad, running a pawnshop in a fading downtown, or my mother, growing more and more bitter about the way her life has shaken out every year.

Knowledge is power, Diane always says.

What would she do?

What would Harper do?

They'd attack. Go on the offensive.

If I had something else on Harper, something that would

give me leverage, I'd be in a better place to bargain. I could take her up on her offer, without having to cater to her every whim for the rest of my life. But I have nothing, unless I can get more from whoever sent me the video in the first place.

I hear voices in the hall. As I creep over to the door, I spot Bill and Richard, deep in conversation, flashlights bobbing.

"The wires are gone. It's the damnedest thing. Need to get someone out here, probably, but let me show you," Bill says.

"That's fine," Richard says. "But I'm not sure we can do anything now." I hear a slam. Then silence.

I lock the door and fling myself on the bed, pushing aside my purse. The poetry book is tucked inside, the envelope with the birth certificates sticking out. I'm lucky no one noticed them when Zach dared me to spill out the bag's contents.

Lying back, propping myself up on the pillows, I move one of the candles to the nightstand and open the envelope holding them. Diane has been pressuring me to find information on the family, and now I need real leverage on Harper, but all I've managed to uncover this weekend is Zach's middle name. Something snags as I slide out the pages, and I hear paper tear. "Shit," I mumble. A small old newspaper clipping got stuck in one of the corners of the envelope, so frail it tore in half when I pulled on the stack of papers.

I carefully wiggle it out and put the two halves together. It's in French—a small news item dated July 18, 1975, three inches in length, dense text, no photos. The headline reads:

Femme Tuée dans un Accident de Voiture Enflammé à Monte-Carlo

I took a few years of French in high school but did not retain enough to read the article in full. Scanning it, my heart leaps to my throat when I spot the words *Celeste Sonoma* and *morte suspecte*.

I rifle through my purse for the glass key chain I found in the box downstairs.

Monte Carlo. 1975.

I open my laptop on the desk. I still have some battery life left, not that it matters since there's no internet connection. I wonder if Diane has looked into Celeste since I sent her that message. There may be answers out there, just a few clicks away, but I can't reach them.

I automatically click my email tab and notice an exclamation point in my outbox. *Shit.* The message to Diane never went through.

I press the key chain into my palm. Katrina Van Ness knew this Celeste. Maybe met up with her in France. According to their birth certificates, they were born less than a year apart, which means they would've been around the same age, late teens, two young Americans abroad. They must've been close friends if she kept these mementos all these years.

But then Celeste was killed in a car crash in 1975. A questionable car accident—*morte suspecte*—if I'm reading the article correctly.

1975. The year, according to Elle, that Katrina arrived back on US soil, showed up at her family's old estate, and decided to revive the winery.

Was she grieving a friend's death?

Or was she running from the same danger?

THE PARTY GUEST

I was right—it is different being on the inside.

In some ways, I feel like I've walked into a dragon's lair, tiptoeing around the treasure hoard Katrina's collected for decades, the mass of gold photo frames, jeweled statues, sparkling glassware, dark bottles, beaded pillows, feathers plucked from exotic birds. Items with no purpose other than to sit and be admired and gather dust. I never understood the need to accumulate things, to have all that weight and baggage. To leave it behind for others to deal with when you are gone. To me, these rooms are just rooms, simple lines and boxes; the stuff inside is meaningless.

"You're seriously sitting there trying to tell me we're related?" Harper asks. "Is this some kind of joke? Is Richard in on it?"

The rain continues to pelt, and there are other sounds, too, from deep within the house.

"I never joke, Harper. We are cousins. Makes sense, doesn't it? You always like to tell me how I remind you of you."

She glares at me. "We are nothing alike."

She's acting tough, but I can sense the mask is slipping. Harper's starting to panic. And when she panics, she makes mistakes. When she worries, she lashes out at someone vulnerable, like her employees. It makes her feel better. Classic bully syndrome.

I sigh. "Believe what you want, but I'm right about this. I first suspected we were related before I even met you. One month, my dad's account didn't have enough to pay his medical bills. When I looked into it, I discovered it was your mom who'd been sending him money—and she'd recently died. The timing added up. When I confronted my dad about it, he admitted they were related. I was shocked, of course. There was no proof, but I felt there was some truth to it. And we were desperate for the money. So I tried to contact your brother, but he ignored me."

"Payments?" Harper asks, narrowing her eyes. "So this is about money."

"Harper…" I take a sip of my wine. It's good wine, I'll give them credit. "Isn't it always about money? You of all people should know that."

Her fingers are digging into the back of the couch like she's trying to tear through it. "You're right. I should have known. Because if it was about anything else—if any of this was the truth—you would've talked to me about it. Like a normal person."

"I did try to talk to you about it. I came to meet with you at VNity in June, a few months after my dad died." I shake my head. "But instead, you mistook me for the temp."

I'd gone dressed in my best suit so I could make a good impression. I'd seen Harper's videos, read her blog. She was a force. I knew if I had any chance at all of convincing her of my story, I'd have to look my best.

There was no one at the reception, and I was able to sneak in behind an employee who had an ID to unlock the door. I walked past rows of desks, where young women typed away on laptops or phones. The place smelled like the greatest spa in the world. There were posh green couches in one corner, and in another, a black marble bar with makeup mirrors and sample products stacked in tiny boxes.

A woman with blond hair extensions to her waist stopped me halfway down. "Oh, you're here! Right this way," she said, clearly thinking I was someone else. I didn't correct her.

She led me to the back. We stopped at an office, Harper's office, with its two purple doors propped open by wedges shaped like high heels.

"She'll be right with you. Help yourself at the coffee bar." The woman disappeared, and I was left in this decked-out office that was larger than my friend's apartment I was crashing at in Brooklyn. I sat in a purple chair across from a large gold slab desk, my palms sweating. There were two TVs and a Peloton. A coffee bar. A private bathroom. Calming piano music pumped through invisible speakers.

"You walked in, chewing on a stylus pen, and barely looked at me," I tell Harper now. "You said you had no time to train me, remember? You said that I had to learn on my own and asked if I was ready for that."

I could've explained then. Spilled who I really was, what I was doing there. But I knew, meeting her cool, confident gaze, that if I did, she wouldn't believe me. She'd call security to drag me out. So a new plan formed. To work there. Get close to her. Earn her trust. Get the proof I needed.

I carefully set down my wineglass on the coffee table.

Harper's staring at me, shock written in the lines of her face. "But I trusted you," she says, and it's the softest I've ever heard her speak.

I don't like this Harper as much. All the bravado has dissipated, and without it, she's just an ordinary person. Plain, even—her head a bit too square, her hair a bit too thin, and that same large, long nose her mother had before the plastic surgery, that my dad had too.

"I was—I am—good at my job," I say simply.

Harper's confused, but she's starting to put the pieces together, I can tell. She just doesn't like the picture they're creating.

"Maybe this will help." I remove the papers from my computer bag—nicely tucked in a folder to keep them safe—and hand them to her. "This is the full report from Discreet DNA testing. I only sent you part of it as a teaser—figured it would be easier to explain everything in person. There's your column, there's mine. They specialize in paternity testing, because apparently men love to wiggle their way out of responsibility of their own flesh and blood, but they will test for other relations. A fourteen-percent match is actually pretty amazing, from what I understand."

Harper barely glances at them, then flings them back at me. They flutter ungracefully to the floor in front of the couch. "What kind of nerve do you have, coming here like this?" she says to me, all venom. She's gathering momentum back now, I can see. When Harper gets angry, she's a tornado, sucking everyone and everything into her funnel if they don't watch out. "Scaring the shit out of me with those text messages, the weird unsigned gift, trying to scam us? Impersonating someone else to get a job? Do you even know how many crimes you committed—and wait—" She gets in my face, and I witness it dawning on her. "How in the fuck did you even get my DNA?"

I smile. It infuriates her when I stay calm, unruffled. "You keep a toothbrush in your office bathroom. I admire the good hygiene actually. So many people just let their teeth stain in the name of caffeine."

"You lying bitch," she hisses. "You're a fraud. And a thief. And it was you who released that video, wasn't it? To sabotage me?"

I don't give her the satisfaction of reacting. Instead, I absorb it, bottle it inside. Raise my chin up to her. "No, that was someone else." I make a clucking noise in my throat. "You really have a way of pissing people off, Harper."

The rain is still pounding steadily against the windows, but there's another noise, a dull thud. Harper looks hopefully at the doorway, but when no one shows, she turns back to me.

"I'm calling the cops right now."

"Be my guest," I say. "I'm assuming you know the local police number by heart? Or wait, maybe you can call 9-1-1. And tell them what, though? What's your emergency? Although, I suppose they could transfer you to the local police department. Where, again, you'd have to figure out exactly what to tell them to make them come all this way in a storm, especially if the roads are impassable. But yes, go do that. I'm sure they'd love to tell everyone they know a wacky Van Ness story. Of course, you don't really need the bad press right now, do you?"

"I want you out," Harper says. "You're fired. And I'll make sure you'll never get another job in New York, or anywhere. If you're not in jail, that is."

And now the Harper I know is back. The one who fights when she's in a corner, claws flying.

"I don't think I'm ready to go just yet," I say. "You're going to sit. And you're going to listen to me for once. You're all going to listen. And then you can fire me, though I expect a generous severance pay. Very generous. Because if you don't, I will destroy you. And your entire family." I raise my voice now. "I don't know who's there, but you might as well come out now. I know you're listening."

There's a loud click, and the full-length mirror hinges open.

In the passageway stands Richard Van Ness.

ELLE

I roll up the blueprints and toss them in a corner. I need to find a way out of this room. But the only other escape is the small window above my head, and there's no way for me to reach it. The one movable piece of furniture is a flimsy camping table, aluminum, with thin legs, meant for a couple of plates, or a lantern, or cocktails.

It's not meant to hold a person's full weight.

But it's my only chance.

I push it against the wall, under the window. If I set a foot on either end of the table, distribute my weight across it, maybe it won't collapse immediately. I lift one knee up to test. The table wobbles, but stays upright. I try to add my other knee, carefully hoist my body on, and then slowly stand.

The window is small, recessed into the stone, but it's just big enough that I think I can wiggle through it. If I can figure out how to open it. There's a slide lock, rusted over, and when I start to tug at it, the table shakes dangerously. I stop, dig one hand into the small ledge of the window to steady myself, then try again.

I pull, again and again, but the lock is so small it's hard to get a good grip. I lean to the side, tugging as hard as I can, and my fingers slip. The table groans, tips. I manage to clutch, briefly, the stone ledge before I fall, hard, and the table falls over with me. It makes a clattering noise, and sharp pain roars in my hip.

I curse, cry out, as I lie there on the floor. I could just stay here, give in, accept the consequences of my mistakes. But I hear my father—*you do give up on everything, don't you?* See Penny's smug smirk as she tells the Van Nesses I betrayed them. My anger brews again. If Mom were here, she'd throw me a steely look. *Rewards come to those who work for them.*

I stand. Find the table and right it. Luckily, it's still intact.

I prop it up again. Climb up. Grasp for the lock and realize that my previous struggle wrenched off some of the rust. I pull again, careful this time not to shift my weight, and it begins to unhinge. I can feel it give. After a few more tugs, the lock slides free and I shove the window open.

Cold wind rushes in, but now it's not freezing; it's life-affirming. I take a deep breath, feel the air rush into my lungs and sting my throat before grabbing on to the frame and hoisting myself out. I mentally thank my physical trainer for all those pull-ups.

The metal window frame cuts into my hands, but soon I'm free. I slowly stand and step out from the bushes, make my way past the side porch to the back of the house. The garden is getting pummeled, muddy pools everywhere, but I barely feel the rain.

I run up the terrace stairs to the back door. Turn the knob and push, but it's locked.

"Help! Zach! Richard! Help!" I slam on the glass, but the kitchen is empty.

No one can hear me.

HARPER

My twin steps out of the mirror's passageway. He seems calm.
Or defeated.

"Ah, Richard. I was hoping it was you," Penny says. "After all those emails I sent, the calls I made that went unreturned, it's nice to finally chat, isn't it? Like a family reunion."

The way she says the word *family*, like it's heartwarming, makes me want to dig my nails into her eyes.

"Penny was the woman who tried to get money from you?" I ask Richard in disbelief. "And you didn't tell me?"

Richard shrugs. "I didn't know it was her."

He crosses the room but makes no move to sit.

"I'm assuming it's you who cut the wires on the generator?" He pulls out a pack of cigarettes and lighter, takes a puff. I can tell he's working hard to stay composed.

Penny laughs. "Things are so much more atmospheric in the dark, aren't they?"

"I'm tired of this bullshit," I say, bringing the conversation back to what matters. "Why the hell would we pay you?"

"Harper..." Richard warns, but I don't have time for him.

"No, honestly, why would we pay you one cent?" I ask. "Even if we are related, which I highly doubt, and which, by the way, was discovered illegally, who cares? So, what you're saying is our grandmother had an affair decades ago? Covered it up?" I throw my arms out wide. "Do you think that's going to matter to us? A baby out of wedlock is hardly a scandal these days."

There's a commotion in the front hall. A door opening, slamming. Low voices, and then Elle's. "I absolutely will not calm down."

In a few seconds she appears in the doorway, her hair matted to her head, wet and dripping. She's wearing different clothes, and her shoes leave wet trails on the hardwood.

Zach and Lucas hover behind her, also soaked to the bone.

"My god, are you alright?" Richard rushes over to her.

"I am *not* alright," she yells. She points a finger at Penny. "She almost killed me."

Penny rolls her eyes. "Hardly."

My husband walks over to the bar and pours a glass of wine for Elle. She takes a shaky slug, then glares at Penny.

"She locked me in the basement," she says, clutching Richard. "She's unstable! Don't trust one word that comes out of her mouth!"

"In the basement?" I ask, assessing Penny newly. What the hell is going on here?

"She's been watching us this weekend," Elle continues. "She has the blueprints to the house."

"*You* stole my blueprints?" I ask Penny. Fuck. So that's where they went. I'd brought them to the office to give to our Realtor the next time we met. "And you're the fucking squirrel I keep hearing in the walls?"

"I made copies of your keys, too," she says dismissively. "You brought all the estate keys with you to the office, Harper. I just needed twenty dollars and a quick stop at a key-making kiosk."

She says my name, but it's Elle she's focused on.

They're conducting a stare-down to rival the ones I have

with Richard. There's a tension snapping between them as if they know each other. But I can't remember ever even introducing them.

"I'm not the only one who's taken valuable information from the VNity offices," Penny says carefully. "Right, Elle?"

Elle's face deepens to the color of my favorite port.

"What's that supposed to mean?" I ask.

"I've got another birthday present for you, Harper." She gestures at Elle. "There's your rat. Your own sister-in-law betrayed you."

Elle? It was *Elle*?

"Are you fucking kidding me?" I say. *"You?"*

She stands there silent, twisting the hem of her sweater.

I feel like I've been wandering around in the dark, in one of Mother's terrible games. The blindfold pulled off, only to realize everyone's been staring and pointing and laughing at me this whole time.

"How could you?" I ask Elle, advancing toward her. "You're the one who released that video?"

Elle sticks out her chin and narrows her eyes. With her wet hair and streaky makeup, the movement is less fierce than she probably intended, but still jarring for Miss Sunshine.

"How could *you*?" she says. "You stole my idea. I trusted you, and you've been rubbing it in my face for years. And then you never even acknowledged everything I did for Mom. You just took credit for that, too."

Elle's eyes flash with an anger and bitterness I've never seen in her. It throws me for a moment. Is she that petty about a vague idea she had years ago, one she never made any moves to pursue? She never had any intention of starting her own business—she was just jealous when I had the balls to do it. When she confronted me after I announced VNity, accused me of stealing her idea, I thought she was just looking for someone to blame for her lack of initiative. I didn't know she was harboring the kind of resentment that would lead to sabotage.

"You blame me for everything, Elle, but you're not as perfect as you like everyone to believe. By the way, it was Linnet who left you that broken vine. But sure, blame it on me. Make me the villain, because that serves your narrative."

Elle's quiet, but Penny makes that clucking sound in her throat again. "I'm not even sure I want to be related to you people. You're not very nice to one another."

"Related?" Zach asks.

He's been so quiet, I forgot he was in the room. I forgot all the guys were here—Richard next to the coffee table, cigarette still burning in his hand; Lucas, near the bar cart, still dripping water from his raincoat and surveying us all with a blank expression. And my baby brother inside the doorway, looking confused.

"Yes, Zach. We're all being enlightened at the same time," I say. "Turns out not only is our sister-in-law trying to sabotage me, but I've also got an assistant who is a liar and a thief and trying to extort us."

Penny laughs, smooths down her pants, picks off a piece of lint and flicks it to the ground. "Not trying, Harper. Going to. I'll leave here tonight with three million dollars. If I don't, then I'll destroy your family."

My eyes settle behind Penny, across the room, on my purse, where my gun waits.

LAUREN

There's something going on downstairs.

I hear yelling. Elle shrieks.

So they found her.

I creep down the hallway and listen at the top of the stairs. They must be back in the sitting room, with the high, echoing ceilings and giant ominous drapes. At first I think it was just the acoustics dramatizing normal sound into commotion, but I hear Zach say impatiently, "There is no way this is happening right now," and I rush down the stairs. Shit. What if Harper is telling him about the blog?

I stop in the doorway. Everyone looks upset. Zach is red in the face, his eyes darting around the room, like he's not sure who to be most pissed at. Elle is drenched, her hair clinging to her cheeks, hands clenched into fists. Lucas is throwing back a drink, and Harper and Richard are, shockingly, stunned into silence. And then I realize why the room seems more crowded— because there's an extra person here. A woman in black. She's small-framed, with a pointy, slightly upturned nose that makes her seem bossy.

The woman's face is twisted with pure hatred.

Whatever is happening, it's apparently not about me, but Harper's next words give me a chill.

"I'll ask again, Penny, what the hell makes you think we're going to give you three million dollars?"

Penny flings a wrapped gift box at her. "Open it. Go ahead."

Harper takes it, holds it out like she's carrying a dead bug. For a second, I think she's going to whip it at Penny's head, but then she lifts the lid and withdraws a file.

"Medical records?" Harper asks, flipping through the papers without really looking at them.

"Look, Penny," Richard says, adjusting his glasses. "That card you sent had no proof of anything. We didn't know any of this until now. I'm sure if your lawyer contacts our lawyer, we can work—"

"Lawyer? I don't have a lawyer," she says with disdain. "And even if I did, I'm done with all the hoops. I've jumped through enough."

Penny seems familiar, but I can't quite place how I know her. There's something off about her, though. She seems confident, like she's got a royal flush and she's just dying to lay down her cards to show us. But there's also fear in her posturing, an imbalance. If I spotted her at one of the parties Diane sent me to, I'd zero in on her. There's a secret screaming inside her, but there's also something broken there too.

"*What* card? *What* money? Is someone going to let me in on all this *knowledge* you seem to have?" Zach says.

He keeps glancing from one twin to the other. He's in the dark, as always, and I think again of Zach almost drowning in the lake. How Harper saved him. Even now, she moves closer to him, as if putting herself between him and Penny. Maybe she really does want to protect him.

"Zach, stay out of this," Richard says dismissively.

"I will not. I'm sick of being cast aside. I'm a member of this family, too."

It's like I've turned on the television for the last ten minutes of the finale of a soap opera I've never seen, my eyes glued to the drama playing out before me.

"My dad had a younger sister," Penny says calmly, as if they have all the time in the world, and the rest of the room quiets. "He adored her. They took care of each other because they had to. Their mom wanted to be an actress, always had money problems, men problems. His sister got sick of it all. She ran off when she was eighteen. My dad heard a year later that she'd died in an accident. He thought that was the end of the story."

Penny pulls out a faded color photo of a little girl sitting on the ground, a feather boa wrapped around her neck. She's smiling up at the camera, one arm out as if striking a pose.

"I couldn't find any other pictures of her. My dad…well, I think he might've destroyed them. He always felt she abandoned him. But after he died, I found this one of my aunt Celeste in a box of papers."

I'm startled by the name. "Celeste?"

Everyone turns to me.

Harper glares. "What are you doing here?"

Penny stares at me.

"She was your aunt?" I ask her, walking farther into the room. "Celeste Sonoma?"

Harper hands the papers to Richard, who glances quickly at them. "These are all just old bills and letters to people we don't know," he mutters.

"Who the hell is Celeste Sonoma?" Zach asks no one in particular.

I speak before I can think better of it. "She and your mom were friends in Europe. She died in a car accident." I stop, tug at the ends of my hair. "I think."

Zach looks confused. "Lauren?" He takes the papers from Richard now, frowning.

"How the hell do you know this?" Harper says. She's shaking. "Are you two working together? Or you three," she adds, thrusting her thumb at Elle.

Elle flinches. "Penny helped me get the video of you to leak, but that's all it was. I swear. I have no idea what this is."

Video? Elle was the anonymous tipster who sent me the story?

Penny is still staring at me strangely. "How do you know about my aunt?" she asks.

And now it dawns on me who she is. She came on stage to apologize for Harper's absence that night at the ambassador event. She was matter-of-fact, cold, definitive. I remember thinking nothing must get past her. And now she's here asking for money and talking about Celeste?

"I don't," I say. "I—I found her birth certificate. In an old book in the library."

"Well, these files explain why," Penny says. "They'll show the truth about this family's history, not that any of you will be happy to hear it."

"Bullshit," Richard says.

"I think you better go now," Harper says to Penny.

But it's Zach who moves. He lunges toward the fire and tosses in the files. The flames roar with delight.

"We're done here." He stands close to Penny to intimidate her, the fire flickering behind them.

There's a heaviness to the air, like we're all in a pot that's about to overboil.

"It's okay," Penny says, unaffected. "They were just copies. I've got more."

Elle slams her empty drink on the table. "You heard him," she says. "Get out."

She crosses the room toward Penny, but my brain is too busy trying to put the pieces together. Katrina and Celeste were friends in Europe. Katrina was a rich orphan heiress. Lonely, maybe? Looking for a friend. Someone to take under her wing, teach the ropes. Someone like Celeste, a runaway from America ready to start a new life, just like me when I moved to the city earlier this year.

And then a tragic accident stopped all that.

I remember the French article, that word *suspecte—suspicious*. I thought maybe Katrina had been running away from the same danger Celeste had faced, but what if it was the opposite? *Did Katrina kill Celeste?*

Out of the corner of my eye, I see Elle brush past Harper and give Penny a surprisingly hard shove. Penny stumbles back, but stays upright. She glances at the hearth, at the eagle statues, but before she can make a move, Elle shoves her again, but Penny's ready for her this time and braces herself, pushing back.

"Enough!" Richard bellows. He marches forward, grips his wife's arm, pulls her away. "Everyone's lost their minds here," he shouts. "We don't act like this. We are Van Nesses."

Penny throws back her head and laughs. "But see? That's where you've got it all wrong. None of you are Van Nesses."

HARPER

Not Van Nesses.

Penny's words burn into my brain like a hot coal. She's bluffing. She's lying. She has to be. She's not making any sense, blabbering on about her aunt, wrapping yellowed files as a gift. I don't even recognize her anymore.

The papers she brought are burning. Zach destroyed them. He's telling Penny to leave. He thinks it's over, just like that. Problem solved. Or if it's not, he thinks Richard or I will take care of it. There will always be someone Zach can lean on. Someone to save him from drowning. Dig him out of the financial holes he falls in. Call to him from the darkness of the woods so he can find his way out.

Isn't that what family's for?

I can still hear distant rumblings of thunder, but the worst of the storm is passing. It's already done its damage, though. So has Penny. In this light, her face looks like a waxwork, the fire casting shadows under her eyes. I imagine her melting from the heat, her features dripping onto the carpet, one by one, until she's just a puddle.

I need a drink. Normally I'd ask Lucas to fix me one—half the time he already would've without even asking—but he's keeping his distance. I walk over to the bar cart and pour whiskey into a glass, no ice, and shoot it. *It's still my birthday*, I think, and want to laugh hysterically.

The gift box Penny carried in is on the coffee table, the gold ribbon glinting in the firelight. I should toss it in the fire too. I swoop over and lift it, and that's when I notice another file at the bottom that Zach missed. I pick it up, pull out a hospital record dated 1970.

When she was fourteen years old, Celeste Sonoma had a broken fibula from a fall that required surgery on the inside of her right leg. Affixed to the file is a photo of the leg with jagged stitches running up the side.

Penny isn't lying.

Zach waves his hand in front of my face. "Harper? What are you doing?"

I show him the hospital record. Those jagged stitches. The scar it would leave.

"Just like Mother's," I say.

Mother never wore skirts above the knee. Or shorts. She was self-conscious about her scar, the harsh zigzags on her otherwise smooth skin. When we asked where it came from, she'd just say, "Stupidity."

Now it all makes sense. Mother's evasiveness about her childhood. I always assumed she just hated to think about her parents dying so young. Even she had feelings.

But it was because she had to hide her past.

"She was a fucking fraud," I murmur.

"What?" Zach asks, irritated. He's ready to yank these papers from me, too.

But it's Richard who takes them and reads them.

"Do you get it now?" Penny asks. "Your mom—my aunt—was clever, I'll give her that. She knew when a good opportunity presented itself."

"No, I don't get it. I don't get anything," Zach says.

"Celeste Sonoma didn't die in that car accident," Penny says. "Katrina Van Ness did."

"It was a case of stolen identity," I tell Zach flatly. "Our mother was a low-class scam artist."

"Harper! You're starting to sound jaded like me," Penny tsks. "I wouldn't say a scam artist. More of an opportunist."

She goes on to explain, but I'm already putting it together in my mind. The police or the hospital must have gotten it wrong, and there was no such thing as DNA testing back then. Maybe Mother was even in the car but survived, or maybe the two of them switched identities for fun. But when people assumed it was Mother, Celeste Sonoma, who died, she must have decided to go with it. She'd evidently had nothing to lose. She had a rich heiress's passport and an estate where none of her family had lived for years.

"She just stepped right into a brand new world, and no one ever questioned her," Penny says.

Mother certainly had the balls to try something like that. She must've assumed she'd never get caught. Or maybe she was shocked when it did work.

My life began and ended at age twenty, Harper. Someday you'll understand.

I always thought Mother meant that aging is both a good and a bad thing. Good because it means experience and wisdom. Bad because beauty fades.

But now I know what she really meant.

One life of hers died. And another began.

"It's sad to realize you aren't who you think you are, isn't it? To think you have it all and then lose it—poof," Penny says.

This house, this land, our money is not ours. My last name is not mine. It's all been a lie. Our whole lives have been a charade. No wonder why I always hated this place, why I always felt like I didn't belong here. It wasn't just Mother's cruel games.

"Why are you doing this?" Richard asks. My twin looks pale, sick. It's starting to sink in for him, too.

Penny is serious now, no more taunting. "My father's dead because of you. Because of your greed. Because you couldn't re-instate the payments that your mother had sent him for years and years. After his stroke, he was getting good care in an assisted living facility. But when those payments stopped, we couldn't afford it anymore. I had to transfer him elsewhere. That place was a hellhole. Do you have any idea what it's like to see some-one you love suffer?" She stops, recoils at the thought. "What am I saying, of course you don't. You have no clue what we went through, and you don't care. He was only there for six days when he had his heart attack. They didn't find him for hours."

Zach squints, looking truly baffled. "How is that our fault?"

"It's all your fault." Penny clenches her fists like she wants to strangle Zach. "A few thousand dollars a month means noth-ing to you people. But it meant *everything* to us. My dad never told a soul about your mother. I don't know how they got back in touch. Maybe he saw her in the news and realized who she was. Maybe she contacted him because she felt guilty, or wanted someone to know the truth. Whatever happened, he was loyal for decades. He kept her secret. And then he gets rewarded by dying in that miserable place."

"But we didn't know any of that," Zach continues, scratch-ing his head. "If you'd told us, I'm sure we could've worked something out."

"I did tell you! I wrote a letter. I emailed. I left voice mails. And all I got was a cold, useless form letter from your attorney that *he* had sent." She points at Richard.

Now I remember telling everyone at dinner the other night about this, how we'd scoffed at the sob story. *You can't open the door even a sliver with these people, or they'll slip right in and refuse to leave.* Richard promising he'd taken care of it.

I feel a tightness in my chest and shake it off.

This is not our fault. But I can see that doesn't matter to Penny. She's created a narrative, and we are the villains. She's good at that. At VNity, she was all about the brand, about the messaging, about making people believe. And now she's convinced herself that we're to blame for her father's death. That it's our fault she couldn't take care of him. She's lost it. But part of me can almost understand it, this desire to blame everyone but yourself. After all, I'm the one who caused Mother to get sick. I didn't follow the rules, I jinxed her.

"Everything has been handed to you all your lives. And you piss it away. You don't give a damn about anyone else. And it's all lies. You deserve none of this. But don't worry." Penny strides over to me and pats my arm like I'm a child. "No one has to know. It's time for me to take something for a change. And then I will go away."

She played us well. I let her into my inner circle, as much as I let anyone in. She had access to my emails, to my office, to my keys. To my DNA.

"If you don't give me what I want, then the world is going to know your entire family is a fraud."

There's a whirlwind of activity. Zach dives at Penny, who throws herself behind me and then behind a chair. I use the distraction to grab my purse, wrestle through it, my hands trembling.

I pull out the gun. Elle sees it and screams, and Zach turns and snatches the gun out of my hand before I can even lift it.

"Hey!" I shout.

He points it at Penny, his eyes focused as she squats behind the chair like it's a shield. I feel a twist in my gut, like we've just crested the top of a roller coaster and there's nowhere to go but down.

"Zach, no!" Lauren shouts from behind him.

Zach holds up his other hand. "Stay back, Lauren. All of you. This has gone far enough."

"Zach, dude." Lucas has finally awakened. My husband had been standing in the shadows next to Lauren, but now he steps forward. "Put that thing down."

"Zach, think about this," I say, trying to sound calm. My brother has that same warlike look on his face as he had on the porch when he was angry about selling the house. "Are you really going to shoot her?"

"I'm not going to do anything," Zach says, waving the gun. "She is. She's going to walk right out of here and go back to the rock she crawled out from. Enough with the threats and blackmail and the lies."

"It's not a lie! I showed you the proof!" Penny says, but I can sense her nerves now, that she knows she's no longer in control.

"You didn't," Zach says, his tone icy.

Richard steps in front of him, puts his hand on Zach's chest. "Stop it, Zach. Now."

"Get out of my way. She's an intruder, Richard. She broke into our house, and this is self-defense."

It's like we are kids again, running around the estate. Zach saying he wants to do one thing, Richard trying to control it all.

"I'm handling this," Richard says.

"Oh are you? Like you handle everything else? Like you're handling selling this house? It's your fault this is happening, that she's even here. She's right—you've always been stingy with money. Selfish. Self-righteous." Zach narrows his eyes, determined to be the hero, to put Richard in his place for once. "You've always treated me like a little kid. A nuisance. I'm never good enough to consult with, to give an opinion. None of it. You're not our father. You never will be. Get out of my way, Richard."

At that moment, Penny takes advantage of the distraction and kicks the chair at Richard. He topples into Zach, and the gun skitters across the room.

"Good fucking work," Zach says as he tries to push Richard

off him. "You think you're so smart, but you ruin everything."
He swings to throw a punch, but Richard grabs his wrist and
rolls off him.

There's movement, clattering behind us in the far corner of
the room. Then Elle screams again. She's near the door mirror,
and in the flickering light, it looks like she's wearing a pale scarf.

But it's not a scarf. It's Penny's arm around her neck. And in
her other hand, Penny has the gun trained right at Elle's head.

"Story time is over," she says. "Give me my money. Or someone's going to get hurt."

THE PARTY GUEST

I move back against a wall, the gun in one hand, Elle in the other.

"Just stay back and Elle won't get hurt." I look to Richard. "I want my money. And then I'll leave."

"Oh god, just shoot her," Harper says viciously.

"Shut up, Harper," Richard says. Then to me, "I can't get you that kind of money right now. It's the weekend."

He reminds me of the doctor at the hospital I tried to talk to after my dad had his stroke. The one who was too busy. The one who I begged to help us, and who only shook his head, uncomfortable, and picked up his clipboard. *There's nothing more I can do right now*, he said, and left me to sob alone.

There's always more you can do. If you're willing, if you care. If you're incentivized.

"You can. Don't try to tell me you don't have a safe here with cash."

"We don't," Richard says.

I feel my heart flutter as panic sets in. But I can't let them see. I tighten my grip on Elle's neck. I don't know how to get rid of her. I was supposed to have the upper hand. I had no idea Harper had a gun. There are too many of them, and only one of me.

"Then I want the egg," I say.

They all look at me, puzzled. Elle whimpers.

Richard holds his hands up in surrender. "Look, I'll get you what you want. As soon as the bank's open on Monday I'll have it wired to you. Okay?"

He's lying. I can see it written all over his face. How stupid does he think I am?

I shake my head. "No. Not good enough. Give me the egg. Tonight."

"What egg?" Harper asks. "We have no idea what you're talking about."

"She does," I say, dragging Elle back. Three million seemed like plenty to pay off my bills, settle debts, and run away. Start fresh. But the egg will do, too. It may even be worth more than that.

I spy Zach inching toward me again, and I turn Elle and myself toward him. "Do not move any closer," I say.

Elle's hair keeps swinging in my face. "Okay," she says. "Okay. I'll give it to you. It's upstairs. Just please, don't hurt anyone."

Richard suddenly looks down at my feet, his features arranging into surprise. I follow his gaze, and that's when he dives at me. A sharp pain pierces my shoulder, and I drop the gun and let go of Elle. I roll quickly and get up, dashing behind the couch, cursing.

I can feel tears pocketing in my eyes, which just makes me angrier. I'm related to these people. They are my *family*. Their blood is my blood. We are the same, and yet look at us. There's a void like the Grand Canyon. What makes them so much better than me? I think of my dad, of the fear and defeat in his eyes when I left him for the last time, in a small, cramped room, only a light-blue curtain separating him from his "roommate" on the other side. It could've been different, all of it.

"I've told people," I shout from behind the couch. "Others know about this. If something happens to me, the truth will still come out."

Zach steps around the couch, staring down at me. "You're lying," he says. He grabs my arm, drags me up, the gun in his other hand.

Desperate, I elbow him in the stomach, catching him off guard, and while he's reeling, I kick at his hand. Out of the corner of my eye, I spot Harper's husband rushing toward me. He collides into me, hitting me hard in the side and knocking me down. I feel something give—a rib breaking?—and a vase behind me topples over. Shards of glass smash all over the floor.

Zach shakes the pain out of his hand and then walks calmly over to the gun. Cocks it.

Lying on the floor, panting amid broken glass, I know I've lost. The three men are standing over me, panting. Angry.

This isn't like in the movies, where I can withdraw a fancy weapon at just the right moment. This isn't the movies at all, where the good guys win and the bad guys lose. This is life, where it's not about who is good or who is bad, but about who has the power, who has the money.

"This ends now," Zach says.

"Zach! No!" Harper shouts.

She moves toward him, hands out, and he startles, jumps. His finger pulls the trigger. The gun goes off, the noise splitting my eardrums. I feel something erupt in my chest, my back. I'm dying. There's no pain, only numbness. I'm frozen. I can't move.

But there's no pain.

It's then I realize. Somehow Zach missed everyone and hit the table behind me. Splinters of wood explode on my back.

Bodies press at me. I thrash like a wild animal, trying to

get their hands off me. Grasp a large shard of glass and thrust it out in defense.

I expect to be shot at again, in my chest, my head—somewhere. But what I don't expect is my shard of glass to hit skin.

Richard's throat, to be exact.

ELLE

I can't comprehend the scene before me. It didn't happen. It's not real. It's just a game of charades. Or a movie. I can press rewind, go back, cut the film and add a different ending.

There's blood. So much blood.

Harper screams. Richard's on his back, his hands clutching at his throat. Making awful noises. Lucas rushes over to him, bends down. "Jesus Christ," I hear him say, as if from a great distance, because the roaring in my ears is so loud.

I can't look.

It's not real.

"We need to stop the blood." Lucas's voice chokes up. "Zach. You have to help."

But Zach's in shock. His mouth keeps opening and closing like a goldfish.

It's Lauren who moves. She quickly takes off her scarf and passes it to Lucas, whose fingers are already blood-streaked.

Penny stands, drops the glass, slick with blood. Richard's blood. She's staring at her hands as if she's never seen them before.

"I didn't—I…"

Penny backs up, away from us. Her eyes are wild. An animal, trapped.

Something about it makes me snap back to reality.

"What have you done!" I scream at her.

"No! It was—"

"You killed him! You killed Richard!" There is nothing else for me now but white-hot rage. The fire of a thousand suns.

I run for the gun.

"Elle!"

I'm not sure who says it, and I don't care.

But before I can even aim it, Penny's gone, disappeared into a dark hole.

It takes my brain a few seconds to process it. The secret passage behind the mirror.

The rage propels me forward. I climb into the hole. The passage is so narrow. My feet pound, like I'm going to break through the floor with every step. I don't care. I run as fast as I can, down the hall and up the steep stairwell. This is what Mom would've done. If anyone came after her family, her children, she'd hunt them down and kill them, no questions asked.

Penny's at the top of the staircase, scurrying around like a panicked squirrel. Stuck. She doesn't know how to open the bookcase door. I can hear her breath, rapid. She's sobbing.

I've got her.

But then I don't. The bookcase opens. She staggers into the upstairs hallway.

And runs.

I follow. She stops short at the stairs, gazes down, then makes an abrupt turnaround. Our eyes meet for a split second. I can see the terror in hers. I almost feel bad. Almost. And then I remember the sounds of Richard gurgling downstairs and the rage returns.

I hold up the gun.

She dodges toward the office doors.

I enter just as she's crossed the room for the balcony. She opens the door, leaving bloody palm prints on the glass. The cold, wet air rushes in, spits in my face as I trail her outside.

"Stay away," she yells, her voice quickly swallowed by the wind. She's in the corner of the balcony, breath heaving, hands up. She keeps glancing between me and the darkness below her.

I lift the gun again.

"It wasn't supposed to happen like this," she says. She's crying now.

I'm crying, too. I wipe at my face furiously, try to remember what I learned in my self-defense class in college, terrified of the power of the weapon in my hand.

She hops onto the railing, a desperate rat, looking for any means of escape. She's perched there on that narrow, slick surface—it must only be a few seconds, but time slows down again. She wavers, tries to catch her balance, grasp the railing. She finds it, seems to grip it for a moment, but then a stronger gust of wind howls through.

Her mouth opens to scream.

And then she tumbles back.

Thunder rumbles in the sky.

I drop the gun. Fall to the ground.

SUNDAY

One Day Later

HARPER

From the front terrace, we watch the red-and-blue lights of the police cars pulsate in the distance.

"They'll be here soon," I tell Zach, handing him the wine bottle.

He takes a swig.

It's nearly dawn. The storm's over. All that violence and damage and rage—here, then gone. The fire department has already hacked up the fallen tree and carted it away.

But there's a gaping black hole in my chest that no one can see.

I keep replaying the moment before Richard's death. I called to Zach, distracted him. If I hadn't, maybe things would've ended differently. Maybe Richard would still be alive.

You messed up, Harper. It's your fault Richard's dead.

Zach puts his arm around me. "It's going to be okay. We'll get through this."

Zach's a Hallmark card with his meaningless platitudes but it's strangely relieving to hear him say it anyway.

"You're shivering," he says. "We should go inside."

I resist his tugging. I never want to set foot inside that house again.

"Well, at least let me go get you a coat." He leaves before I can protest.

The police cars are closer now. I hear the ominous, droning whine of their alarms.

I recognize I'm dealing with Richard's death in a very unhealthy way. Then again, I'm not sure there's a healthy way to deal when your twin gets murdered in front of you. If there is, someone should fucking send me an email, because I can't think of one.

I resist the pull of the black hole swirling inside. Everything should be in order, and right now, I need to be strong for all of us.

The door opens behind me, but it's Elle who steps out with my raincoat and a hot cup of coffee. She hands them to me wordlessly. Part of me wants to stay cold, but I shrug it on and belt it tight at the waist. Sip the scalding, bitter liquid.

"I know you're blaming yourself," she says, tucking her hair behind her ear. She showered at some point, changed into jeans and a thin sweater, but didn't bother to dry her hair. "And you shouldn't. If anything, it's my fault."

I stare at her profile. Elle's face is puffy, her eyes bloodshot. I've only seen her like that one other time. The day Mother died.

I take another drink. The coffee splashes and burns my upper lip.

I should tell Elle it's not her fault either. Maybe if I was a different person, this would be our moment. The part where we each reach out, start to forgive, put things aside and start new.

"The cops are going to be here soon. You know what to say, right?" I ask. "You've got the story straight?"

Elle glances at me. I can see the pain in her eyes, the tears welling up. Finally, she nods. "Harper, I—"

But whatever she was going to say is cut off by Zach's return. He folds her in his arms and she starts crying again. "Shh," he whispers, like he's soothing an infant. "It's gonna be fine." Elle wipes her eyes, smiles gratefully at him, and goes back inside the house.

He raises an eyebrow at me. "And what about you?"

"I'll be fine, too."

There's a crunch of gravel, and then my husband comes around the corner of the house. He joins us on the terrace, hands in his pockets. "Mission accomplished," he says.

"Thank you," I say gratefully.

We haven't talked about Todd yet, about our marriage, about what's going to happen. But the way he's stepped up, maybe that's one glimmer of hope in this otherwise shit-filled nightmare.

"What's going to happen now?" Zach asks. He sounds like he's eight years old again, looking up at Richard and me for guidance. I can still picture that little boy who jumped in the lake, knowing he wouldn't be able to keep himself afloat. The panic of realizing he had no way to save himself. And me knowing I was the only one who could.

Now I have to do it again. I have to jump in the water and save us all.

"Like I told you, like I told everyone, we tell them the truth," I say, and my voice is surprisingly calm, steady. The hot coffee is working; I feel more alert. "Penny was an unbalanced stalker who came here this weekend to hurt me. She's been spreading lies and rumors about me and she took it too far." I wait for him to meet my eyes. "She killed our brother."

Zach's face is whiter than I've ever seen it. "I mean about the rest of it," he says. "About what she told us."

You're not a Van Ness. You never have been.

We all know what's at stake if Penny's story ever comes out. With the bloodline clause in the will, we'd have no legal ownership of this house, this land, the winery, if the fact of our mother's fraud ever became public. There would be investigations, lawsuits, public ridicule—it would make my VNity bad press look like puff pieces. I might even lose VNity altogether.

Lucas did his best to find whatever of Penny's he could in the basement room she locked Elle in. Her laptop and her real phone are somewhere safe now, and he'll wipe any incriminating files, figure out what damage might be done. But we don't know what's in her car, wherever that is, or who else she might've told, what other plans she may have set up.

"We do nothing," I say firmly, hoping it's true. "You need to make sure your fiancée knows that."

"Don't worry about Lauren," he says, running his hand through his hair.

I haven't told Zach—or anyone—about Lauren's little "career," and I won't have to if she keeps her end of our deal. But I know the stakes have changed after all that's happened, after everything we've learned, and I'll need to stay one step ahead.

"I just can't believe it," Lucas says as the police cars come up to the driveway, their sirens blaring. There's an ambulance, too. It looks like a goddamn Fourth of July parade. "She just walked right into this house and said she was Katrina Van Ness, and everyone believed her?"

"Mother was always good at getting people to do what she wanted," I point out.

There must not have been many people to convince either. The estate had been basically abandoned for years—the last Van Ness, Katrina's grandmother, had died in the early '70s, and the family's attorney hadn't seen Katrina since she was a baby. It was easy—too easy—for Celeste to step into her shoes. She must have lain low for a couple of years, hired a winemaker and learned the business. Met Dad, who taught her how to invest. Had us. Divorced. Lived a lie.

"None of this is ours," Zach says, kicking at the porch rail. "It never has been."

I lean against it. I wish we'd never come back here.

Maybe Mother felt the same way. Maybe she wished, sometimes, that she'd never come here. Or maybe she thought it was the best decision she ever made. After all, she got money, power, land, fame. The only price she had to pay was to look over her shoulder, sometimes, hope no one would ever discover the truth.

And now she's passed that shadow on to us.

We watch as the officers pull up. Doors slam. They head toward us, the squawk of their radios punching the thick air.

"I'm going to go warn the others," Lucas says. He glances at me, hesitates, then kisses me on the cheek before disappearing inside.

It's a good thing, too, since right after he leaves, the officers yank someone out of the back seat of the cruiser. Looking disheveled is Todd Christie. He's calm, talking reasonably to the officer even though he must be upset. "As I told you already, this is a grave misunderstanding. She will tell you."

"Ma'am?" the officer says. "Do you know this man? He says you employed him. Says he went for a hike and got lost and caught in the storm."

"More than a hike," Todd says. "As I told you, I'm a wellness instructor. I have a YouTube channel. I was scouting locations." He slumps against the officer's grip. "Please tell him, Harper. I thought they'd come to rescue me, and instead they think I had something to do with some crime."

Part of me would love to see Todd Christie hauled away in handcuffs, but I don't have it in me after everything that's transpired. "Yes," I say wearily. "He's with us."

"Let's go inside," the officer says, climbing the steps.

The others are already walking the perimeter, collecting evidence. Instinctively I turn around for Richard's guidance, and then remember he's not there. Will never be here again.

As we follow the detectives inside, I grab Zach's arm and tug him back. Quietly, I say, "Penny was wrong. We are still Van Nesses. Always have been, and always will be."

It seems like something Richard would've said.

LAUREN

I go along with it, like I've gone along with everything this weekend, trying to be a good sport. Trying not to upset anyone, trying not to get in the way, trying to be helpful where I can. I help Linnet heat up the dinner from the night before, and we set it out, but no one except Lucas eats any of it.

Harper steps in to take charge, cold-blooded as ever, making sure the stories are straight and the variables are accounted for. I admire her ability to cleave off one part of herself and focus on the details, put her emotions aside. Rally the troops. I suppose it's how she rose to the top, how she's so successful. I suppose that's how her mother was, too.

Once the cops come, the hours pass like years. None of us have slept, and my eyes begin to feel like they are seventeen pounds each. I'm dragging. My bones are hollowed out, heavy, tired, but I plug on, handing out the coffee Linnet brews, swapping dinner for breakfast that also goes uneaten, finding a stash of tissue boxes in a supply closet.

I've been through this before, the solemn procession of death and grieving. My father's brother died when I was young. I remember all of us going through the motions, washing dishes, feeding the dog, everything seeming so odd in its regularity.

And this is the second time this family has done it this year. I want to be there for Zach, but we're avoiding each other, exchanging only the necessary words. I tell myself this is because we're all on display, surrounded by police, with a secret to keep, that Zach needs some space.

Sometime just after daybreak, Lucas approaches me on the back terrace, the only place I could find to escape from it all. The police have already questioned us. Much of the house is a crime scene we aren't allowed in.

"I'm going for a walk," he says. "Want to come?" He throws me a small smile, and the warmth of it weakens my resistance. "Come on, it'll do you good. We can assess the storm damage."

Lucas and I don't talk much. What happened between us seems so faraway now, an old memory not worth the effort of recalling. The wet ground sinks slightly with each step. The bitter air feels fitting. It wakes me up. I can't imagine ever sleeping peacefully again, any of us, not after what we've seen.

The storm has done a number on the estate. Downed branches everywhere, small twigs and larger thick branches knocked from the trees and impaled upright in the ground. Occasionally Lucas will lift a low-hanging branch to keep it from hitting me, or break up a large one that fell, but mostly it's just the sound of our soggy steps to keep us company.

Despite the mess, the vineyards seem untouched, the craggy wrinkled vines still reaching out, swooping over each other, lined up in rows like little soldiers. The sky has cleared, a bright blue morning. It's going to be a beautiful day. It's always beautiful right after a storm.

"Do you think it'll be okay?" I finally ask Lucas.

He takes a while to answer, and then he nods. "Yeah. Yeah, of course." He pauses, pulls back a long green vine in my path and lets me pass. "I guess you're the only liability left?"

"What do you mean?"

"I mean, you're the only outsider who knows." He gestures

toward my ring. "Though I guess once you two are hitched, we won't have to worry about you anymore."

"Worry about me? I would never—you don't have to…"

"Oh, I know. But it's kind of interesting, isn't it? We're all sort of…tied together now. Aren't we?"

My phone makes a loud sound. A text message. It's Maisie, finally. Five exclamation points.

OMG! I told you you'd get what you wanted!!!!

Above it, I spot the photo of the ring I'd sent her an eternity ago, when everything had been different.

I look over at Lucas as I slide my phone back in my jacket. The media has so far been kept at bay, but it's only a matter of time before the story gets broadcast everywhere. Before Maisie hears about it.

And what will Diane say? How much would she pay for *this* story?

I glance over my shoulder at the estate, all the land, the vines, think of the many barrels of wine waiting to be bottled and stored. So many riches here—that's what Celeste, Zach's mom, must've thought when she showed up all those decades ago. She didn't have the right to any of it, but it fell into her lap, and she took the opportunity when she saw it.

Lucas nudges me. "This way," he says.

We're walking toward the main entrance to the Van Ness Winery, I realize. The very entrance Zach and I passed on our way here three days ago. The gates loom ahead of us, sealed shut, a police car on the other side with its lights flashing.

As we turn, following the bend of the road, we both stop. Noticing it at the same time.

The concrete Van Ness sign, with their name and logo carved into it, has been broken in half, right through the name.

"Damn," Lucas murmurs, crouching down beside it. He

traces the jagged break with his fingers. "Lightning must've hit it. Well, that's done for."

"Not necessarily," I say. I stand back, assessing it.

The break was clean. Someone could most likely press it back together and no one would ever be able to see the crack.

TWO YEARS LATER

LAUREN

The drive is eerily familiar. The curvy roads, the cows, the fields. The nervous flutter in my stomach.

I didn't think I'd ever come back to this house, and yet, here I am.

Remember, Brady, you're here for business.

I pull into the private drive. The gates are open—Elle knows I'm coming—and I drive straight through, take the uneven gravel road slowly. The vineyards are lush now, the grapes full and heavy, testing the weight of their vines. Gnats and flies pulverize into tiny bits of goo on my windshield.

Keeping my eyes on the road, I instinctively reach for my leather bag, feel for the digital recorder I'll use to conduct the interview. It's more of a formality at this point to interview other members of the family, but I'm covering my bases, and Elle insisted we do it here.

I stop in front of the house. It casts a long shadow over my car, the drive, the lawn where we played games in the dark. I'm early, but I can't bring myself to go inside yet.

Zach.

We tried to make it work for a few months. I quit the blog and Harper didn't rat me out to him. But it became clear we weren't going to last. Sometimes living through something horrible can bond people together, but in our case, it pushed us apart.

It was for the best, I remind myself.

I get out of the car and press my hand against the cold stone pillar at the edge of one of the garages. Even after everything that happened here, this place takes my breath away. I could have been part of this family, could have had all this and more. Maisie still thinks I'm crazy for not trying harder to work things out with Zach.

My new job as a features editor is a dream one. Harper kept her word; in exchange for staying quiet about their family's history, she helped my career take a sudden upturn. My parents are proud of me. Maisie and I share a charming apartment in the West Village. But there's a part of me that wanted to come back here. It's why I hard-pitched the idea of writing about Harper on the two-year anniversary of past events: I don't want this door to close.

I sling my bag over my shoulder and head for the entrance. In some ways, these doors will never close. I know so much about this family. Whenever I worry about my choices, about what the future might hold, like now, I remember the two-inch-high safe deposit box in the basement of a nondescript bank in Maurville. The smallest piece of real estate, but just enough room for copies of two birth certificates and an old newspaper clipping.

Though the rich can get away with anything, in the end, knowledge is the most lasting form of power.

ELLE

The doorbell rings.

I twirl in front of the mirror, admiring my maxi skirt one last time before heading downstairs to answer it. I hope Lauren notices the work I've been doing on the house. Slowly renovating, redecorating, putting my stamp on it. A modern geometric patterned rug to replace the traditional Persian carpet in the entryway. The crystal chandelier swapped for a more modern metal light fixture. And we completely gutted the sitting room where everything happened.

When I open the door, Lauren has that same friendly, slightly curious expression I remember, but her shoulders are slung back with a confidence I don't recall. It reminds me to be on guard.

I hug her, always the gracious host. "My gosh. It's been so long. You look great."

"So do you," she says. "Thank you for talking with me. I promise this won't take long."

"Well, I wouldn't think it would. You said it was mostly about Harper, after all." I smile thinly.

"A profile, yes," she says, tugging the ends of her hair. "But I prefer to get background from the people who surround her, know her best."

I almost laugh. I haven't seen Harper in months, ever since I moved here full-time. She won't step foot near this place. She could've sold it to the highest bidder—Richard's share of the estate and the winery was divided between her and Zach given the bloodline clause. She and I will probably never forgive each other for our past misdeeds, but Harper always had a soft spot for her little brother and let me buy out her portion.

"It's such a nice day. Let's sit on the terrace," I say, leading Lauren to the back of the house.

She fills the silence with chatter. "So your business seems to be doing so well!"

I watch her face, but she seems sincere. "It's really more of a hobby…"

"You were just named one of the top ten shops on Etsy, Elle. That's a little more than a hobby. I keep pitching you at *Beauty Plus*," she presses. "I'd love to do a story someday, help it take off in a different way."

She's lying. We both know my small business selling lotions is not interesting enough for her magazine.

Still, I'll play the game, play nice. For the good of the family. For the good of our secrets.

I slide the back door open, and we step out. "I'm happy where I am now. I've got other responsibilities, as you know."

As if on cue, a giggle interrupts our chat. I shade my eyes from the sun to see Zach in a crisp white shirt and R.J., his bright red pants bunching around his diaper, running across the gardens toward us. Or rather, stumbling, since R.J., still fairly new to walking, falls every step or so, dotting his knees with grass.

I join them down in the garden.

"Momma!" R.J. holds out a chubby fist, opens his fingers delightedly to reveal the tufts of grass in his hand.

"Hi, baby," I say, pulling him to me, kissing the top of his

sweet head, which smells like baby powder. Lauren trails behind, and I can feel the awkwardness grow.

"We've been giving the lawn a haircut," Zach says to me, a
big grin on his face.

I kiss Zach, too, and he snakes an arm around me. It really
is true what they say: Sometimes good things can come out
of tragedies.

When we part, Zach folds Lauren into a quick hug.

R.J. wiggles away from me, puts his hands up to his uncle,
who scoops him up and twirls him around. My son squeals, his
head thrown back. I can't help but warm at the sight of them.
R.J. looks like his father more and more every day, a sweet tes-
tament to his memory. But it's fitting that Zach looks so much
like his brother did.

"Did you want to talk to both of us? Or one at a time?" I
ask Lauren.

"One at a time is fine," she says, still observing Zach and R.J.
She bites her lip. This must be stirring up old feelings for her.

"Why don't you two start then?" Zach says. "I'll entertain
this monster."

As we step back onto the terrace and into the same Adirondack chairs where we gossiped the first time we met, I think
how funny it is the way things end up.

Lauren sets a recorder down between us. A red light illuminates, the timer starts counting.

"People keep saying that Harper's reinvented herself over
the last couple of years. Would you agree?" Lauren asks, sitting
back in the chair like we're old friends.

I give her the softball answer she's looking for—how resilient
Harper is, how she always manages to bounce back, even after
tragedy. But in the back of my mind, I think about that word.
Reinvention. I've been thinking about it a lot lately. I wonder
how Celeste must've felt when she took Katrina's name, if she
always felt like an actress playing a role or if, after a while, it

just became who she was. I think about how Penny must've felt working closely with Harper, all the while deceiving her. Or Lauren, using a fake name to write her articles. They each shed their former selves, pretended to be someone they weren't, to try to get what they wanted.

I turn away from Lauren and gaze out at the perfectly manicured gardens. Maybe all of us are like this, creatures compelled to hide who we really are to become someone else. I suppose in the years since Richard died, I've reinvented myself as well.

Because I was always destined to be a Van Ness.

And I will do whatever it takes to stay one.

BEAUTY PLUS SEPTEMBER COVER STORY

Harper Van Ness on Life, Beauty,
and Her Second Resurgence

By Lauren Brady

Harper Van Ness compares herself to a Phoenix. Every few years, she burns up and re-emerges from the fiery ashes stronger, smarter, and more beautiful.

It's a powerful image—but then again, Harper Van Ness is a powerful woman. And each time her life reaches a breaking point that would've ruined most anyone else in this world, she manages to turn it around into a win.

"Like this coffee, I've gone through some really tough shit," she admits with a laugh as she sips her cup of kopi luwak—the beans of which work their way through the digestive systems of Indonesian Palm Civets to create the world's most expensive luxury coffee.

But she's not overstating the trauma she's been through. Two years ago, pancreatic cancer killed her mother, and later that same year, a stalker ambushed Harper on her family's private estate and killed her twin brother before dying by suicide. Though she doesn't like to talk about it—she distances herself as much as possible from the Van Ness name these days—Harper admits that the past certainly affects all her daily decisions.

"I truly believe the things we go through help to make us stronger," she says earnestly, those famous blue eyes twinkling with emotion. "All that darkness—there's a light ahead, and we just have to strive for it."

The beauty mogul, indeed, seems to keep getting stronger. Sitting with her on the balcony of her new rooftop condominium in Manhattan, it certainly feels like Harper is on top of the world—literally and figuratively. The scandal over her mistreatment of employees two years ago seems long behind her, and she has not only revamped the way she hires and trains her workforce, but also has re-doubled her efforts to make sure she's reaching and empowering women everywhere. She rebranded her beauty company VNity to reflect the personal nature of all she does. Now simply called HARPER, the company produced $25 million in profits last year and is only growing further.

"It's really important to me to have products, to have a line, that's really meaningful," she says. Each time she starts talking about her company, her face lights up with passion. "Especially as we age, women become invisible, we matter less. And other places, they want to sell you a magic pill to erase all your problems. We will never sell you a pill. It's all about a lifestyle, a re-love of yourself and your life. One thing I've learned is you need to embrace you and make that you the best it can be."

At almost 37, Harper says she feels free to "do what I want and say what I want," but there are definitely topics she won't address. Some of these include if she'll ever consider plastic surgery, who she votes for, and details of the events that transpired that fateful weekend at her family's estate in upstate New York.

Her younger brother, Zachary, who she remains close with, is happy living there full-time as their wine business thrives. The family recently donated an undisclosed amount of money to crown the Richard Van Ness School of Business at their brother's alma mater. However, the loss of her twin brother devastated the siblings, and Harper admits she hasn't fully dealt with it and may never be able to. Since Richard's murder, she hasn't returned to the estate.

"Too many ghosts," she says, her voice raspy, as she shakes her head as if to clear whatever images have materialized.

Harper approaches each passing year with hope and a new way of thinking about beauty and life. She works out, eats plant-based, and tries—key word, tries—to cut back on alcohol. Life with her husband of nine years, tech entrepreneur Lucas Quinn, is "hectic but fab," in her words, and she laughs self-consciously as she says this. The couple doesn't have children—never wanted them, Harper says—but they did recently acquire Monte, a Golden-doodle puppy named in tribute to how the couple first met at a casino. In addition to being adorable, Monte is also lucky: the dog has his own custom-made fainting couch, only eats homemade dog food, and is pampered weekly at a doggy salon.

"It's definitely surprised us how much we spoil him," Harper says with a laugh. But for Harper, surprising herself is a kind of mantra to live by. "Life is so boring if you stay in the same lane everyone expects you to."

She uses her own mother as an example and role model. "Mother never caved to the pressures of the kind of woman she was 'supposed' to be," she says, mentioning Katrina Van Ness's ability to grow the family's business assets while mothering three children on her own after her contentious divorce from their father. Harper says that each morning she wakes up and repeats the same advice her mother used to give her:

"In the end, you are who you make yourself to be."

★ ★ ★ ★ ★

ACKNOWLEDGMENTS

I have joked that I have the worst process when it comes to writing books, but after this one, I can confidently say I'd win all the awards in this category. To that end, I need to thank all the people involved in this process who didn't stab me (yet) as I worked to the bitter end on this story. That starts, of course, with my wonderful editor, Melanie Fried, who is irritatingly always right and, fortunately for me, very patient. I also need to thank the rest of the Graydon House team who have worked to bring this book into the world and into readers' hands—Diane Lavoie, Ambur Hostyn, Justine Sha, Sean Kapitain, and everyone else on the marketing, publicity, sales, subrights, and production teams who work behind the scenes. And my fantastic agent Michelle Richter, who constantly reminds me, "You can't edit the thing if it's not on the page."

Given the winery setting in the book, I had to do some "research." (Tough job, but someone has to do it.) Thank you to Elizabeth Harris and Kevin Switz at Stone Tower Winery, Sarah Blagg at Bully Hill Vineyards, Eliza Andrews, and Logan Sweet for all your knowledge and help with my wine research—any errors here about wine and growing grapes are all my fault.

Special shout-out to the Chessie Chapter of Sisters in Crime

Power Write lunchtime group—especially Ellen Byerrum, Deanna Fowler, Jeffrey James Higgins, Smita Harish Jain, Jane Limprecht, Adam Meyer, Jeanmaire Remes, and Lauren Silberman. I would definitely have not gotten through this without seeing your faces daily.

Thank you to my "partner in joy," Alice Henderson, for all the wonderful emails and texts about writing, AI-generated hilarity, commiserations and encouragement, and everything else. Your unending curiosity and passion for what you do inspires me! We need more people like you in the world.

Thank you to Karen Kitching, for giving me some time in Almost Heaven to draft the early versions of this book. And to my writing group, Art Taylor and Brandon Wicks, for the cocktails, critiques, and good conversation. Thank you to my early readers, especially April Kaminski and Bernadette Murphy, for your keen eyes and perspective. This book is better because of you both. And my other writer friends who make this crazy business worth it, especially Ed Aymar, John Copenhaver, Carol Goodman, Alexia Gordon, Sherry Harris, Alma Katsu, Shannon Kirk, Alan Orloff, Hank Phillippi Ryan, and LynDee Walker.

I have the good fortune of *not* having family like the Van Nesses, and I'm most grateful to all my family's support and love. This book, like everything I write, goes out to them, especially to my dad, my brother, my husband, Art, and our son Dash. The wine would not be as sweet or as complex without you all in my world.

THE WEEKEND RETREAT
PLAYLIST

"Thunder"–Imagine Dragons

"Super Rich Kids"–Frank Ocean, Earl Sweatshirt

"Royals"–Lorde

"Red Red Wine"–Charles Mann

"Rich Girl"–Lake Street Dive

"Here Comes the Rain Again"–Macy Gray

"Running Up That Hill"–Placebo

"Common People"–Pulp

"Beautiful People"–Ed Sheeran, Khalid

"Yellow"–Coldplay

"Stormy Weather"–Etta James

"Poison & Wine"–The Civil Wars

"November Rain"–Guns N' Roses

"I Wanna Be Rich"–Calloway

Find it on Spotify: bit.ly/SongsForTheWeekendRetreat